A TOKEN OF

LOVE

Other Non-Fiction Books
By Delia Halverson:

Helping Your Child Discover Faith
Helping Your Teen Develop Faith
Teaching Prayer in the Classroom
How to Train Volunteer Teachers
New Ways to Tell the Old, Old Story
How Do Our Children Grow?
Helping Children Care for God's People
Leading Adult Learners
Living Simply, Simply Living
32 Ways to Become a Great Sunday School Teacher
How Do Our Children Grow? (revised edition)
The Gift of Hospitality
My Cup Runneth Over (Most of the Time) *
*Meditations by the Sea**
The Nuts & Bolts of Christian Education
Side by Side: Families Learning and Living the Faith Together
Teaching & Celebrating the Christian Seasons
Teaching Prayer in the Classroom (revised/expanded)
Children's Activities for the Christian Year
Teaching the Lord's Prayer
*Growing the Soul: Meditations from My Garden**
Let the Children Give
*Lessons I Learned From My Grandchildren**
What's in Worship?
Ready, Set, Teach!
Creating Holy Spaces (with Karen Appleby)

*Devotionals are indicated by **

A TOKEN OF
LOVE

Delia Halverson

To Ann,
such a great
neighbor!
Delia
Halverson

MOUNTAIN ARBOR
PRESS

**Mountain Arbor
Press**

Alpharetta, GA

ISBN: 978-1-6653-0009-4 - Paperback
eISBN: 978-1-6653-0010-0 - ePub
eISBN: 978-1-6653-0011-7 - mobi

Library of Congress Control Number: 2021903173

Printed in the United States of America   022321

∞This paper meets the requirements of ANSI/NISO Z39.48-1992 (Permanence of Paper)

To all those great people
who helped me enjoy my years
in the Dakotas,
including my husband and family.

Contents

Chapter One

Gravel crunched beneath the wheels as Amanda slammed on the brakes. She stared at the sign: Stoney Butte, North Dakota – population 92.

A long way from home, she thought, *a long way from my previous life. I wanted a new start and a small town, but is this really a place I can bury the past?*

At the kitchen table in Atlanta, this town did not seem so far away. But after two days on the road to Minneapolis and another day and a half to the northwestern edge of North Dakota and Stoney Butte, Amanda felt she had entered another world.

She looked around. She had seen few signs of life since she left the paved road twenty miles to the east. Ahead of her lay a deep riverbed rimmed with large trees, their leaves rippling in the wind. These were the only trees obvious for the past twenty miles, except around an occasional farmhouse. Nothing to the south except a cut-bank in the low hill, not even a tree. To the north, only some strange spiky plants and a barbed wire fence. Across the bridge to the west she saw a cluster of several houses. *This is it, the end of the universe.*

Amanda clenched the steering wheel with sweaty palms. Her fast heartbeat echoed in her ears. She turned to the large calico cat in the carrycase beside her. "Well, Aggie, we're actually here. But

I'm beginning to have second thoughts about coming to this god-forsaken place, even to get away from the past."

This uneasiness felt so different from her usual, confident self. In the past her decisions came quick and exact. Now she just wasn't sure about anything. Maybe she should turn back. *No. It's too late to turn back, and certainly too far. I can't travel those desolate roads again right now.* If nothing else, she needed to honor the contract she had signed. A few strokes of the pen had committed her to teach a full year in the two-room school of Stoney Butte, North Dakota. Well, she wanted a place to start anew, away from the stress and people who knew her past, and it certainly looked like she'd found it.

Easing off the break, Amanda drove toward the bridge that spanned an almost dry river. She crossed the bridge to begin her new life.

The road curved past a gas station, and she drove down what must be the main street. According to the directions she received from the school board, she assumed that must be the general store on the left. Well, at least she could get bread and milk here. From the looks of the sagging corner porch, the building appeared to be 100 years old. And there, at the next corner, she saw the white schoolhouse.

She pulled the new 1973 Volvo in front of the two-room schoolhouse, killed the motor, and looked around. The building needed a coat of paint, but it looked sound enough. Large windows on either side of the building reached almost from the ceiling to the floor. That would give the rooms plenty of light. There was a wide porch across the front with four steps. Amanda thought of the handicap requirements that were being implemented in the Atlanta schools and hoped that none of the children had physical handicaps here, or they would have difficulty with the stairs. She noticed that the roof was tin. She'd not listened to rain on a tin roof since her childhood visits to her grandmother's house in the mountains of north Georgia. That would bring back fond memories.

Several trees shaded the yard, cooling the area for the children's play. She would have to learn the names of trees in this area and teach them to the children. The few trees she'd seen certainly looked different from those in Georgia. On one side of the schoolhouse a swing hung from a high branch of a tree, the wooden seat moving in the wind. Knee-high weeds grew on the other side where she expected to see the mobile home. Where was her promised home?

Exhausted, she closed her eyes and sank back into the seat.

"Ms. Davidson?"

Amanda bolted upright and looked into the face of an older woman, her skin weathered, crow's feet spreading on either side of sparkling blue eyes surrounded by graying hair. "Oh, you startled me."

"You are Ms. Davidson, aren't you?"

"Yes, I'm Amanda Davidson."

"I'm Sue Biscoff, chair of the school board," the woman said. "We're so glad you're here. How was your trip?"

"Wonderful, except for the long drive across North Dakota," Amanda said, opening the door and stepping out of the car.

"We're used to the distances around here," the woman said with a smile. "Tend to forget that new folks see it different. I suppose you're wondering about where you'll live."

"I thought I might have read the letter wrong."

"You had it right," said the chairwoman. "The mobile home was damaged in route. Not too smart a driver, when it comes to our gravel roads. We made him take it back. The new one won't be here for several days. Meanwhile, you're welcome to stay with us. My husband and I live west of town, just across the Montana line."

"Thank you," Amanda said in relief. She did not like the idea of staying in the home of strangers, but after driving through town she realized she didn't have much choice. She hadn't even seen a hotel in the town she'd driven through twenty miles back as she left the highway.

"I do have a large cat with me," she said. "Will that be a problem?"

"Not at all. We're used to all sorts of animals at the ranch. We have a couple of cats ourselves. Would you like to take a tour of the schoolhouse now, or do you want to wait until you've settled in? The opening date for school is still two weeks away."

Amanda thought for a moment. "After the long drive, perhaps it's just as well that I wait until tomorrow to tour the school. Then I can unload the boxes of things I brought for the classroom. You say your home is just out of town?"

"You can follow me. We should get there about the time Josh gets back from Williston. He had to go for some veterinary supplies. With no resident vet in this area, we have to take care of most of the animal's medical problems ourselves."

Amanda started the engine and pulled out onto the road behind the dusty blue station wagon. They turned down the main street in the direction that Amanda had come. Then just before the sharp curve in the road, Sue turned right and drove west, past several houses and out of town. The dust from the road billowed up behind the station wagon, forcing Amanda to close the car window and turn on the air conditioner. She thought if she didn't die of the dry, hundred-degree weather in this country, she'd die of lung congestion from the dust.

Just a few miles out of town they crossed the Montana state line. At the next mailbox, Sue turned the station wagon into a road, pulled over to the side and stopped. She got out of the car and came back to speak to Amanda. "I'll just check the mailbox. I'm sure Willard John's been by with the mail. You can drive on ahead. The house is just over that draw. Go ahead and park under the trees, and I'll be right along."

Amanda pulled around Sue, rumbling across the cattle guard and down the road. She crested the hill, and a neat, white house spread out among a few trees. It was obvious that the trees had been planted, because there were no other trees nearby. The patch of trees was like a fountain, in the midst of a desert. Gratefully, Amanda pulled up under a tree and turned to her cat, Aggie. "Well, old friend. It looks like we're at the end of our road, at least for now."

Sue Biscoff pulled up beside the Volvo and got out of her car. "Let me help you with something. I see Josh's truck is here, so he must be back from Williston."

Amanda followed Sue through a gate, past a bright blush of flowers, toward what turned out to be the back door of the house. The path to the front door appeared to be seldom used. Obviously, this home welcomed guests with informal hospitality.

As they stepped across the threshold, Amanda appreciated the cool air. After the furnace-like heat outside, the air-conditioned interior renewed her spirit. "The air conditioning is a relief from your intense heat," she said. "I never expected it to be so hot up here."

"Most people only hear about our sub-zero winter weather, but we often have temperatures over 100 degrees in the summer. Air conditioning is one thing Josh and I are privileged to have. Not too many folks have it around these parts. Everyone says our summers aren't all that long. But we find that the air conditioning revives us and gives us energy for what we must do on the ranch. Your mobile home will be air conditioned, but I'm afraid the schoolhouse isn't. You'll only have a couple of weeks, at the most, before things cool off. In fact, some years we have frost by the end of August."

As Amanda set Aggie's carry case on the floor, she looked around the kitchen. The room seemed to reflect Sue's sunny personality. Tiers of white sheer ruffles billowed over the windows, and a large antique pedestal table sat on the braided rug, along with six straight-back chairs. The flowers in the large basket on the table looked as if they had been picked that very morning, and fresh bread was cooling on a rack beside the stove.

"Let me show you to your room, and you can rest a little before supper," Sue suggested. "Josh must be down at the barn finishing up some chores."

Amanda welcomed the time to rest alone in the room. It had been a long trip, although she stopped early enough each day to relax in the motel rooms. Finally arriving at her destination, the stress of the hours of driving alone left her exhausted. Perhaps it was best that her home was not ready. She might have tried to unpack everything right away, and then she would really have worn herself to a frazzle.

After opening Aggie's carrycase so that she could explore their room, Amanda lay on the bed, closed her eyes and coaxed each muscle to relax. Her next consciousness was that of voices coming from the kitchen. She turned over and looked at the clock. Six-thirty! She must have fallen asleep. She looked into the mirror and saw dark circles beneath her dark brown eyes. Quickly she freshened her face and fluffed her short, dark hair. As she approached the kitchen, she remembered that she had only munched in the car for lunch. The scent of roasting chicken sprang excitement to her stomach.

"Amanda, I hope you rested well." Sue greeted her.

"Evidently too well," Amanda responded with a smile. "I must have fallen asleep. What can I do to help?"

"Nothing right now." Turning to the man that Amanda had not seen, Sue said, "Amanda, this is my husband, Josh."

Amanda looked into a pair of dark brown eyes below a two-toned forehead. She recognized the tell-tale signs of a man who spent much of his time outside, with a hat on his head. He was tall and lanky, but with muscles as firm as a trainer in any suburban Atlanta gym.

"We're glad you are here," said Josh. "I'm sorry your home wasn't ready, but our home is your home for as long as you need. We can store what you don't need right now in the spare room at the schoolhouse. Then you can get to it when you want."

"Thank you," responded Amanda. "You have a very welcoming home."

"Sue gets the credit for that," said Josh. "It is a home we enjoy and one we like to share with others."

By the time Josh helped Amanda bring in her additional bags, Sue had supper on the table. Mashed potatoes and corn on the cob accompanied the roasted chicken. Fresh tomatoes and cucumbers completed the meal. When Amanda complimented Sue on the vegetables, she told her that they all came from their garden.

"I'll be happy to share with you," she said. "We always have much more than we can eat or freeze. With supermarkets fifty miles away, we grow a large garden and pack our freezer full for the winter."

"Thank you," said Amanda. "I thoroughly love gardening. I imagine gardening in North Dakota is quite different from gardening in Georgia. If I put in a garden next year, I'll have to get your advice." Silently she thought, *If I'm still here.*

As the meal progressed Amanda began to relax and asked Sue and Josh to tell her a bit about themselves and the town of Stoney Butte.

"I grew up on this very ranch," Sue began. "My parents settled here in 1920, and I was born on the ranch three years later. They only had a small one-bedroom shell of a house then. They added a couple of rooms to it later, but after we took over the ranch and our children were born, we tore down the small place and built this. The children are married and live a distance away. Stoney Butte's not a bad place to grow up. Everyone knows everyone else, and there's plenty of room to roam."

"I can see that," commented Amanda. "I've never seen so much open country. It's quite a change from the congestion of Atlanta. How did you two meet?"

Josh picked up the story, "I'm from western Montana, and Sue came to Missoula to attend nursing school. She was looking for the big city life, although Missoula is no large city, compared to Atlanta."

"It seemed large to me," intersected Sue. "In comparison to Stoney Butte, it was a metropolis."

"I was studying agriculture at the University of Montana, and a friend introduced us," Josh continued. "We dated for about six months, and by that time we knew it was a done deal that we were destined to be together."

"The rest is history, as they say," Sue closed out the subject. "About the time Josh graduated, my parents were killed in a tragic accident between here and Miles City, and since I was the only child, we came back to run the ranch."

Recognizing that Sue had no desire to fill in any more details, Amanda asked no more questions. The conversation turned to the weather and the prospects for the start of the school year. Sue and Josh filled her in on some details about various students that would be in her class, but Amanda only listened with half an ear. She always preferred to make her own decisions about people instead of accepting the judgments of others. She'd been that way throughout her teaching career. In fact, ignoring a teacher's warnings had been the start of her problems back in Atlanta. But Amanda still preferred to make her own decisions.

When they finished the meal, Amanda helped Sue clear the table and set the kitchen straight. Her hostess made her feel comfortable, and she began to relax after the grueling drive from Atlanta.

Just as they were moving into the living room with a cup of coffee, the phone rang three short rings. Josh went to the hallway, and Amanda could hear his voice as he spoke to someone. When he returned, he said, "Evidently most of the town knows that you're here, Amanda. It's gone through the party lines."

Sue smiled at Amanda's puzzled expression. "You may as well get used to our telephone system," she said. "We have a private system with party lines up and down on both sides of the North Dakota and Montana border. When there's news, it travels fast across the wires. Our telephone operator usually knows about all there is to know about everyone, and she's always ready to share her knowledge."

"Is that the only telephone system in the area?" Amanda asked.

"Yes," answered Josh. "The Watsons own the phone company and so far, have managed to ward off the larger phone companies that tried to purchase the company and upgrade the equipment. Bertha Watson operates the switchboard, and her husband, Neman, works the lines. Actually, our system usually works when others fail because it's so simple, and Neman keeps the lines repaired promptly. The amazing thing is that Neman is blind, but he can repair any line in the country. Bertha takes him to the problem line and sees that he gets up the ladder. Then when he's finished, he puts a call through to her at the switchboard, and she returns to take him back home. She has a way to hook the system up to a special number in the closest town just in case there is an emergency while she's away from the switchboard. The two of them operate the business out of their home, so they can handle it between themselves."

"I didn't know any party line systems still existed," Amanda mused.

"Well, it works for us. You just have to remember that anything you say on the telephone might become the knowledge of everyone in two counties." responded Sue. "You see, most of us have rubber buttons. Listening in on someone else's telephone conversation is called 'rubbering'. If more than two people pick up the phone on a party line at once it cuts the volume so that it's difficult to hear. When you push the rubber button you can hear what's being said but cannot talk yourself. That restores the power, and everyone can hear. It's convenient, but it really cuts down on your privacy."

"I guess I'll have to learn to live with a less private life," commented Amanda. "It's certainly different from what I'm used to."

"It does have its advantages, at times," said Josh. "All the phones are crank phones, and if you have an emergency you can ring two long rings and everyone on the line knows to pick up the phone because someone has an emergency. In this remote country, the neighbors are more helpful than any emergency crew that has to travel fifty miles to get to you."

Suddenly Amanda saw her future. She had run away, looking for an escape from her life. Now she was committed to a year in a place on the edge of the universe where everyone knew your business. What had she done?

Chapter Two

Neil Welburn stepped out the door of his small house by the Methodist Church and headed for his car. He'd promised Hannah Gill he'd be at their house by noon for dinner. He would enjoy a meal that wasn't his own cooking. Besides, this was the best time to talk about the church budget with Otto. Ranchers began their day early, and by noon they were ready for a relaxed, hearty meal. He looked at his watch. Just time enough to stop and visit Mrs. Glaser on the way to the Gill ranch.

Pulling into the gravel street he mused over his decision to serve in this community. He felt he had no choice. After four years in the Coast Guard, he had dedicated his life to follow God's call. Although he was still in his probation period with the Methodist Church, following God's call meant he went where the bishop sent him. When he entered seminary, he visualized serving a neighborhood church in the outskirts of a larger city where there would be an opportunity to date young women and enjoy some cultural venues. Sure, the Dakotas had a few larger cities, but there weren't many churches in towns as small as Stoney Butte. Actually, he had the responsibility of two churches. Stoney Butte was the largest, with 42 adult members. It was also the one with a parsonage. The other church, Prairie Creek, was simply perched on the side of the road, about 15 miles across the Montana line. He felt God wanted him to serve here, and so he accepted the small town. There were certainly enough folks in these parts who needed to hear the law of the Lord.

On the edge of town Neil turned into the yard of a small house, smaller than his parsonage. Emma Glaser had lived here for the last 15 years. Before that she and her husband worked on the Bates ranch, just south of town. Her husband had died there. Emma had no family that anyone knew of, but the whole community of Stoney Butte called her "Miss Emma" and considered her family. Until recently she graced the doors of the church every time they opened, and she visited everyone who fell ill whether they were members of the church or not. A crippling arthritis now kept Miss Emma home most of the time, so Neil tried to stop in to see her as often as he could.

Miss Emma opened the door with her usual cheerful smile. No one knew her exact age, but the wrinkles in her face told of the summers she had spent in the hot sun and dry Dakota winds. Her hair, cut in a pixie cut, was as white as snow.

As always, Miss Emma had the coffee pot ready, and she invited him into her tidy kitchen. There were red and white checked window valances that matched her tablecloth. The chairs were outfitted as if they were dresses with buttons down the back, a belted sash, and a neat collar around the top. Neil noticed a slight tremor as her gnarled hands poured his cup of coffee.

When she settled into her chair at the kitchen table, she asked, "Have you heard about the new teacher?"

"I knew we were getting one, but I didn't know she was here yet." he replied.

"Don't you listen on the telephone? It's been the subject of every conversation since she arrived yesterday afternoon."

Neil smiled. He still had trouble picking up the phone if it wasn't his ring. "You know I don't listen in on other conversations," he said. "I know there's no biblical law against it, but they didn't have telephones when the Bible was written."

Miss Emma's laugh rang true. "Bible times were a lot different in many ways. I dare say Jesus would have different ideas about a lot of things today."

"Now, Miss Emma," he began. "You and I often disagree about things in the Bible. I don't want to get into that now."

"That's true," agreed the old woman. "Anyway, the new teacher is supposed to be a real good-looking woman. She may be a little older than you, but I imagine you'd enjoy her company."

"Don't you go trying to set me up," he replied. "In this town I'll meet anyone new soon enough."

Miss Emma's eyes twinkled as she smiled. "She came from Atlanta. Maybe she has enough culture to interest you. I hear Atlanta is an up and coming cultural center."

"You sound like my grandma now, Miss Emma. She's always telling me that I'll not be happy until I'm married. I wonder just why this new teacher agreed to come and teach in this little town."

Miss Emma's mouth twitched as she seemed to pause in a moment of thought. "Well, it's really not for us to wonder. Whatever her reason, it's her business and her business alone."

After a bit more conversation about the news around Stoney Butte, Neil finished his coffee and bade Miss Emma goodbye. He stopped to visit the woman every time he passed her way, but he always made his visits short. From experience he'd learned that she could hold her own in any biblical debate, and the longer he stayed, the more likely they were to get into a heated argument.

This was hard on the ego, since she only had an eighth-grade education and he was a seminary graduate. How could he shepherd his flock if he couldn't exhibit leadership? Miss Emma never forced her opinions down anyone else's throat, but she didn't hesitate to make her own beliefs known. For her generation, she had a very liberal theological view of life.

When Neil reached the Gill ranch it was almost noon. As he pulled into the yard, he saw Otto coming from the barn to the house. Otto was not as tall as most men, but he was solidly built. His graying hair stuck out around his faded, dusty hat, and his arms were tanned from hours in the North Dakota sun.

Exciting smells met the men as they walked through the kitchen door. It was a neat room with bright yellow curtains and a large table with ladder-back chairs. "You're just in time, Neil," said Hannah. "You guys go ahead and wash up, and I'll have dinner on the table by the time you're through."

As they sat down at the table, Otto asked Neil to say the blessing. It was not unusual for people to ask the pastor to pray, and it did make him feel that his calling into ministry was important. He thanked God for the food, prayed for rain which had been scarce this summer, and asked for blessings on their discussion of the budget. Neil felt he'd prayed a good prayer, using all the "Thee's" and "Thou's" that he had grown up with.

During the meal Hannah asked, "Have you met the new teacher yet?"

"No, I haven't," said Neil. "Everyone's been telling me about her, but I haven't even heard her name. I don't think anyone knows much about her except that she's from Atlanta."

"Well, her name's Amanda Davidson, and she came with high recommendations from her school superintendent in Atlanta," said

Hannah. "In fact, she was principal of an elementary school the last two years. Although she has grown children, she's pretty young to have been a principal. Can't quite figure out why she'd leave that position to come out here and teach in a two-room schoolhouse, but I'm glad she did. It's mighty hard to find folks who will live here unless they grew up here."

Otto spoke up, "Most of us who grew up in this country don't want to leave, and many who do leave end up coming back. Even Bill Bates came back after seeing half the world. Bill may have come back because he felt obliged to carry on the ranch after his parents were killed in their plane accident, but he seems happy to be here now. He does take off on long trips from time to time, however. I just hope that not too many people realize how peaceful and calm the Dakotas are, compared to the rest of the country."

"Well, maybe Amanda Davidson will come to church on Sunday and you can meet her." said Hannah. Then her eyes lit up, "You know, Neil, the Labor Day dance is coming up and you could invite her to go with you."

Here it is again, thought Neil. *Amanda Davidson's only been in town overnight and already everyone is trying to get us together. If I'd only been assigned to a suburban church, I wouldn't have these busybodies trying to match me up.*

After dinner, and Hannah cleared the table, Neil pulled the budget out of his briefcase. Because they were a small charge, the two churches were considered a mission, and Neil received his salary from the general church. The small Stoney Butte congregation still struggled to keep up the building and parsonage and pay the utility bills. Right now, both the church and parsonage needed a coat of paint, but there certainly wasn't enough money for that.

Otto nodded as Neil explained everything he proposed. When he left, he had Otto's agreement on presenting the budget at the next church council meeting. On his way home, his mind reverted back to their conversation just after they had eaten. *Who is this Bill Bates, and where does he go for up to six months at a time? It sounds rather fishy to me. No one seems to know where he goes and what he does. When he gets back to town, I want to meet him.*

Chapter Three

"Are you the new teacher?" asked a voice from the door of the schoolroom.

Amanda looked up from her last box of supplies to see a freckled-faced, red-headed boy with a sheepish grin.

"Yes I am. And you are?" she asked.

"I'm Joel Karr. I'll be in the first grade this year!" exclaimed the boy with excitement in his eyes. "I've been waiting six whole years to be in the first grade, and you'll be my teacher."

Amanda walked over to the young boy and sat down at a school desk, looking into his eyes. "That will be exciting for both you and for me. Where do you live?"

"I live with my grandparents just down the street in the back of the store," the boy answered. "My grandparents run it. We have all sorts of things if you need to buy anything."

"Oh, I'm sure I'll need to buy lots of things at your store once my home gets here," Amanda assured him.

"Yeah," he said. "They pulled your trailer in and tried to get Mrs. Biscoff to take it even though anyone could see it was beat up. But Mrs. Biscoff is smart. She stood right there and told them to take it back and bring one that was perfect. I heard her myself."

Joel pulled himself up to his six-year-old height and puffed out his chest in pride.

"Well, I'm sure glad she did," said Amanda. "I wouldn't want to live in a beat-up trailer."

"Well, some folks have to live in a beat-up trailer, like Marilyn and Mandy," the boy said. "But my grandmother said when the school pays for a new one, they had better bring a perfect one."

"Your grandmother certainly is right," Amanda assured him. "Who are Marilyn and Mandy? Do they go to school?"

"They sure do. They'll be in the second and third grades this year. They're bigger than me, but I'm going to catch up with them because I drink all my milk," boasted Joel.

Amanda smiled to herself as she went back to unpacking her box. Joel watched silently for a few minutes and then asked, "Is it okay if I swing on the swing outside when no one is on the playground?"

"Certainly, just be careful and don't get hurt."

"I won't," he cried as he dashed out the door. "I really know how to swing good."

Amanda finished unpacking the box and looked at her classroom. It certainly wasn't like any classroom she'd taught in before. There was a pot-belly stove in the corner instead of a central heating system. Three bare light bulbs hung from the ceiling instead of a bank of florescent lights. But just as she expected, the high windows let in the afternoon sun. The ancient teacher's desk was big and bulky and none of the drawers were deep enough to accommodate file folders, but there was plenty of room for supplies. She made a note to buy a small filing cabinet on a trip to Williston, or perhaps order it from a catalog. Ten old student desks sat in three horizontal rows in front of the teacher's desk, and a long row of pegs on the back wall took the place of lockers. Shelves above the row of pegs were adequate for holding the children's lunch boxes. Someone had hastily written names on the wall above the shelves. The whole room could use a coat of paint, but she had brought some colorful alphabet strips, maps, and posters. They made the room a little more cheerful.

Amanda opened the door that led into the room for the upper class. She expected ten students in the first through fourth grade, and the fifth through eighth grade would have eight students. Eighteen children in the total school. In Atlanta her classes often had twice that number of students. The other classroom looked even more drab than hers. She'd been told that Ione Wirth was a single woman who taught the class for the past 29 years. Amanda hadn't met her yet, and she wondered about her method of teaching. She realized that there might be problems if they differed in educational philosophy. Amanda had been a principal for the past two years and was accustomed to setting the pace for the learning of the whole school. Now she feared that the other teacher would try to pull rank and dictate her teaching methods. Once again, she wondered just what she'd gotten herself into.

Too late now, she thought as she closed the door between the classrooms. She picked up the empty box, slit the tape that held the bottom, and flattened it. Her side of the small storeroom behind the classrooms was the perfect place to store the flattened boxes. She might need them if this tiny community was too desolate for her. Several other boxes held seasonal supplies, but her room was now ready for the students.

Amanda picked up the student books she'd set aside to take back to the Biscoff ranch. It had only taken a few days to set up her room, but now she had to prepare lesson plans for different classes.

Fortunately, all ten students were in three grades. She only had to worry with three lesson plans.

She locked the door to the schoolhouse and decided to make one stop on her way back to the ranch to rent a post office box, since there was no mail delivery in town. It was really surprising to have a post office in such a small town, but all her correspondence had been addressed from Stoney Butte, North Dakota, so there must be one somewhere. Now it was a matter of finding it. She also wanted to locate the town hall that Sue had mentioned when she told her about the Labor Day dance that was coming up.

Amanda began driving up and down the few streets of the town. Besides the grocery store and a gas station, she noticed a saloon and a small café that was closed. There were several vacant buildings, but she couldn't find anything that resembled a town hall. One unpainted cement block building on a side street was large enough for a dance, but the windows were boarded up. When she drove north, she soon ran out of town, noticing what looked like a fairground just off the road. There were several buildings of bleached wood and a fenced-in arena. Beside the arena was a larger fenced area with some cows.

Turning around, she headed back through town, back past the store and saloon. She turned down the one street she'd missed earlier and discovered a one room church, Methodist, according to the sign over the door. Circling the block, she came back to Main Street. Just as she was about to turn west and head for the ranch, she noticed the flag by the service station. Then she realized that the post office was attached to the side of that building.

After arranging for a post office box and purchasing a few stamps, Amanda made her way back to the ranch. As she pulled into the yard, Sue motioned for her to join her in the garden. The scent of freshly watered ground pleased her senses as she walked between the rows of beans where Sue skillfully handled the hoe.

"I have great news," Sue said with a smile. "Your new home will be delivered early tomorrow morning. The company called and said it's on the way. Now if they just have a driver who's capable of navigating our gravel roads."

"That will be nice," said Amanda. "I'm sure you'll be glad to get me out of your hair."

"Oh, it's been nice to have you with us these few days. I really wish it had been longer. But then we'll have lots of opportunity to get to know each other."

Recalling what Joel had said about a beat-up trailer, Amanda asked, "What do you know about two of my students, Marilyn and Mandy? Joel Karr came by my classroom today and mentioned them."

Sue leaned on her hoe. "They are sweet girls, having to carry far too much responsibility for their ages. Their father, Wenzel Swenson, works for a small lumber mill about ten miles northwest of town. They cut a little timber off the butte there. The mill supplies mainly lumber for out-buildings and fence posts. They don't have drying kilns, so the lumber is usually sold green, right off the belt. The company barely makes enough to meet the payroll of a few employees, and that's meager earnings. The girls' parents, Myrtle Mae and Wenzel, grew up in Minnesota, they seem to like the community and say they wouldn't live anywhere else now. Myrtle Mae has been sick off and on most of the time she's been here. Right now, she's struggling with what seems to be the beginnings of Multiple Sclerosis. Consequently, much of the housework falls on Marilyn and Mandy. They live in a trailer just behind the Methodist Church. It's in pretty bad shape, but it's all they have. The girls not only cook and take care of the house, but they work a small garden and sometimes must take turns staying home from school if their mother is bad off. I've never seen children with more determination than those two. Both girls have their mother's attitude. They seem to find something positive in everything that comes their way."

Amanda thought for a moment about a pair of sisters in her previous school. They too had had a positive attitude, but their father looked for any opportunity he could to turn their attitude negative. His treatment of the girls had been a part of why she moved as far away from Georgia as she could. She wondered if she'd learned not to intervene in family affairs after that experience. But then she couldn't just sit back and let something happen that she knew was bad for children. *Please, God,* she thought, *don't let me step into another situation like that here.*

Later in the evening, Amanda asked Sue about Joel. "When Joel talked to me at the schoolhouse today, he said he lives in the back of the store with his grandparents. Can you fill me in a little about him?"

"That was a bad situation that has turned out well after all. Joel's mother got pregnant out of wedlock, and everyone was so shocked. It was the talk of the town for a while, but our previous pastor calmed it down, especially when Joel's mother brought him to her parents and simply disappeared. I know it's still a sad situation for Delmer and Leola, but they do love Joel and he seems to be a well-adjusted little boy. Everyone in town certainly loves him."

Amanda remembered situations similar to that in Atlanta when the child had been shunned. She said, "This community seems to accept people no matter what their background. That's a healthy attitude."

With a twinkle in her eye, Sue said, "That's why we like it here so much. It's almost a world to itself."

Chapter Four

The next morning Amanda drove to town to see her new home. The air was fresh, and before her spread a brilliant blue sky, much like the advertisements for the big sky country of Montana. She hadn't realized just how different this would be from the movies she'd seen of the mountains of Montana. This was truly the big sky country, and the flat landscape seemed to go on forever. Although the land rolled and dipped at places, there were no high hills to try to see over, no trees blocking the view, and certainly no buildings jammed against each other. There was a sense of rightness about it, conveying a calmness that city life missed.

As she drove into Stoney Butte, she realized that the delivery of her home caused quite a furor of activity. Beside the school building sat the new trailer, looking like a rodeo queen in the midst of an arena of trucks. Men moved about, carrying boards and tools from their trucks to where they were sawing and hammering. Several of the men were digging a shallow ditch just below the edge of the trailer.

Amanda turned the car around and parked on Main Street in order to keep it out of the way. When she walked up to the schoolyard Josh greeted her with a grin. "What do you think of your new home?" he asked.

"Wow!" she replied. "Looks like a castle right now, surrounded by a moat. What is the ditch for?"

"We're putting an insulated skirt around the trailer," answered Josh. "Sue and I had one like this around the trailer we lived in at the university in Missoula, and it really kept the floor warm in the winter. We'll build two walls below the trailer, about six inches apart, and fill the gap with sawdust. The lumber mill northwest of town donated the lumber, and they're just glad to get rid of the sawdust.

"Most of the men you see working here are either fathers of students or connected to the school board in some way. One member of the school board, Bill Bates, isn't here. He's out of town. We are really glad you're here and want to make you comfortable in your new home."

"Thank you," said Amanda. "I really appreciate all these men taking time from their work to do this for me."

"Well, that's one thing about ranching," said Josh. "We can pretty much arrange our schedules, except when we have an emergency or it's calving and lambing time. Would you like a tour?"

Josh introduced her to several of the men as he led her up the steps and across the small porch they had constructed for her new home. It was not one of the modern, double wide models that were called "Manufactured Homes", but it was adequate for her. She took a deep breath as she went through the door and everything smelled new. The furniture had all been unwrapped and set in place, and it looked ready for her to move in. To her surprise, she liked the walls and drapes.

"Who selected the furniture and drapes?" she asked.

"You can thank Sue for that," said Josh. "She did all the leg work on the purchase."

"She sent me on ahead," Amanda said. "She was finishing up some baking. I think she's bringing something for these hard-working men."

"Several of the women brought rolls and coffee for us when we first started," Josh told her. "Most of the men had already spent a couple of hours doing chores before they got here. About noon we'll break for lunch, and Sue and some other women will spread a feast."

Josh called to one of the men to help Amanda bring several of her boxes from the school storeroom. Josh introduced him as Neil Welburn, the minister of the church. As they walked to the schoolhouse, Amanda stole a better look at Neil. She guessed that he was a bit younger than she. His auburn hair shone in the sun, and his muscles easily filled the polo shirt. She would never have guessed him to be a preacher, according to most of the preachers she had known. Any woman would notice this man in a crowd.

"How long have you lived in Stoney Butte?" she asked.

"I just came here in June after I graduated from seminary," Neil answered. "I spent several years in the Coast Guard before I recognized God's call to become a preacher. I had thought I would serve a church in a larger city, but this seems to be where God wants me now."

"Sometimes things really change in our lives," suggested Amanda. "A year ago, I expected to live in Atlanta the rest of my life."

"So, what changed your mind?" asked Neil.

"Just circumstances," she answered. "I was looking for a change, and this job caught my attention. I didn't know much more about North Dakota than the facts I taught my classes in geography. But here I am, and school starts on the day after Labor Day. I hope I can get my home squared away and the lesson plans for the first couple of weeks finished before then."

"You'll make it. Have you met many people in town?"

"Not many, Sue told me about the Labor Day dance next Saturday. Maybe I'll meet more folks then. I've been pretty busy getting my classroom set up."

"I understand that most everyone in the area turns out for the Labor Day dance," Neil informed her. "I doubt that I'll be going since it's on Saturday, and I have to preach at two churches on Sunday."

"Where's your other church?" asked Amanda.

"It's Prairie Creek Methodist, about 15 miles across the Montana line," he answered. "It's not in a town; just a country church. Of course, most folks would call the one here in town a country church, but the local people consider it the town church. I hope you'll join us for services on Sundays."

"Maybe I will," she said. "I didn't attend much in Atlanta. My parents belonged to a very strict church when I was growing up, and by the time I was a teenager we had lots of arguments about religion. Once I was out of my parents' house and on my own, I found it better to keep my mouth shut and stay away from churches."

Neil responded, "I spent many years not going to church. Then in the Coast Guard I had a buddy who led me to Christ, and I've had such joy in my heart ever since. Have you ever had a serious discussion with anyone about Christ?"

Amanda scurried into the school storeroom and picked up a box before answering. "Oh, I've had a good many discussions, particularly in my teen years, but everyone simply told me just what to believe, and I wanted to make up my own mind. Then I got out of college and married. After that, my teaching career and family took up all my time and energy. There is a Methodist seminary in Atlanta, and I always thought I might take a course or two there, but I never got around to it."

Neil grimaced as he walked beside her with a large box. "Oh, I've heard of that seminary. It's just as well you didn't take any classes there. They question much of what is in the Bible. At my seminary it was very simple. They interpreted the Bible for you, and you never had to question anything. You just had to remember that the Bible is the literal word of God."

After she and Neil brought all the boxes from the storeroom, Neil again invited her to church on Sundays. Amanda politely thanked him and told him she would come sometime. Neil's words about questioning the Bible gave her even more questions than before.

Since all the men were working outside, Amanda began putting things in cupboards and drawers. It had been hard to decide what to bring. She was downsizing from a three-bedroom house to a trailer with two bedrooms, if you could call the second room a bedroom. She had asked them not to put a bed in it because she wanted to use it as a study. If she had guests, she would sleep on the sofa and give the guests her bed.

Just as Josh predicted, Sue and several other women arrived a little before noon with all sorts of food. Sawhorses were set up on the school porch and boards placed across them. Amanda turned to Sue with questioning eyes, "Is it common to greet a new person in town this way?"

Sue answered, "Yes, it is when we know about it ahead of time and especially when we've been waiting and anxious to have a new teacher. Sometimes a new family moves into a vacant house without our knowing that it will happen. In fact, I just heard that the Stewart Cazer family moved into town, and surprisingly no one seemed to know they were coming back. Stewart is the nephew of Melton Cazer who owns the sawmill just north of town."

The women covered the makeshift table with large red and white checked cloths and laid out the feast. Amanda had never seen such an array of food, everything from fried chicken and ham to fresh creamed corn, sliced tomatoes and green beans, plus several cakes and pies. As she watched the men filling their plates, she recognized the importance of food in this country. The meal not only refueled these hard-working men, but it really connected the people.

Amanda told Sue, "It seems everyone in town and all the surrounding ranches has brought something to this feast. This is a true definition of a community breaking bread together."

Sue's smile spread across her face, and her eyes sparkled. "This is the way we live out here. Something like this is as special to us as a rock concert in the city. You'll notice that everyone brought their families, and this gives us a chance to talk to each other and see how the children have grown. Almost everything that happens in this country is a family affair, and every minute of it is not only anticipated but also cherished for years afterwards."

By late afternoon, the insulated skirt around Amanda's new home was in place and painted to match the trim of the trailer. The refrigerator held leftovers from the noon meal. As the men cleared away the scrap lumber and stowed their tools in their trucks, families began to come from all directions. Each family had a sack full of groceries for her.

"Are they really bringing all this food for me, the new teacher?" asked Amanda.

Sue said, "We call this a 'pounding'. It comes from an old tradition, where everyone brought a 'pound' of something for their new neighbor."

Amanda was overwhelmed. "There is so much food here that I feel like the general store myself. I won't need to visit Joel's grandparents' store for some time except for fresh essentials. They even put a supply of meat, cream, and eggs in the refrigerator."

Sue laughed at her surprise. "The meat, cream and eggs came straight from the ranches, so you can be sure they are fresh."

Amanda said, "I'd really like to thank all these people for the work they've done and all the food they brought. Can I do that now?"

Sue found Josh and asked him to call the people together. Amanda stood on her new porch and looked out at her new community. "I came here really not knowing what to expect, but I certainly didn't expect this great a reception as a schoolteacher. I look forward to teaching your children, and I know I will love them like my own. I also want to thank each of you for what you have done for me today. I now have a lovely home with lots of good food to welcome me. Each time I eat one of the items you brought to the pounding, I will remember this day and thank you from my heart. Please let me know when I can return the kindness you've given me today."

After everyone left, Amanda drove to the Biscoff ranch to retrieve Aggie and the last of her clothing. It was dark when she parked beside her new home. Stepping out of the car, under the canopy of stars, she came to appreciate the attitude of awe that the psalmists so aptly portrayed. She recognized that her understanding of the star-studded sky had been far different from that of the psalmists, but beyond any question this view of the stars expanded her appreciation for all of creation. In this tiny town, at what seemed to be the end of the universe, Amanda felt at peace with herself. Just maybe, she had made the right decision after all.

Chapter Five

Amanda awoke to the gentle kneading of Aggie's feet. This was her usual alarm clock, but it surprised her to see how quickly the cat seemed to adjust her internal clock. Amanda was still struggling with the change to a new time zone. She began to click off all that she intended to accomplish that day. She had more boxes to unpack, some letters to write, and Neman Watson was to install her telephone. She was anxious to meet the owners of this small telephone system. She also intended to find out just where the town hall was located. For a town so small, that building seemed to be a hidden mystery.

As she finished her breakfast, an old truck pulled off the road and parked beside her car. A robust woman and a man with a white cane stepped out of the truck. If the man hadn't had the white cane, Amanda would never have guessed that this middle age man was blind. He did wear sunglasses, but he held his slightly balding head high and walked with determination. Amanda thought that he must be very familiar with the whole community of Stoney Butte. As Bertha introduced herself and Neman, Amanda looked into the bright eyes of a woman who seemed to know her business and was definitely interested in yours.

"We're Bertha and Neman Watson," she said with a smile. "We'll be fixin' your new telephone."

As Neman worked, Bertha began her inquiry. "I understand you're from Atlanta. Had a friend in high school who up and decided to go to Atlanta to find herself a southern man. Never did hear just what happened to her. She never came back for our high school reunions, and her folks moved out of town. Did you ever hear of Matilda Beckworth down there?"

Amanda smiled back. "I can't say that I ever heard the name, but Atlanta's a pretty big city, and she could have lived in another part of town."

"Well, she talked about going to beauty school and eventually opening her own salon," Bertha responded. "Maybe you didn't go to her salon."

"Atlanta itself has grown so large that all the neighboring towns meet," Amanda replied. "Sometimes it can take an hour to drive from one part of the metropolitan area to another."

"My lands," exclaimed Bertha. "And we thought it took us a long time to get places out here. Did I hear that you were principal of an elementary school in Atlanta? Just why did you decide to come way up north and teach in our small school?"

Amanda was beginning to wonder the same question herself, but she wasn't about to give this news broadcaster the complete reason for her decision. "I felt I needed a change, and your advertisement caught my eye. Guess it was an opportunity to get to know a different part of the country as much as anything else."

During their conversation Neman's deft hands had installed the crank telephone in the kitchen. "Well, I'm finished here," he said.

With those four words, Bertha took over the instructions, "Has anyone explained how our telephone system works?"

"Sue and Josh gave me some information on it," Amanda responded, "but I'm sure there will be questions when I start using it."

"It's really pretty simple," Bertha continued. "Your number is 9678, and you're on the same line with the schoolhouse. The school has one long and one short ring, and your phone will have three short rings." She pointed to the black button on the front of the phone. "This is the rubber button so that you can listen without draining the line. When you want to make a call you just crank the phone here with a long ring, and I'll pick up at the switchboard. If you want to call the school, you crank it one short and one long ring. Then I know you're talking to someone on the line and not calling the switchboard. After Neman connects the wire at the pole, I'll give you a ring and you can see how it works. Then if you have any questions we can go from there."

Next Bertha helped Neman run the wires from the trailer to the pole by the road. After seeing that Neman was safely up the pole and perched in his working position, Bertha backed the truck and returned to the switchboard. It only took about fifteen minutes before the three short rings chimed from the phone. Amanda answered, and Bertha asked if she had any questions so far. Bertha insisted that Amanda try to ring her several times before she concluded that the telephone lessons were accomplished.

When Bertha returned for Neman, she brought a small telephone directory. After they left, Amanda looked through the directory. The rural families were identified by their route and box numbers, but any town families simply said, "Stoney Butte". Amanda realized this would not help her locate the exact houses of those families who lived in town. This she'd have to learn by trial and error.

Her next plan was to find out about the town hall. Since everything in town was so close, she felt foolish driving around looking for the thing. She would simply have to swallow her pride and ask someone. She'd felt comfortable with Leola Karr when she came to the pounding the previous day, and the proprietors of the general store seemed the appropriate place to start. She looked around the kitchen trying to determine just what she could buy at the store. The pounding had filled her cupboards with almost everything she might need except cereal and milk, so that would camouflage her mission.

Grabbing her purse, Amanda headed down the block. This was the first chance she really had for a close look at her immediate surroundings. In the block of the general store was an old, abandoned storefront. It might have been a clothing store at one time, but now dried grass fell against the edges of the building and several windows were broken. A truck pulled up in front of the general store, and a man went inside. The streets were vacant with no other moving vehicles in site. She thought about the difference in traffic in Atlanta and Stoney Butte. No hum of traffic in the background. No horns blaring with road rage. No traffic lights and speed bumps.

As Amanda stepped inside the store, she noticed the neat shelves and display cases. They reminded her of the nursery rhyme about a general store that she'd loved as a child. The first lines came to mind, *Someday I'm going to have a store with a tinkly bell hung over the door...* As a child, she had even dreamed of having such a store someday.

As Amanda came through the door, Leola's smile spread across her face. "Good to see you, Amanda. What can we do for you today?"

"Well, the community did such a good job of supplying my cupboards, so all I actually need is some milk and cereal."

"Gallon or half gallon?" Leola asked as she reached into the old deep cooler beside her counter.

"Half gallon is plenty," Amanda responded. "Do you have Cheerios?"

"Sure do!" Leola said as she pointed her toward the shelves in the center of the store. "I keep plenty on hand. That's one of the favorites of kids around here."

Amanda brought her Cheerios to the counter and stood beside the tallest man she had ever seen. She thought that any professional basketball coach would like to have him on the team.

"Amanda, this is Willard John," said Leola. "He just stopped in to get a Coke and some cookies before heading out for the rest of his mail route."

Willard John tipped his western hat. With a grin that spread from ear to ear. He said, "Pleased to meet you, Miss Davidson. I'm sorry I couldn't help with your trailer yesterday. You know the old saying about the mail. Even helping a lovely lady get her home ready isn't a proper excuse for not delivering the mail."

"Thank you, Willard John," Amanda said. "I'm sure the U.S. government sees the mail delivery as a priority. Plenty of people turned out, and they did a great job."

An idea took root in Amanda's mind, and she asked, "Have you ever talked to the school children about your job?"

Willard John's eyebrows raised in a question. "Why would I do that? Everyone on my route knows me, even those not on my route. Why would I talk to the school children?"

"I like to help children recognize the helpers in our community, and I plan to invite various people to come to the classroom and tell about their jobs."

"But all I do is deliver the mail. I enjoy it, but it's no great job."

Amanda smiled, "That's just what I want to get across to the children. Everyone's job is vital for our community to function. I would like to have you come and talk with them sometime. Can I count on you?"

"I guess so," he answered with apprehension. "You'll have to tell me just what to say. I'm not much of a speech maker."

"We'll go over it ahead of time. When I've gotten the class settled and have a better idea of our schedule, I'll get back in touch with you, and we'll lay out plans."

After Willard John left Amanda told Leola, "I'd like to plan a time for you and Delmar to talk with the children too. Since the school is so close, we might even make it a field trip so that the children can see some of what you do behind the scenes."

Pride spread over her face as Leola responded. "What a great idea. It would be good for the kids to know that my job is more than just taking their money when they buy something."

After Amanda paid for her purchases she said in an off-handed manner, "I understand there's to be a Labor Day dance Saturday at the town hall. Just where is the town hall?"

"Oh, it's right down the street," Leola pointed. "It's the large building just east of here on that side street. The volunteer fire department keeps the fire engine in one side of the building, and the other side has a big hall with a stage and even a little kitchen. That's where we have any community activities. Do you plan to go to the dance?"

"I'm thinking about it," said Amanda. "I've never been to a community dance before."

"We'll throw a dance for almost any occasion. A dance makes a good excuse for everybody in this county and the next to get together. I do hope you'll come."

As she walked back to the trailer she thought, *So the boarded-up building is the town hall. I'd never have guessed that.*

Chapter Six

Amanda looked into the full-length mirror on her closet door. The blue dress with the white sash seemed appropriate for a Labor Day dance. After thinking about the dance hall with the boarded-up windows, Amanda had decided to wear a sleeveless dress. Her bare arms showed off the healthy tan she'd sweated for all summer. She decided, however, to take her white stole. It was still very warm in the daytime. In fact, the locals claimed that this warm temperature was unusual for Labor Day. The nights were another matter. It had already dropped to 49 degrees one night.

As she left the bedroom, she saw Sue's station wagon pull up outside. She gave Aggie a final pat, grabbed her purse, and locked the door behind her. Settling in the seat, Amanda said, "I really feel strange riding to the dance when it's only a couple of blocks away."

Sue responded, "This way you don't walk into a room of strangers. You've met some of the people in town, but there will be a host of folks from the country."

Josh smiled at her in the rear-view mirror. "You certainly look nice. You'll be the belle of the ball."

Amanda smiled back. "Thank you. I may be from the south, but I've never thought of myself as a southern belle."

Sue laughed. "Our dances aren't much like the fancy balls you would have in Atlanta, but we do enjoy getting together."

As they turned the corner by the town hall Josh said, "We may have to go back to the school to park."

Amanda understood what Leola meant when she said everyone in the county would be there. The vacant lot across from the town hall was a solid mass of cars and trucks parked at every angle. Amanda thought it looked like parking at the Dogwood Festival in Atlanta, only the trucks far outnumbered the cars and there was neither rhyme nor reason to the way they parked. Josh managed to find a place in the lot, and the threesome made their way through the maze of trucks toward the hall. A lone light bulb shone beside the door, inviting a frenzied party of fat moths and various bugs.

As they crossed the street, strands of music came from the building along with laughter and bits of conversation. The old boarded up building no longer looked lonely. As Amanda stepped through the door, a colorful patchwork of skirts and shirts met her eyes. Denim was definitely the formal wear for this community, denim and boots for men, and a few of the women besides.

A parade of bare light bulbs marched across the ceiling like tiny moons, ending at the stage where a five-piece band held court between the sagging curtains. Amanda recognized Willard John as one of the two guitar players. A woman played bass, and a couple of guys played banjo and fiddle. On the stage in front of them was a jar with bills in it, the method of payment for the band. Amanda made a mental note to be sure to add to the jar sometime during the evening.

The whole community seemed to have gathered. Adults of all ages sat in chairs that lined the walls, and children scampered across the dance floor, dodging the dancers. In one corner sat a large wood-burning stove, the primary heat for winter months. Narrow hardwood boards made up a floor that would rival any dance floor in Atlanta. Although it had no shine to it, shuffling boots kept it smooth as satin. In the stove corner, however, Amanda noticed that the boards had curved, evidence of a previous leak in the roof. The dancers made a point of avoiding that corner. Two large floor fans created a small hurricane for those in front of them but did little for the general stuffiness of the room. Open windows would certainly have been an advantage.

Just inside the doors Sue and Josh stopped in front of an older woman, seated among several teenagers, with a preschool aged girl on her lap. "What a special treat to have you with us tonight, Miss Emma," said Sue. "You must be feeling pretty good."

Miss Emma's eyes twinkled with welcome. "Well, I just had to come out and meet our new schoolteacher. Besides, this is the last weekend before Lloyd and Ethel go back to high school in Williston, and they promised to pick me up and take me home early."

When Sue introduced Miss Emma, Amanda looked into sparkling eyes that flashed a welcome. Her face reminded Amanda of the wrinkled apple-faced dolls she'd bought when she traveled through north Georgia with her family as a child. The wrinkles etched a road map around her smiling brown eyes and mouth.

"We're happy to have you with us, Amanda," said Miss Emma. "I hope you'll keep these kids' minds open to new ideas. They need to be able to think for themselves."

Amanda looked into the woman's eyes. "That's what I enjoy doing," she said.

As they moved on Sue said, "Miss Emma is loved by folks of all ages. The young people particularly enjoy her since she talks with them about things that interest them. I don't think she's traveled much, but she seems to have a wealth of knowledge about what's happening in the world. She keeps the bookmobile busy and can even get into some serious theological debates."

Several seats down from Miss Emma sat a man whose shape reminded Amanda of a fire hydrant. Sue introduced Otto Gill, and his wife, Hannah. She said, "These two are strong leaders in our little church. Otto is the treasurer, and Hannah leads the women's group."

As they moved on around the room, Sue introduced her to a couple with a young boy. "Amanda, meet Willis, Wilda, and Jimmy. You remember I told you that Bill Bates is on our school board. Willis runs his ranch and does double duty when Bill is away. They live on the ranch too, and Willis hires a crew to help him."

Jimmy spoke up. "I'll be in the third grade this year, and you will be my teacher. I'm excited that school will start. I don't see my friends as much during the summer."

Amanda gave the boy a big smile. "I'm pretty excited about school starting too. You will have to help me with names, because I've not met most of the students."

True to their promise, Sue and Josh ambled on along the walls, introducing her to most of the adults in the room. Amanda's head began to spin with names. She knew that many were related in some way but trying to keep them straight only made matters worse. Her usual method of remembering names seemed to rush out the door. She began to run out of associations. The jeans and western shirts had too much similarity, and the faces began to bleed together.

After circling the room with introductions, Josh asked Amanda if she would like to dance. Never having danced to country music, she mentally questioned her wisdom in coming. She accepted Josh's offer, and they moved onto the dance floor. The beat of the band was steady and strong, and Amanda found herself caught up in the music. The flow of dancers along the outer edge of the dance floor seemed to move in a counterclockwise direction around the room, while those in the middle found their own paths. Josh guided her into the flow around the edges, and Amanda wondered if this pattern was an unconscious decision among the whole community. This division allowed the less experienced dancers opportunity to dance with no fear of bumping into one another.

When the music stopped, Josh led Amanda to the side, and Willard John stepped to the microphone. "All right. Now it's time for you kids to have your own dance. It doesn't matter if you have a partner or not. Just come on out and dance the Crocodile Rock!"

As the music began, children poured out from among the crowd. Amanda recognized Joel Karr dancing with a couple of grade-school girls. She wondered if they were Marilyn and Mandy. Nearby several young children twisted and stomped to the music. One of them appeared to be hardly old enough to walk. As she looked across the room and saw Miss Emma patting her foot and nodding her head to the music, Amanda recognized the occasion as a true intergenerational community experience, creating joy for all ages.

After the children's dance, the band took a break and Josh and Sue asked Amanda if she'd like something to drink. Looking around, Amanda saw no indication of a refreshment table, but Josh led them out to the parked car. Josh opened the back of the station wagon, and Sue spread a cloth on the tailgate. She opened a cooler and lifted out a plate of hors d'oeuvres and glasses.

"The only place to get a drink in Stoney Butte is the bar," explained Sue. "The bar is so crowded that we usually bring our own drinks. Some folks go to their cars and just pass around a bottle of liquor and then a bottle of some sort of chaser, not bothering with glasses. But we prefer to either mix our drinks or have wine. What is your choice? We also brought some sodas."

"A glass of wine is fine with me," said Amanda. "This is almost like a picnic with good friends."

Sue smiled. "We thought you might as well get acquainted with our version of hospitality at the dances. Although we have a small kitchen in the town hall, there's no running water, and so we have to haul gallons of water when we use it. Someday maybe we'll drill a well like the one you're hooked up to at the school. There is an outhouse behind the building, but most folks in town just walk home if they need to use a restroom."

"At least the walk is close enough for me," commented Amanda.

The rest of the evening went smoothly, and by the time the band played the last number, Amanda had learned her way around the dance floor, even dancing in the middle of the room with more accomplished partners. She hoped she would remember the names of most of the men she had danced with as well as the women she sat and visited with.

After Sue and Josh dropped her off, Amanda sat on the sofa with Aggie recalling the evening. She realized that most families either couldn't afford babysitters or had to travel several miles just to pick up and take babysitters home, and so the children naturally became a part of the dances. Toward the end of the evening quilts had been spread in the corners of the dance floor, and young children slept as soundly as in their own beds. After the last song was played, parents lifted the children into their cars without a single child's waking cry. This had become their life.

There was a world of difference between the formal balls of Atlanta and the family dances of Stoney Butte. Was this the other end of the universe?

Chapter Seven

The next morning Neil Welburn pulled up to his usual parking place between his house and the church. He had opened the building and turned up the heat before going to preach at the Prairie Creek Church. He looked around, recognizing all the cars parked near the church. This would not be a big congregation. He supposed that some of his flock stayed in bed this morning after the dance last night.

When Neil stood in the pulpit and faced the congregation, he was surprised to see Miss Emma sitting between Lloyd and Ethel, the teens who would be returning to high school in Williston on Tuesday. They must have picked her up this morning so that she could attend the service. When Neil first came to Stoney Butte, he was surprised to see fifteen-year-olds driving. Then he learned that the driving age was low in the Dakotas and Montana because teenagers needed to drive in order to work on their ranches, and many of them had to drive themselves to school.

Mentally, Neil reviewed his sermon plans, thinking how he and Miss Emma often disagreed theologically. He planned to use verses from the 30th chapter of Numbers, in the Old Testament, where God commands Moses to send 12,000 men out to destroy the Midianite nation, including men, boys, and women who were not virgins. He knew that he would probably get a rise from Miss Emma after the service.

During the first hymn, as was his custom, Neil counted the number of worshipers. Twenty-two today; the number was a bit down. He noted that Ms. Davidson had not come to church. Perhaps she was recovering from too much indulgence at the Labor Day dance. Sue and Josh were in their seats, however, and they usually attended the dances. He probably should add dancing to the list of things that God frowns upon if such events draw folks away from church.

At the close of the service, Miss Emma stopped to speak to Neil as he stood at the door. He reached out and shook her hand. She squeezed it and said, "I somehow don't believe that you and I worship the same God, Neil. The God that I've come to know would never demand that a nation go out and totally obliterate another country. I think those people were just looking for affirmation of their own vengeance. They just didn't understand the true, loving God that I know. Or maybe they were just growing in their understanding of God."

Today Miss Emma didn't wait for a reply. She gave him a smile with her twinkling brown eyes and walked past him to Lloyd's car. The teens followed her, and they drove out of the church yard. Neil knew that Miss Emma's words weren't meant to be cruel. She didn't have a cruel bone in her body. The twinkle in her eye told him that he'd just hit on something they didn't agree on.

As Lloyd and Ethel drove Miss Emma home, Ethel said, "Miss Emma, I can't believe you talked that way to the preacher. He's the one who speaks from God."

"Well," she said, "sometimes we don't hear God the same way. I really believe that in many of those Old Testament stories the people believed they were following God, but their understanding of God had not developed as far as ours has today. Can you imagine Jesus telling an army of men to annihilate a whole country of people? What did Jesus say about loving our neighbor? And I don't think that just meant the person in the house next door."

Ethel thought for a moment. "That's why I enjoy being with you. You don't accept what other people say without thinking about it yourself. And you also listen to our ideas."

"Let me add one more suggestion," said Miss Emma. "Instead of considering the Bible as a literal statement of history and science, or thinking that every word is literally true, think about it as writings that tell about how we, as people, have grown in our understanding of God. If you went back into other records of history, you'd find that the scripture Pastor Neil used this morning fits right into the moral thinking of people of that day. They believed that God was only concerned about their own people and had no real concern for people of other countries or races. But Jesus taught and acted differently."

Lloyd asked, "Where did you come up with these understandings, Miss Emma? Did you go to seminary at one time?"

"No," she laughed. "But I had a good friend who was not afraid to talk with me about things and didn't just accept what someone else told him. Our conversations really made me think, and I think they helped him grow."

"Well, I hope that I can keep growing in my thoughts about the Bible the way you have," said Ethel.

Miss Emma replied, "Just remember to always find out the circumstances of the scriptures when you read them. Sometimes that means reading some books that tell of the customs and the cultures of that time,"

Lloyd glanced at Miss Emma. "We're studying about some very ancient ruins in school right now. The dating of those ruins doesn't seem to correlate with the timing of creation that we've heard from the pastor."

"Yes," answered Miss Emma. "That's another area where Pastor Neil and I don't agree. Most of the time, we just agree to disagree. All of us have a right to our own beliefs. I feel that our faith is our relationship with God, and our beliefs are simply what we believe. For me, it's better to keep faith and beliefs separate. Pastor Neil does seem to have a deep relationship with God, although our beliefs differ. Now that I'm retired I have even more time to talk with God. I know you two are busy with school but remember that you can talk with God in your mind at anytime and anywhere. Just keep your mind open to thinking through what other people tell you about their beliefs. You must make up your mind yourself about those, and not be dictated by others. When the pastor, or anyone else, says something that bothers you, just give it time to mull in your mind. I'll be happy to listen to your thoughts and questions any time. I can't give you pat answers, because those have to be your choices."

After Lloyd and Ethel dropped Miss Emma at her house, Ethel wondered, "Who do you suppose Miss Emma was talking about when she said she had someone in the past who really made her think and dig into her beliefs? She's lived in Stoney Butte all her adult life. Could it be someone who lives here?"

"You're right, she worked on the Bates ranch after she married. Speaking of Bill Bates, what do you suppose he does on those long trips he takes?"

"I don't know. I've wondered that myself many times. Do you suppose we'll ever find out?"

Chapter Eight

Early that morning Amanda had rolled over in bed, reaching for Aggie. The September sun beamed through a frosty window. She was not accustomed to frost this early in the fall. Perhaps she should consider a television so that she could better keep up with the weather. She supposed rabbit ears would not work this far from a station, but she had seen several houses with antennas on the roof or on poles. This would be something to consider after her first paycheck. But then, she could always use the radio. Maybe that would be best.

Slipping into her warm robe, Amanda turned up the heat on her way to the kitchen and the coffee pot. Tuesday would be the first day of school. Last week she had met Ione Wirth, the teacher in the older children's classroom. She seemed pleasant enough, but her room reflected a different style of teaching. Would this cause a conflict? In her thirtieth, and probably last year of teaching, would she feel it her obligation to push Amanda to teach in the manner she used? As Amanda poured herself a cup of coffee and found a comfortable chair, she hoped that she was simply looking for trouble where no trouble lay.

Suddenly her thoughts were interrupted by three short rings. She stood up and walked into the kitchen for the wall phone. She answered with a cheery greeting, "Hello, this morning."

"Hi, Mom." came the familiar voice.

"Kurt! How good to hear your voice. You just made my morning."

"I forgot the time difference. It's almost noon here. Hope I didn't wake you."

"Oh, no. I've been up long enough to make my coffee. I went to the Labor Day dance last night but wasn't out too late. Only had to go three blocks to get there."

"Was it a big one?"

"Quite different from our dances in Atlanta, though you never enjoyed going to the ones your father and I did. They had a five-piece band with guitars, a bass played by a woman, a banjo, and a fiddle. Real western. It took me awhile to get the hang of dancing to the rhythm."

"That doesn't sound like you've run away from everything like you said you would."

"I never said I was running away from everything – just certain things."

Remembering the party lines and the operator on the telephone, Amanda said, "I have to tell you about the telephone system here. We have party lines, and anyone can listen in on your conversation without your even knowing it."

"Oops. I wondered why I had to go through an operator. I guess I shouldn't call you my Run-Away Mom, should I?"

"Just be aware that there's a potential for listeners. You also can't afford long distance calls like this. I know your budget is limited. Have you had any gigs to play for lately besides your night club job?"

"No, in fact my immediate future is something I called you about. I wanted to tell you that I've signed up for a stint in the Peace Corps."

Amanda sat down suddenly. "What! You did what?"

"I signed up for the Peace Corps. I don't want to be drafted."

"But, Kurt, the president is talking about making the armed forces volunteer. Don't join the Peace Corps just to avoid the draft, because I think it will go volunteer."

"I'm not joining just to avoid the draft. I want to give my service, and I don't want to do it in a military situation. I'd really like to go to the Congo. Oops, I forgot the country has a new name, Zaire. Do you remember Richard, my friend who plays the drums?"

"Yes, I remember him. Are you getting mixed up with the Civil Rights Movement?"

"No. I have done a couple of sit-ins, but I'm not officially involved. Anyway, my friend Richard discovered that his roots go back to the slaves that were brought here from that country. He's been looking into the situation there, and they gained their independence in 1960. Richard and I joined the Peace Corps together. We both feel that working to help other people in a peaceful way is more important than the military."

"Oh, Kurt. That sounds so dangerous, even if it is with the Peace Corps. Are you sure this is what you want to do with your life? Although you got your degree in education, I thought you were really dedicated to your music."

"I can certainly use my music in the Peace Corps. I just know this is the direction I need to take right now. Don't worry, Mom. I'll be fine, and you can know that I'll be happy doing this, no matter how difficult it may be. After all, you had to run away to North Dakota when you felt it was your direction."

"Yes, I suppose you must follow your own star. You're an adult. Have you told your sister? What does she think?"

"Ashley thinks I'm crazy, but then you know how she is. She's all into her own equal-opportunity-for-women phase. She will wear herself out trying to climb the corporate ladder and won't enjoy a bit of real living."

"I guess you're right there. When do you leave for training, and when will you know where you're going?"

"We leave next week. Won't know just where we're assigned until we finish our first phase of the training. We may need to learn French, or the language of the country where we'll work. The official language of Zaire is French because it was a colony of Belgium. We'll have to see just where we'll be assigned."

"Well, you know I'll be thinking about you. Write and keep me informed. These phone calls can get expensive, but I'm glad I was able to talk with you about this."

"Yes, I suppose I'd better sign off. When is the first day with your students?"

"That's the day after tomorrow, the day after Labor Day. I'm looking forward to it."

"That's good. I'll be thinking of you on that day too. I'll write to you when I know my address. I love you."

"I love you too, Kurt. Please take care."

After she hung up the phone, she poured another cup of coffee and looked across a couple of vacant lots from the schoolyard, to the little white church. The service seemed to be over, and cars were pulling out of the parking lot. Amanda wondered if she should have gone to church, but she was certainly happy to be home for Kurt's call. Maybe she needed to think about the different directions she and Kurt were now taking with their lives. She'd definitely felt that she needed to take this contract to teach in this tiny town at the end of the universe. Was this a "God thing"? Was God nudging Kurt to make this dedication to the Peace Corps? She just couldn't believe that there was a God who had a plan for your life. She had made the decision to move to North Dakota herself, and Kurt had made his decision, even though Richard's influence had weighed in on that. It was just too much to think about right now. The first day of classes was enough to occupy her mind.

She got up and looked in the refrigerator for the eggs and bacon that had been a part of her "pounding".

Chapter Nine

The first day of school dawned bright without frost. Amanda was ready when the big bell in the front yard tolled the beginning of the school day. One of the eighth-grade boys was enjoying his responsibility of ringing the bell. Ione had told her that they reserved this privilege for the eighth graders, hoping that it would keep some of them in school a little longer. Many of the children saw absolutely no advantage to school beyond learning to read and do enough math to assure they weren't cheated when they bought or sold something. Amanda hoped she could instill a love for learning in the students of her class.

She stood at the door greeting the students as they entered. She had made large name tags and placed them on their desks. These indicated where they should sit, at least for now. When they had hung up their coats and placed their lunch boxes on the shelf, she asked them to find their seats according to their names. She told the older children to help the first graders read their names.

After the students settled down, she began her introductory talk. "Good morning, children. We'll be working together this year, and I want to get to know you better. That's the main thing we'll be doing today. All of you know each other, but I'm new to Stoney Butte, so you're going to have to help me. We'll do our introductions in a way that you would introduce someone to a friend. I'll put you together in twos, and I want you to talk to each other and find out something about the other person that you don't know. It might be something that they did this summer, or it might be a new animal or a new game they learned to play. You will also need to think about just what you already know about the other person, because remember that I don't know much about anyone. Then you will introduce that person to me. I'll show you how we do it once you've talked together."

The students practiced introductions the rest of the morning, and Amanda began to learn about the likes and dislikes of her students as well as some of the work, activities, and events that filled up their days. After lunch she pulled a book out of her bookcase and asked several of the older students to take turns reading a story to the younger students. This gave her an idea of their reading ability. To close the day of introductions, she asked each student to draw a picture of something that made them special, and they posted them around the room.

After the students left, Ione came into Amanda's classroom and asked, "How did it go? Did you get to know the students a little better?"

"That's the main thing we concentrated on today. I do have grades from last year for the returning students, but I like to get a better understanding of each student myself. Although I'm working with a wider age range than in my previous classes, it's nice to have a smaller number. In Atlanta our classes often number in the high twenties or even thirties. I hope to be able to tailor the curriculum to each individual student."

"I've been teaching these children so long that I feel I know them like they're my own children, or perhaps grandchildren, since I taught most of their parents," said Ione. "Maybe my teaching isn't as effective as it should be since I've done it so long. I seem to get into a rut and just repeat things over and over."

"Maybe we can brainstorm different ideas throughout the year," suggested Amanda. "I'm sure you have some ideas that will help me."

Later, as she reviewed the day, Amanda thought about Marilyn and Mandy. While most of the children told about rodeos and games, as well as work at home, the introductions for these girls told only of their work at home. Marilyn, the third grader, was introduced by another third grader. He said she had worked in the garden most of the summer, but he also said that she found butterflies almost every day she was in the garden and watched a mother bird feed her babies in the tree behind their trailer. This affirmed what Sue had said about the positive attitude these girls had about their hard life.

Mandy was interviewed by Joel, and he said that she canned vegetables from the garden. She liked to see the different colors of the vegetables in the clear jars. Then Joel added, "The vegetables in our store aren't in jars, but the pictures on the cans are different colors." This brought a laugh from the class. Mandy seemed to have a great appreciation for the little things in life. Amanda was anxious to get to know their mother, because she felt certain that the woman's understanding of life had a great influence on her daughters.

Most of the introductions helped Amanda get a grasp on the children, and she had taken numerous notes. Her class was small enough she hoped to pay a visit to each household sometime in the near future. That shouldn't be too hard, considering the size of the class, and some of the students were siblings. It would give her more insight into how to approach the children as she taught.

Chapter Ten

Bill Bates slowed to make the deep curve in the gravel road. It had been six months since he traveled this road, but he still knew it well. The landscape was so different from the many roads he'd traveled during the past six months. It had been a positive six months, and he felt he had made progress. Now he was back on the prairie.

Although he grew up in this country, the contrast made it an entirely different world. He thought about the people in the little town of Stoney Butte and the surrounding ranches and remembered them as friendly as the ones he'd worked with for the past six months. He would enjoy a conversation with Miss Emma. She was like a second mother for him, especially since his parents died. How many times had he sat on the stool in the big ranch kitchen and talked with her about people, and also about God? He knew their conversations made a big influence on his decision to make these trips. However, he was the one who chose to keep his destinations and purpose secret. Most everyone in Stoney Butte would not understand just why he did this.

As he pulled into the ranch road and drove under the BB Ranch sign, his old home seemed to greet him. He noticed that Willis was mending a fence as he neared the house. Willis and Bill went way back, even to the small two room schoolhouse years ago. They had bonded as no others. He was anxious to find out what had happened since he left six months ago. He had been in and out of the Stoney Butte life more times than he could count.

After high school Bill wanted a bigger city life, and so he went to the University of Minnesota and majored in horticulture. At first, he enjoyed the Twin Cities, but shortly after he graduated, he headed back to the prairie. He liked the openness of the Dakotas and eastern Montana, but he missed the vegetation so much that he convinced his father to build a greenhouse so that he could start a business. The greenhouse was a great success, although he had to bring in most of the soil and then transport his flowers and trees to Williston, Bismarck, and Miles City to sell. Over several years he had built up his company so that he could leave it now in Willis' care and take the trips that he felt were so important. Willis was not only a great manager of the greenhouses, but also took care of the ranch that Bill inherited. Willis hired a good crew to work with him, and between the two enterprises Bill made enough money to finance his other interest.

Willis and his wife, Wilda, were the only persons who knew just where to locate Bill, should an emergency arise during his time away. They lived on the ranch and managed it well.

"Hello, stranger!" came Willis' usual greeting. "We've missed you in these parts."

"And I've missed everyone here," responded Bill. "How are Wilda and the young one?"

"Couldn't be better. They'll be glad to see you. Wilda said she's cooking your favorite supper tonight. Bless her, she knew you'd be here in time. Jimmy is in the third grade now. You won't believe how he's grown since you left!"

Both men were in their late forties, but neither had married until Willis met Wilda at a horse auction several years ago. When

Jimmy was born, Bill immediately became a favorite "uncle". He especially missed the tow-headed guy this time while he was away.

As Bill grabbed his duffle bag, Willis began to catch him up on the latest news. "The new schoolteacher got here a few days ago. I helped set up her trailer and then saw her at the Labor Day dance. Quite a nice-looking gal, about our age I would guess. Of course, Bertha is keeping up on all that goes on around town, including who's talking about the schoolteacher. She said that she has a son who called her on Sunday. We have a new preacher too, and some of the folks are trying to hook them up together. Hearing a few of his sermons, I doubt that it will work. He's pretty fundamental in his beliefs, and she's from Atlanta and didn't go to church on Sundays. You'll have to form your own opinion about that match."

Bill laughed, "I'm no matchmaker, and you know I believe that everyone has the right to his or her own decisions."

Willis slung his arm around Bill as they headed for the house. Bill was anxious to take a shower before dinner. He looked forward to relaxing and enjoying Wilda's cooking. The meal turned out to be as good as he remembered, quite different from what he'd become accustomed to in the past six months.

After dinner Bill listened to Jimmy tell about his new teacher, and then he and Willis retired to the office at Bill's house, to go over the ranch and greenhouse affairs. Willis never contacted him during his absences unless it was something major, but when he returned Willis always caught him up on the business. Everything seemed in order, as he expected. He felt fortunate to have him running the ranch during his absences.

This year Willis said they had a heavy spring snow which caught everyone by surprise, but the BB Ranch came through it fine. Several ranchers lost sheep, since they huddle together in a crevice when it snows. The snow drifted several feet, covering the animals. Willis helped one rancher dig his sheep out of the wet snow, but the storm brought a real loss for many ranchers. The roads were blocked for three days before the county dynamited and the plow could get through. The community of Stoney Butte was accustomed to this, and everyone stored up for such occasions and shared with neighbors when necessary.

When Bill asked Willis about Miss Emma he said, "She's her same lively old self. Lloyd and Ethel took her to the Labor Day dance, and she tapped her foot the whole time. They've been taking her to church most Sundays this summer. I know she'll be glad to see you."

"That's one of the first things on my list. Is there anything you need me to attend to in the morning? If not, I'll head to town to see her."

"No, you go on to town and let folks know you're home."

Bill laughed. "I wouldn't have to leave the ranch to do that. All I'd have to do is pick up the phone. Bertha has known my voice ever since I tried to play pranks on her as a child."

"Those were some fun days," said Willis with a smile. "I don't know how much longer Bertha and Neman can hold off the bigger companies that want to buy them out. Then kids will no longer be able to make prank calls to Bertha."

With the business of the ranch and the news about the community finished, Willis returned home, and Bill headed to bed for some much-needed sleep.

Chapter Eleven

The next morning Bill drove the six miles into town. As he crossed the bridge into Stoney Butte, he thought how the town had changed in the last 15 to 20 years. When he was a child there were more people living in town, with a clothing store and a small bank. They were all closed now, except the grocery. Buster Dooley still had a gas station, but it was rebuilt, and the post office operated out of half of the building. Of course, there was still the bar, and Dean and Laura Bagley still opened their little café during the summer months with good home cooking. They usually left the day after Labor Day. Bill thought they about broke even, but Laura loved to cook, and they did quite well during the rodeo in mid-August. He'd missed the annual fair and rodeo this year, but he had other things to do. Once again, Bill thought about the difference between his little town and the people where he'd spent the past six months.

As Bill drove the three blocks to Miss Emma's, he remembered the story about her growing up years. She was born of a single mother, and everyone in her hometown continually asked her who her daddy was. She hated to be asked, because she had no idea who he was, and her mother would not tell her. On the first Sunday that they had a new pastor at their church, her mother had gone out of the building ahead of her. When she approached the pastor standing at the door, he said, "Hi, little girl. Who is your daddy?" Everyone waiting to speak to the pastor seemed to freeze.

The pastor recognized the tension and said, "I know who your daddy is. You're a child of God." Miss Emma told Bill how that changed her life. After that she held her head high when anyone asked her and said, "I'm a child of God." And, as she put it, she's been a child of God ever since.

Bill relished in the stories the old woman told, both about her childhood and about the world in general. She always read the papers and mourned over those who were deprived, whether near or far away. Bill thought her heart was as big as the whole world.

Miss Emma must have had a premonition that he was back in town, because as soon as she opened the door Bill smelled his favorite cookies, snickerdoodles. He remembered rolling the messy dough balls in sugar before placing them on the cookie sheet in the big ranch kitchen. *Memories are made of this.* He hoped that the children he'd been with for the past six months would have fond memories as they grew older.

"You are a sight for old eyes," greeted Miss Emma. "Don't know when I've been more anxious to see you. I need someone to talk to who won't put me down."

"Who's been bullying you, Miss Emma? Tell me and I'll set them straight."

Her smile deepened the wrinkles of her face as she said, "Guess it's no one in particular, but I just need some good conversation like we always have. That new minister is nice enough, but he and I don't agree on lots of things, and we've sort of called a truce about conversations of any depth."

Bill smiled. "Yes, I hear we have a new preacher. Is he a young sprout?"

"Not so young, but his spiritual ideas haven't matured much, very literal in his interpretation of the Bible. He spent several years in the Coast Guard and had a conversion experience that he throws in our face from time to time. Went to a conservative seminary and is not yet fully connected with the conference. Not sure he will make it if he doesn't begin to think for himself.

"But, enough about him for now. Tell me how you are doing. Did you keep well during these past six months? Are you getting enough to eat? Have you been sleeping well?"

"Oh, Miss Emma," said Bill as he gave her frail body a hug. "You are still my second mama. Don't know how I'd get along if I didn't know you were here worrying and praying for me. Who's taking care of you?"

"Shaw!" she responded. "I don't need anyone to take care of me. Besides, little Joel brings me the groceries I need from his grandparents' store, and Lloyd and Ethel take me to church most of the time. Can't ask for much more at my age."

Miss Emma took a milk bottle from the refrigerator and set a plate of snickerdoodles in front of Bill. "Now, sit down and tell me what you've been doing these past six months."

Milk and snickerdoodles had always been their way of catching up, and Bill took his time filling her in on his latest adventure. She understood all his struggles. In fact, it was because of her influence that Bill spent months away from home each year. He would always be indebted to her for helping him find this pleasure in life.

Bill shifted in his chair. "Now, you tell me about the latest gossip here in Stoney Butte."

"Pretty much the same as usual," said Miss Emma. "There is a new teacher at the schoolhouse from Atlanta. Can't understand just why she left a big city to come to our little town, but she seems pretty nice. I understand she's a widow with grown children."

"Now where did you glean that information?" asked Bill.

"The usual place, over the telephone. Where did you expect? I did meet her at the dance the other night, and she was very nice. Was a good dancer too, once she got the hang of our western style of dancing. You'll have to meet her."

"Don't you go hooking me up with some southern belle. You know I'm more liberal than southerners, thanks to you."

Miss Emma's eyes lit up. "We've had some good conversations over the years, haven't we? You've been a good listener when I needed to express my opinions."

Bill put his hand over hers on the table. "You've expressed your opinions, and those opinions have given me fodder for thought. But you never pushed your ideas on me. I'd not be the man I am today if we hadn't had those discussions."

"Oh, Peshaw," she said. "You had that good man inside you all along. It just took time for it to come out. But seriously, I do want to get to know this teacher better myself, and I'd like for you to meet her too. I'm not sure if it will be at church, however, she hasn't been to a service yet. Maybe she heard just how dogmatic this new preacher is."

He laughed. "Well, in this little town of 92 people, I think it's pretty likely that this new teacher and I will meet somewhere or other."

The visit with Miss Emma refreshed Bill's soul. He knew that others would tease him about the new teacher, but he had a few items he wanted to purchase at the store. He had bought some things on his way home from the airport. He wanted to give

Delmer and Leola his business, so he always went to the little store for what he knew they carried. He'd get some canned vegetables, rice, and other staples.

Delmer was restocking the shelves when the little bell tinkled as Bill opened the door. "Well, look who's here," declared Delmer. "Leola, come on out here and see this foreigner." Leola came in from the back room with a smile on her face and open arms. He had been a favorite of hers ever since he was a tiny boy.

"We heard you were back," she said. Bill knew just how she'd learned that – just like all the other gossip in their little town.

"I don't know how we'll keep up with the news if Bertha and Neman ever sell out to a big company," Bill said.

"That won't happen until they can't physically do their work," Leola said. "Bertha couldn't stand to live around here and not know everything that's happening."

Delmer and Leola must have known not to ask Bill about his trip. Those trips had gone on for so many years that everyone just knew that there was no reason to ask because they'd just get the same answer: the trip was "fine", no details. Those trips were Bill's secret, and no one had been able to crack the nut to learn just where he went nor why. He always looked rested when he returned, and although everyone speculated, the specifics were beyond the community's questioning.

As Delmer was filling out the list of groceries, Leola naturally brought up the new teacher. "Joel really likes the new teacher," she began. "She has some ideas about teaching that are different from what this school's used to. She even asked us if we would come to her class one day and tell about what we do to keep the store running. I also heard her ask Willard John if he'd tell about being a mail carrier."

Bill looked surprised. "You mean Willard John will talk to the kids at school? I've hardly heard him say more than three sentences at one time, even when we were in school. She must have a way of asking."

"Well, she just said she wanted the children to have an idea of what different jobs involved and for the kids to learn about the work that people do," explained Leola. "She does have a lovely smile too. That certainly helps."

"How is she getting along with Ms. Ione? She should be about to retire. It seems she's been teaching since God made dirt," Bill said.

Delmer piped in. "Yes, this may be her last year. We've not heard of any conflict there, but so far Mrs. Davidson's been pretty quiet about that. And you know Ione. She just doesn't talk about anything."

By the time Delmer finished filling Bill's order, he'd pretty well caught up on all the gossip of the little town. Happy to be filled in, Bill headed for the ranch. Now any time someone started to give him some gossip, he could say he's already heard it and ward off a long gossip conversation.

Chapter Twelve

Amanda stepped out the door of her new home into the brisk fall air. When she'd left Atlanta, they were experiencing record heat. Now, several weeks later, she shivered in the North Dakota fall air. She made her way across the few yards to the schoolhouse. As she entered her room, she recognized sounds of Ione moving around in the other classroom. She stepped into Ione's room and noticed one wall covered with pictures drawn by the students. "These are interesting," she said.

Ione replied. "When I saw what you'd done to get to know the students, I thought I'd ask my students just what they'd like to do when they finished school. I was surprised that I got some new insights into these students that I thought I knew so well. This picture shows that Jason wants to be a doctor, and I had no idea that he had an interest in that. Of course, he's made good grades in his science courses, but a doctor?"

Amanda laughed. "These kids can certainly surprise you sometimes. I'm going to have some of the people in the community come in and tell us about what they do for a living. Would you like to combine our classes for that? And maybe we can have a doctor come out from Williston to talk to the class. You never know what will come of these children."

"I would like that. Maybe Sue can help us locate people in the medical field, even though she's not been in that career for a while.

You know, Bill Bates has greenhouses where he grows plants. He ships them to large cities. Have you met Bill?"

"No, but I've heard his name mentioned. Isn't he out of town?"

Iona finished wiping the blackboard. "He was, but I heard Bertha say that he's back now. I wonder just what he does when he leaves for such a long time. It's a good thing that he has Willis to take care of the ranch and greenhouses. Those two are pretty smart, but they were a handful when I had them in my class."

The teachers talked for a few minutes about other careers that they might explore with the children. As Amanda made her way back to her classroom, she smiled to herself. *Maybe Ione and I can get along together this year, after all.* She resolved to take it slow and easy and from time to time ask Ione's advice about things. She had always learned from other teachers in her past schools, and she knew there were things she could learn from a woman who had taught in a two-room school for almost 30 years.

When the bell rang, the students entered the room, full of energy. Jimmy excitedly ran to her desk. "Ms. Davidson, guess what. Todd and Timothy are back. They used to live here, but they moved to Dickinson. They're living in the old Byers place. Todd's in Ms. Ione's room, but Timmy is in my grade."

A rather timid boy in outgrown clothes peered out from behind Jimmy. He gave the boy a shove, filling Amanda with a smile. "Here's Timmy. His whole name is Timothy, named after some guy in the Bible. But that's too long a name, so we call him Timmy. I knew him before he moved to Dickinson. Can he sit by me?"

Amanda smiled at the new boy. "We're happy to have you with us. Jimmy is anxious for you to sit beside him. You will need to sit in the empty seat behind him since Marilyn already as her things in the desk beside him. I do want all of you third graders to sit together.

"What is your last name, Timmy?"

"It's Cazer," he said in a quiet voice.

"Are you related to the Melton Cazer who owns the sawmill?"

"Yes'm. He's my father's uncle," Timmy replied.

As the new student went to claim his seat, Amanda realized that he was limping. Perhaps a visit to his home should come before her other visits.

That afternoon, as the children left, Amanda gave each a note for their parents, explaining that she wanted to get to know the children better and would like to visit in each home. She asked for specific times that would be convenient for them.

The next morning, most of the children brought the note back with suggestions for times for a visit. Amanda looked them over and decided that the visit to Timmy's home would be the following Saturday morning. She sent a note back confirming that time.

That afternoon Amanda asked Ione the location of the old Byers place. Ione said, "That family has been in and out of Stoney Butte for years. Timmy's father has hopscotched jobs all his life. This time they're living in the old Byers place just on this side of the Montana line, on the way to the Biscoffs'. You'll recognize it by the big wrap around porch and the broken-down fence."

On Saturday morning as she approached the house, the appearance told her it had not been lived in for some time. Timmy's mother met her at the door and invited her in. There was little furniture in the house, although it was big and roomy. She was led to the kitchen and offered a cup of coffee. She noticed that the mug had a small chip in it but decided to ignore it. Perhaps this was the best mug they had. There was a large wood cook stove, which she suspected to be the only heat in the house. Behind the stove was a large bag of oatmeal. She wondered if this was their staple food. Through the back window she saw a cow, munching on grass.

Timmy's mother apologized for the outside of the house. "We haven't had time to do anything to the outside. The house has not been lived in for several years, and we actually had to take the hose and wash down the whole inside. This is what the previous woman who lived here did every spring." A small giggle escaped her lips. "When we were children, we used to make fun of her yearly spring cleaning. She would move all of the furniture outside and really give it a wash down. Now I found myself doing the same thing, but I don't think I'll do that every spring."

Suddenly Timmy burst through the back door, limping even worse than he had in school. His foot was tied in a flannel bandage. "You did come to visit us. Some of the kids said you'd never visit because we don't have a fancy house."

"Oh, Timmy. Of course, I wanted to see you," Amanda said. "I see that you have a bandage on your foot today. I hope it's getting better."

Timmy's mother said, "He stepped on a nail, and it was fine at first. But then it seemed to be getting festered, so I followed the cow around and caught some of its poop before it hit the ground and made a poultice to put on the red part of his foot. That should draw the infection out."

Amanda quickly swallowed the coffee she had just sipped so as not to spew it across the room. It was hard to keep a neutral face. "I've never heard of that sort of treatment before. Does it really work?"

Timmy smiled. "Oh, yes, ma'am. Mama's done that for both of us boys when we get an infection. Do you want to see what I just made this morning?"

Amanda was happy for the change of subject and followed him to his room. There, laid out on the table, was a map of North Dakota with most of the roads and towns filled in. "Did you make this yourself?" she asked.

"Oh, yes. I like to make maps. See, I've circled the towns where we've lived and darkened the roads we've been on."

Amanda recognized then just why she wanted to visit each home. It always amazed her just what she would learn about a student when she visited their family. She wondered what she would learn that afternoon when she visited Marilyn and Mandy's house. Perhaps she would learn more about their mother's illness.

When Amanda and Timmy returned to the kitchen, Amanda said, "Timmy certainly has a gift for detailing maps."

"Oh," his mother said. "He's always doodling around with something or other with a pencil. He finds something to draw on, even when we're out of paper."

Amanda replied, "Perhaps I can send some scrap paper home with him. That's certainly better than throwing it in the trash, and it will give him something to use for his doodling."

As she left, Amanda decided she would give Timmy opportunities to draw maps on the blackboard during school. His gift for drawing certainly needed to be nurtured. Perhaps he could draw a map of the road they drove when they moved back to Stoney Butte from

Dickenson. Many of the children had never been that far from this little town.

Chapter Thirteen

Amanda had arranged to visit Marilyn and Mandy's home that afternoon. After stopping by her trailer for a quick lunch, she decided to walk. Ione had told her just where it was – close by, behind the Methodist Church. When she knocked on the door of the small trailer, Mandy opened it with a smile.

"Please come in," she said. "Mama has been anxious to meet you. She doesn't get out much, so she's always glad to have company."

Amanda stepped into the tiny trailer noticing the sparse, but spotless interior. The girls' mother, Myrtle Mae, greeted her with a smile and an outstretched hand. She was a small woman with soft, dark curls all over her head, and sparkling eyes. Her smile cut a dimple into her left check. She sat with her legs stretched out on the sofa. Amanda realized that she must be in an early stage of Multiple Sclerosis, because her arms and legs looked normal.

After the girls introduced Amanda, Myrtle Mae said, "I'm a bit tired today. I don't know what I'd do without the girls. Marilyn, will you please get us some tea and those cookies you baked?"

After they had discussed the weather and drunk their tea, Amanda felt quite at home. She asked Myrtle Mae, "Have you lived in Stoney Butte all your life?"

"Heavens, no, I grew up in Minnesota in a small town, in the midst of Superior National Forest. It wasn't much bigger than our little town here, but we did have many more trees and lakes around us. The girls were so small when we left that they don't remember any of it. I've wanted to take them back to see that part of the country, but don't know if it will happen. Stoney Butte is a nice little town for the girls to grow up in. It's friendly, and so far they've had some pretty good teachers in our little schoolhouse."

"Well, I hope I can live up to that standard," answered Amanda.

"From what the girls tell me, you're doing a good job so far. They certainly like you."

As Marilyn sank to the floor beside her mother, she smiled and said, "You even gave Miss Ione a new idea. She had her students draw pictures of what they'd like to be when they grow up."

"And what would you like to be?" asked Amanda.

"I want to do medical research so that I can help people with Multiple Sclerosis like my mother." She put a hand on her mother's arm, which brought a loving smile from Myrtle Mae.

Amanda said, "When we had introductions in our classroom, Mandy told about how much she enjoyed the different colors of vegetables when she helped canning them in jars. I'm sure you have a large garden to be able to can so many vegetables."

Myrtle Mae motioned out the back window. "Yes, the girls help their father plant the garden each spring and work all summer, watering it and pulling weeds. We usually get a big yield. I have to eat healthy foods, and canning them ourselves is the best way to be sure that they are nutritious."

Amanda's eyes lit up. "Those must have been your beans that I received at the pounding when I moved into my home. They were delicious. I'll make sure that I give the jar to Mandy."

"Another thing the girls do is to wash once a week. We took the sink and toilet out of the trailer, built a nice outhouse, and put a washer and dryer in the room instead. In the cold of the winter, it's nice to wash clothes inside and not have to hang them outside to dry. It just made more sense to us."

Amanda decided that the wisdom of that would take some thought, so she just smiled and pushed the idea to the back of her mind for another time.

"What brought you here?" Amanda asked.

"Well, when the girls were still toddlers, and before I began to have symptoms of Multiple Scleroses, my husband, Wenzel, lost his job in Minnesota when his company closed down. His cousin in Williston told him about a job with the little lumber mill here. He actually has more responsibility here than he did there. He's in charge of the tree cutting on Stoney Butte. Have you been up on the butte yet? It's surprising that the only trees that grow naturally in this area are in the river bottom or creek beds and on the butte. It's not as stony as you would think from the name."

"That sounds like a nice place to go. I grew up in Georgia, and I do miss the trees that were everywhere there. I read that if the land that Atlanta sits on belonged to the Forest Service it would have enough trees per acre to qualify for a timber cut. Yes, I would enjoy a trip up the butte."

Mandy piped up. "We'll go with you and show you some of the cool places, if you'd like."

Amanda smiled. "I'd like that very much." She turned to Myrtle May. "I know you don't get out much, but are there occasions when you can go to some town functions?"

Myrtle Mae answered. "Oh, yes. I even went to the rodeo this year. I used a wheelchair and didn't stay long, but it was so good to see other people. If I'm feeling well, I always go to the school play at Christmas."

Amanda looked surprised. "I haven't heard about that. Where is it held? Do both classes combine to put it on?"

Myrtle Mae explained. "It's held in the town hall. I hear you went to a dance there with Sue and Josh. All the children usually have a part in the play. It's a great time for the whole community to get together. Also, in order to raise money, the Methodist Church has an auction just after Thanksgiving. They make handcrafted items throughout the year. Since it's hard for me to get to Williston, it's a good opportunity to do some Christmas shopping. Most of my other shopping I do by catalog."

Amanda mused, "I suppose that I had better start thinking about the Christmas play. We need plenty of time for the children to memorize their parts."

"If you'd like a play that's original, I'd be happy to work with you on it," said Myrtle May. "I used to do a lot of writing when I lived in Minnesota. I even have a typewriter. Never had anything published, but I enjoyed it."

"That would be great," beamed Amanda. "We wouldn't have to pay any royalties that way. I'm sure our school budget is tight. I'll talk to Ione and get back with you."

Myrtle Mae commented, "We may not be living in this trailer much longer. We have a promise of a house from one of the ranches nearby. We plan to move it to a lot Wenzel bought behind the town hall, one big enough for a garden. We almost have enough money to pay for the move."

"That would give you more room, I'm sure", Amanda replied. "I know that the girls will let me know when you're moved."

"Oh," laughed Myrtle Mae, "I'm sure everyone in town will know. The men at the lumber yard have promised to help Wenzel pour the foundation and flooring. We've already contacted a house moving company in Williston to come out and move the house. Our little town will make it a big occasion."

Myrtle Mae changed the subject, "Have you gone to church yet? The girls attend Sunday school every Sunday, and I try to get there several times a year. It's only a one-room church, and Marilyn and Mandy's Sunday school teacher holds their class behind the piano because some of the boys try to distract the preschool class. Our new preacher has only been here a couple of months. I understand he was in the Coast Guard before he went to seminary. I haven't heard him preach yet, but the girls often come home with questions about what he says."

"I'm glad that they listen, and it's always good to think about what's being said and even question it, whether at church or at school," said Amanda.

Marilyn spoke up. "He says that the earth isn't as old as our science books tell us. He says that the books are written just to fool us. I don't think that's right. Do you, Ms. Davidson?"

Amanda took time to think, realizing she was getting into a more theological area than she'd expected. "You must remember that the Bible was written by people who didn't know what we've learned about science, and they were trying their best to make sense of our world and how it came about. Sometimes we need to think in ways that they thought in order to understand just why they wrote certain things."

Mandy said, "I wish you would teach our Sunday school class. You would let us ask questions and think about things."

"Well, that's just the way I think. The Bible has some great things to say about how we should treat others, and it also has some stories of ways that people treated others badly. God gave us a mind, and we have to use it, even when we're reading the Bible. We must remember that the writers of the Bible didn't know a lot of things that we know today. For instance, they thought the world was flat because they knew only the part of the world close around them."

Mandy smiled. "And today we know that it is round. People have traveled all around the world and come back to tell us about it. I like the big globe that you brought for us to see how it is round."

"The globe is one of my favorite things to use in teaching. I find something new when I take time to look at it closely."

"Ms. Davidson, I didn't think you had anything more to learn. Didn't you go to college for several years?" asked Mandy.

Amanda laughed. "You'd be surprised at the many things I discover every day. We just need to keep our eyes and our minds open to learn."

"I know I'll learn a lot this year. I'm excited about that," said Mandy.

The conversation moved to what the girls would expect from their classes this year, and then Amanda left, knowing Mandy and Marilyn a little better. She mused over just what the girls were hearing from this new preacher. Maybe she should go and hear him herself.

Chapter Fourteen

The next day Amanda woke early enough to go to the little white church. Actually, the building had been white, but much of the paint was now peeling off. As she entered, Neil came up to welcome her. He said he needed to speak to the pianist, but he would enjoy seeing her after the service. As he talked to the pianist, Amanda remembered Myrtle Mae's comment that Marilyn and Mandy's class meets behind the piano so that the boys would not distract the preschool class.

As Amanda decided on a seat, she noticed how the sunlight from the window brightened Neil's auburn hair, how his muscles filled out his suit. Although she knew she was older, she was drawn to him. As she sat down, she realized that her attraction to Neil was strictly his looks. Admitting this brought thoughts of her husband. She felt that no one would ever replace the joy she'd felt each time she saw her husband. His untimely death had shaken her, but she was over the shock of the car accident and dwelt on remembering the happy memories now.

Mandy and Marilyn sat in the front row with the man she assumed to be their father. She made a mental note to talk to them after the service.

Just as the pianist began playing the prelude, two men, a woman, and Jimmy from her class slipped into the pew in front of her. She recognized one of the men as a rancher who had helped build the porch for her trailer, and the woman and Jimmy had been among those who brought the meal that day. She didn't remember the names of the adults, and the second man did not look familiar at all.

As they sang the first hymn, Amanda became conscious of the lovely bass and tenor voices of the two men. It might not have surprised her in a church in Atlanta, but the richness of their voices stood out in this tiny church in North Dakota.

The service proceeded with some familiarity, although it had been years since she had attended a worship service. When Neil began his sermon, she listened carefully to hear just what he said. There was nothing she disagreed with during this sermon. She thought that she may need to come additional times to hear anything that Mandy and Marilyn questioned.

When the service was over, she hesitated in the pew since Neil had said he wanted to talk with her. Mandy and Marilyn saw her and rushed back to give her a hug. Then they turned to the strange man in front of her and Mandy said, "Bill! When did you get back?"

A broad smile crossed the man's tanned face as he gathered the two girls to him. "I got home a couple of days ago. I can't believe how you girls have grown while I've been away."

Marilyn said, "Well, you've been gone at least six months. We grow whether you're here or not."

This brought a hearty laugh from Bill. "You still tell it as it is, don't you, Marilyn? Good for you. It is certainly good to have your hugs again."

Amanda was amazed that this man with broad shoulders and a mass of dark curls seemed to enjoy the girls so much. He looked like he was ready to grab them up in his arms and twirl them around if they had been outside. The man that she assumed to be their father beamed.

"How is your mother?" asked Bill.

Mandy replied. "She wasn't feeling too well today, but she felt good yesterday when Ms. Amanda visited us. Have you met our new teacher yet, Bill?"

"No, not yet," replied Bill as he turned to her.

Amanda saw the love for these girls in his dark brown eyes. She thought, *This certainly is a loving town. Everyone seems to be greeting and talking to each other.*

Mandy used the instructions that she had learned at school to properly introduce her to Bill Bates. Then she told her that Bill not only owned a ranch but also had huge greenhouses where he grew plants for people in the cities who didn't have a place to grow them. Her smile disappeared, however, when she said, "But Bill goes on these long trips, and we miss him when he's gone."

Hugging Mandy closer he said, "I miss you too, Miss Mandy."

"Then why do you go on those trips?" she asked.

"It's something that God has put in my heart that I must do," he answered. "Someday, when you're grown up, I may tell you more about the trips."

"Well," she mused. "I guess I'd better keep growing up."

Marilyn smiled as she followed Mandy's lead in introducing their father, Wenzel. Amanda saw that his forehead was lighter than the rest of his face, recognizing the tale tell signs of a man who works outdoors. His straw-colored hair was parted on one side, with wisps around his neck. His smile shot wrinkles beside his deep blue eyes.

Amanda said, "I enjoyed my visit with your family yesterday. I understand you grew up in a Minnesota forest. I'm sure you find it quite different here."

He replied, "Yes, I miss the forest, but when I go up the butte to cut trees for lumber, it gives me a lift."

"We promised Ms. Amanda to show her the butte and all the fun places there," Marilyn said as she looked at her. "Just let us know when you have time to go. I know teaching keeps you pretty busy."

Amanda put her hand on Marilyn's shoulder, "Yes, it keeps me busy, but we'll find a time. I want to visit in the homes of your classmates first. That way I'll get to know all of you better."

Most of the congregation had left the church as their conversation ended. When Amanda turned, she realized that Miss Emma and the two teens who had been with her at the dance were sitting behind her. The teens must have come home for the weekend.

Miss Emma said, "Amanda, I'm glad you had a chance to meet Bill. Mandy, you did a good job of introductions."

"Oh, Ms. Amanda taught us how to do that the first day of school," she said as she skipped down the aisle with Marilyn and her father.

Bill gave Miss Emma a hug and smiled at Amanda, "I'd not be the man I am today without this great lady. She's taught me more than I ever learned in school. She practically raised me. I spent many a day on a stool, helping her in our kitchen on the ranch while her husband took care of the animals." The love between them was evident.

Miss Emma asked if she was going home now. Amanda answered, "The pastor asked me to stay and talk to him."

After everyone else had left the church, Neil came back inside to speak to Amanda. "I'm glad you were able to worship with us today. We're a small group, but the people seem to enjoy our time together on Sunday mornings."

"I saw some familiar faces, and I met some new people today. It is certainly a friendly town."

"I know you're from Atlanta, and this doesn't compare to any large city. I thought you might like to have lunch with me, and we can compare large city living with small towns. The Bagley Café, the only place to eat in town, is closed. The owners go south to escape the cold weather, and they left the day after Labor Day. Would you like to go to the next town over? It's only 20 miles, and there's a little place to eat there. They also serve food at the bowling alley."

Amanda remembered her ride over the gravel road on her way into Stoney Butte. It was an easy decision to make. "I have to work on my lesson plans for tomorrow, so I think I'd better go on home. I thank you, though."

As she opened the trailer door, Amanda heard her three short rings chime from the crank phone. She tossed her purse on the sofa and reached for it. "Mother, what's going on there? You told me that the town had its own telephone service, but I never expected to have to go through an operator to get you."

Amanda remembered her short letter to her daughter. "I guess I didn't tell you all about the telephone system. Yes, we have an operator, and we also have party lines, so others can listen in on your conversation at any time. In fact, that's how much of the news gets around in this little town."

Immediately she thought of some of the members of the church who may have realized she had stayed to talk to Neil. That news must be all over town and to neighboring ranches by now. She was glad she had decided not to go to lunch with him.

"My, gosh!" replied Ashley. "You are in a time warp, aren't you? How is school life there?"

"We now have twenty students in the two classes. A new family moved to town with two more. I only have eleven, and they are all in three grades, so I only have three lesson plans to make. That cuts down on my workload. They are lovely and well-behaved children most of the time. What's happening with you? Have you had any interesting cases lately?"

"Yes, but I think I'd better save those law cases for a letter. The main reason I called was to hear your voice and to tell you that the renters of our house seem to be keeping it up well, at least from the outside. I also checked on your storage unit, and all's well there."

"That's my lawyer daughter, on top of everything. I'm happy to hear your voice too. I think of you and Kurt so often, and I do miss you. Is he still in town?"

"Yes, he's still waiting for his assignment. I can't believe he's going to join the Peace Corps. But then, there's lots about my brother that I can't believe."

Amanda thought, *And he about you! My two diverse children.*

After a little more conversation about mutual friends, they ended their call. Amanda gathered Aggie in her arms and buried her head into her fur. She did miss her children, but they were grown and living lives of their own. Aggie would have to receive her physical loving for now.

Chapter Fifteen

Bill Bates pulled sandwich makings from the refrigerator. He remembered Sundays when Miss Emma had put a roast in the oven before they went to church, and they always had a delicious dinner soon after returning home. Those days were gone, and when he was back at Stoney Butte, his Sundays often felt rather lonely. As he spread the mayonnaise on his bread, he recalled the excitement of Sundays when he was away from home. *Perhaps I should just sell out and leave,* he thought. No, he had too much invested in the ranch, and he truly felt that God wanted him to keep both ventures going. Without the income from his ranch and greenhouses, he could not follow his other calling from God.

He hated not being able to see Miss Emma for several months of the year. She had been his lifeline, not only as a child, but also in his adult decisions. She was the one he went to when he was searching for just what God wanted him to do. She never told him. She only listened; she was a great sounding board for his soul. Although the years were creeping up on her, he felt that God still kept their connection, even when he was elsewhere.

He smiled to himself when he remembered how Mandy had introduced the new teacher to him and how Miss Emma had said she learned her lesson of introductions well. Amanda had turned to him with a smile that seemed to light up the whole room. So many people had mentioned this new teacher, and he could see why. The town seemed to like her. The new pastor, Neil, had asked her to stay until the others left. Bill wasn't overly impressed with this new pastor, but he knew that they often were assigned persons who had just graduated from seminary because they were such a small mission church. He wondered why Neil had asked Amanda to stay to talk to him.

After finishing his sandwich, Bill headed for his greenhouses. He found Sunday afternoons as good times to simply walk through the greenhouses and marvel over the growth that God brought about from the tiny seeds. He remembered the verse from the 13th chapter of Matthew comparing faith to a mustard seed: *Although it is the smallest of all seeds, it grows larger than any garden plant and becomes a tree. Birds even come and nest on its branches (CEV).* The verse had always puzzled him. The only mustard plants he knew were only about one to two feet tall. When he was in college, his curiosity sent him to the university library, and he learned of a mustard bush that can grow 20 to 30 feet tall, with a limb spread of 20 feet. God's world always amazed him. That's why the horticulture course at the university kept him there, even though he didn't like the crowded city. The months he now spent away from Stoney Butte were such a contrast to the surrounding nature of his home. He enjoyed that contrast. Walking through his greenhouses did help him on Sundays.

"What did you think of the new teacher?" Willis startled him from his thoughts.

"She seemed very nice," he replied. "Did you say that no one knows just why she chose to leave Georgia and come to this prairie country?"

"I've heard many answers, but they've only been speculations. Haven't heard anyone say that she's actually told them why, except she was looking for a change and our little ad caught her eye."

"Seems mighty strange to me."

"Many of us have secrets." Willis winked at him. "I guess that's her secret."

"Well, everyone seems to like her, especially the children. Mandy seemed proud as a Georgia peach to introduce her."

Willis said, "I hear she is making visits to every student's home. I'm sure she will find out a lot about our little town that way, as well as her students. Oh, yes, she's inviting several people to talk to the students about their profession. I suppose she will ask you to talk about your greenhouses."

"Delmer and Leola told me about that. She even asked Willard John to talk to the students. Can you believe that? I'll be glad to talk with them. With our Dakota sun, greenhouses are a good venture. I just hope she doesn't try to worm out of me where I go during the months I spend away from here."

"I doubt she will. She seems pretty level-headed to me, not one to seek out gossip. The Cazer family moved back from Dickenson, living in the Byers place. She visited them yesterday, and so far has made no mention of the conditions there, which I'm sure are pretty bad."

"It's nice to know that the new teacher can keep her thoughts to herself. This town is full enough of gossip already."

"Oh, by the way," Willis interjected, "Wilda told me to invite you for supper tonight. It will be a simple meal, but the vegetables come from the garden."

"I will not only get a good meal and company, but a chance to talk to Jimmy again. You are so fortunate to have him."

"I can't imagine what I'd do without him now. Why did it take me so long to have a child?"

"Mainly because it took a while for you to meet Wilda. You'd never have met her here in Stoney Butte, that's for sure. It's a nice town, and my home, but there's lots of world out there beyond the gravel road that leads to this town."

Willis pulled a dead leaf from a plant. "You've sure seen enough of it. If we all took on a mission like yours, we'd be a much better world."

"Everyone isn't cut out for what I do, and God doesn't call all of us to that. Just think of how Miss Emma influenced me. In her adult life she never left this ranch except for an occasional trip to Williston, but she's a wealth of knowledge. I'm sure glad that her health has held up these many years."

"You're right. We all need to follow our own star, and I do enjoy working your ranch and greenhouses."

Just as Willis finished speaking, the sprinklers came on in the greenhouse, and they both ran for the door. "I let time get away from me as I enjoyed the plants you've tended so well," exclaimed Bill as he shook the water from his dark curls. "At least we know that the timer works right."

Willis turned with a smile, and they both went to their houses to find dry clothing.

The evening meal was filled with vegetables, punctuated with the antics of little Jimmy, which suited Bill fine. He went to bed happy to be home, although he missed the people he'd been with for the past six months. His last thoughts were, *This is a good life! I really have the best of two worlds.*

Chapter Sixteen

That afternoon Amanda picked up the phone and gave the handle on the phone-box one long crank. It seemed strange to crank it instead of simply dialing a number. She smiled to herself as she remembered how her parents had talked about crank phones. At the time she had thought this as almost barbaric, but now she was actually doing it herself.

Bertha answered in a short time, although she sounded breathless. "I'm sorry," she said. "There has been so much excitement this afternoon that I can't seem to keep up with the calls. Have you heard about the new baby born in our town? Oh, I forgot, you wouldn't know Alice yet. She's pretty young and just moved here. Her son isn't school age."

Amanda heard a giggle at the other end of the line. Bertha continued, "When her first child was born, she was put under, so she had no idea what her birth pains felt like. This afternoon she laid down for a nap with her son, and when she woke up, she felt like she had to go to the toilet, and so she did. But instead, it was birth pains, and out popped her second son. She had to send her little boy next door to get help. Then they rushed her to the hospital in Williston. My, I bet that was a surprise for her. I also hear that the little boy told the neighbor that he had a 'bloody baby brother.'"

Amanda thought, *This is way more than I need to know about this birth when I don't even know the mother.* It took her a few seconds to pull herself together. *I'd better get used to unusual things happening in this town.*

Finally, she said, "I hope the young mother and baby are doing ok."

"Oh, they're fine. It will be a good story for the baby to learn later, that he was born in a toilet. It did bring some excitement to our little town, and I like excitement."

And you enjoy passing it on, thought Amanda. After a pause, she asked if Willard John had a phone. Bertha assured her that he did, since it was important for him to know if the mail was late or didn't come at all because of bad weather.

"Do you want me to ring him now?"

"Yes, please." *I'd better tell her why, or she might pass on some false information.* "I asked him to talk to the school children about his job, and I want to set up a time."

"Alright, here we go." Bertha connected her line to his, and Amanda heard her give two short and two long rings. There was no answer. Finally, Bertha said, "I'll keep trying and call you back when he answers. He's probably out milking the cow."

As Amanda put the phone back in its cradle, she thought about beginning a journal as she went through this year in the tiny town. But then she mused that no one would believe it and would think she'd made it all up. She'd just sit back and take it all in.

Later that evening Bertha connected her to Willard John.

His response was a nondescript, "Hello."

"Do you remember that I asked you to talk to the students about what you do as a mail carrier?"

"Yea."

"Well, I'd like for you to come this Wednesday and talk with them. Can you do that?"

"Don't know what I'd say except that I put the mail in the boxes."

Amanda had thought that he would need some prompting. "How about telling them just how long you've been doing this, and maybe how you got the job in the first place."

"Yea, I guess I could say that."

"You also might tell them about some interesting things you've seen when you've been on your route. Perhaps some animals, like pheasants, or deer, or maybe you've run into a skunk."

"Oh, that was a terrible one. All the mail smelled like skunk."

"The children would enjoy hearing about that. Did you have trouble delivering the mail during a blizzard when the roads were blocked?"

"That happened just last spring. We didn't even have a mail truck come to town for two days."

"They should remember that blizzard, and you can tell them how you had extra mail when the mail truck did get into town."

There was a pause. Then Willard John asked, "Could you write some of those things down for me? I'm not too good at remembering."

"I'll be happy to do that. The children may have some questions to ask you too. Do you think you can handle that?"

"You may have to help me if the questions are too hard."

Amanda smiled to herself. "Well, the day before you come the students will study about our mail service. We will talk about how letters were first carried by people going from one town to another on personal business, then how the mail service got started many years ago with the Pony Express, and later by the railroads, and how it's carried by truck from one town to another now. When the Pony Express started it cost $5.00 for a half ounce letter. In today's money that would be over a hundred dollars. The Pony Express rider had to weigh 125 pounds or less so that the rider didn't wear out the horse. There were stations along the route where the rider would quickly change horses so that he had a fresh one to ride. He usually rode about 75 to 100 hours, day and night before another rider took over."

"Wow, I didn't know all of that. I wish you'd been my teacher."

"We have books called encyclopedias that tell us a lot of things if we just look for the information."

"The children will know more than I do."

Amanda curled the phone cord around her arm. "You will be telling them what it's like to be a mail carrier today. What is a good time for you to talk to the class on Wednesday?"

"It will have to be early, because the mail truck comes in around ten-thirty."

"School starts at eight-thirty, so let's say you come about nine."

"Ok, if you will write up those ideas and help me if I get stuck."

"I'll be happy to do that. I know the children will enjoy hearing about being a mail carrier. It's an important job."

After Amanda put the phone in its cradle, she began writing down the ideas for Willard John. She had already cleared the date with Ione, and he would talk with both classes. She had made notes of the background material for the other class. She suggested that Ione might have some of the older children look up the Pony Express in the encyclopedias in their room and learn even more about it.

For her first lesson on occupations, Willard John did a great job. She prompted him occasionally, but most of the time he stood on his own. The children really warmed up to him. As the morning progressed, she could see Willard John loosen up. Before he left, he had them laughing with him about some of his experiences on the mail route.

Chapter Seventeen

Several weeks later, on a Sunday evening, Amanda headed out of town to the Bates ranch. Wilda had insisted that her visit to see Jimmy and the family include a supper meal. The weather had turned brisk, and the cottonwood trees along the riverbed were bright yellow. As the leaves twisted and twirled in the wind, she realized there had been wind every day since she arrived in the Dakotas. The wind seemed to blow constantly across the prairie. Sometimes it was just a gentle breeze, and at times it seemed to make her hair stand on end, but there was a constant wind of some sort. They had had several days of rain, and the riverbed was almost full. It gave the air a renewal. Everything seemed fresh and clean. She wondered what the landscape would be like when snow accompanied the wind.

As she approached the ranch, she saw the greenhouses that she'd been told about. This ranch looked better kept than most of them she'd gone to on her home visits. She noticed that both houses had large solar panels on the roofs. Following Wilda's directions, she drove past the larger house to a yellow two-story house near the large barn. A white picket fence surrounded the front yard where the grass was still quite green, despite the recent frost.

Willis met her at the door and invited her inside. Comfortable furniture graced the living room, suggesting one linger awhile among the colorful needlework pillows. The fire in the fireplace took care of the chill and made the living room quite cheerful. And the most delicious aroma wafted through the house.

Wilda called hello from the kitchen. When Amanda turned to greet her, she saw that Bill Bates was placing a large bowl of salad on the farm style table. "We asked Bill to join us," Willis said. "He's always happy to have someone to eat with."

Bill smiled, and she noticed that his dark eyes lit up. "This is a second home for me. Willis is right about my liking to have someone to eat with. Although I love my house, I miss the times we enjoyed big family meals."

"Bill's also a good cook himself," said Wilda.

"Well, that's only with thanks to Miss Emma. I spent many a day in the kitchen with her, learning first one thing and then another," responded Bill.

Miss Emma came from the other side of the kitchen and met Amanda with a big smile. "When I heard that you were coming tonight, I asked to come too. I haven't had a chance to really get to know you, and I think that's something I'd like to do."

Amanda returned her smile. "I've heard so much about you and how you're been here most of your adult life. I'm glad that you're living in town so that we will have opportunities to be together. You can probably help me gain knowledge of the background and personalities of some of my students. I've already come to love them, but I've taught enough to know that I will need the wisdom of someone like you to bring about a greater understanding."

Miss Emma chuckled, "Someone's been talking about me, someone who knows how I love children."

"Yes, you come with high references from Sue Biscoff. She tells me that you've been here through several generations."

"And I've loved them all. It's been a privilege to watch them grow up and develop their own personalities."

Suddenly there was the clatter of small feet on the stairway, and Jimmy came running into the room, rushing into Amanda's arms. "I'm so happy that you're here! Come and see the turtle I have in my room. He wandered into our yard this summer, and sometimes we bring him into the house for a while. But we always let him outside again. He needs to be in his own surroundings. Maybe I can take him to school sometime. I'd be sure to bring him back to our yard where he has a special place he likes to stay."

Bill watched Amanda follow Jimmy up the stairs, asking Jimmy the name of his turtle. He turned to Willis and commented, "She certainly has taken Jimmy's heart. How did the school board find someone like her? I understand she has great teaching skills too."

"She came out of the blue when we put a hiring notice in one of the education magazines. Evidently it was a stroke of luck that she saw our ad and inquired about the position. Her husband died four years ago, and her two children are grown and on their own. She said she wanted a change of scenery and to leave the Atlanta traffic."

"Well, she certainly got both," said Bill. "I've been in Atlanta traffic, and believe me, it's enough to send you packing. She also got the change of scenery, trading wooded hills for our prairie flat land. The mountains are beautiful, but the steep hills are a challenge when there's ice and snow."

About the time Amanda and Jimmy come down the stairs, Miss Emma came from the kitchen and invited them to the big farm-style table. Before Amanda lay the fixings of a feast. This was true beauty for her eyes, as well as her nose.

To her surprise, everyone held hands and Willis asked Miss Emma to pray for them. Miss Emma lifted her head and said, "God, we are here together to welcome Amanda to our community and to enjoy time together. We see before us a lovely banquet that Wilda has prepared, with the help of some of us. We thank you that Bill has returned to our fellowship. We thank you for this food, and for our friendship that draws us closer to you. Amen."

It was a simple prayer, shared in simple language, so unlike most prayers Amanda had heard. She remembered that her son spoke highly of the prayers he had heard in the home of his friend, Richard.

As the meal progressed, she welcomed the delightful taste of home-grown vegetables and the chatter among friends. It had been a long time since she had felt so welcome in a group of people.

Amanda turned to Wilda. "I imagine you grew these vegetables in your garden. They are so fresh, even though we've had our first frost."

Wilda smiled, "They are fresh. Bill gives us space in his greenhouses, and we keep a garden growing year-round. It's a real delight to have the use of it. Maybe you can take a little tour of some of the greenhouses after dinner. There are lights so that we can work the garden at night."

"I'd enjoy that," Amanda replied.

True to her word, after the meal Wilda shooed Bill and Amanda out of the house, telling them she and Willis would clean up the kitchen.

As they approached the greenhouses Bill asked, "Did you have a garden in Atlanta?"

"No, I didn't have room for one, and teaching and raising two children kept me pretty busy. I did, however, shop at a farmer's market near my home. They had fresh vegetables, but I was never sure what chemicals they used to grow them. They also had various produce and meats from other cultures. I enjoyed trying new things. That was fine with my son, but my daughter sometimes refused to eat something new."

Bill smiled at that. "I've had no children, but I'm afraid I was like your daughter at times in my younger years. However, when Miss Emma cooked for us, I loved her so much that I would try anything she cooked, and I found that I liked it. I understand that your children are on their own now."

"Yes, my daughter is an attorney, and after college my son tried to make a go of singing, but now he has signed up for the Peace Corps. He's waiting to be assigned. His friend from Zaire signed up with him. I still can't get used to calling the country Zaire since I learned it as the Congo in elementary school. At any rate, they hope to go to some place in Africa."

"There are many countries in Africa that can really use someone in the Peace Corps. I wish them well."

They entered one of the greenhouses, and Bill flipped on the light. "This is where Willis and Wilda have their winter garden. They are just beginning to reap the rewards of their efforts this season. By using the greenhouses, they usually have three to four harvests a year. The back part of this greenhouse is where we compost and prepare the dirt that we use. We grow vegetables as well as flower plants commercially for the spring market. We also grow shrubs and trees, but that's done outside in order to acclimate them to the North Dakota weather."

Amanda looked around the greenhouse. "I'm amazed that you can do this in this climate. How did you begin such an endeavor?"

"I went to the University of Minnesota, mainly to get away from the isolation of the prairie. I thought I wanted the fast life of the city. Then I realized that my heart was in this country, and I decided to major in horticulture. The greenhouses at the university intrigued me, and I convinced my father to build the first one. Since my parents' accident and death, I've added two more. They've been successful, and now we truck the flowers, shrubs, and trees in all directions."

Amanda asked, "Would you like to visit the school and talk to the children about your greenhouses? I'm having people visit and talk about various careers. This could also have a science connection."

"I'd enjoy that. Maybe we could have a follow-up when they could come out to see the greenhouses themselves. That would be better in the spring."

She looked up at him with excitement in her eyes, "I'm so pleased that you will do this. I fear these children don't have opportunity to know about anything but ranching and lumber. Delmer and Leola Karr will talk to them about owning a grocery store, and Willard John already spent part of a morning telling them about working as a mail carrier."

As they returned to the house, Bill said, "I don't think any other teacher has done anything like this. You are really a hands-on teacher."

"That's the fun part of teaching. It opens the world to these children. They learn so much about the world and how they can be a part of it."

Back at Willis and Wilda's house, she spent some time reading a story to little Jimmy while cuddling him under her arm. All too soon, Wilda took him off to bed, and the adults talked a bit about the weather and what they expected for the winter.

Amanda noticed that Miss Emma seemed to have difficulty keeping her eyes open, so she suggested, "Miss Emma, would you like to ride back to town with me? There's no reason for Willis to make that trip when we live so close to each other."

"I would appreciate that. It seems the older I get, the more sleep I need. If you don't mind, I'll ride with you."

With good-byes and some hugs, Amanda pulled onto the farm road with Miss Emma beside her. "I'm glad you asked to be with us tonight," she said.

"I love those four so much," Miss Emma said. "They have been a part of my life for many years. Kin doesn't have to come from blood. Kin is the circle you create as you live your life."

As Amanda made a sharp curve, she said, "I noticed that two of the teen-agers give you rides to some of the events. It is kind of them to do that."

"Yes, that's Lloyd and Ethel. They board in Williston during the school year, but occasionally they come home for a weekend."

"I will be happy to drive you anywhere you would like."

Miss Emma replied, "Well, there are only a few times that I get out, but I would appreciate it."

Amanda dropped Miss Emma at her home and watched to be sure she got in safely. When she saw the light go on in the little house, she drove to her home. *I feel that I'm becoming a part of this little community. Perhaps it is not the end of the universe after all.*

Chapter Eighteen

The next week went smoothly, and Amanda and Iona discussed the Christmas play. Once they decided on a theme, Amanda talked to Myrtle May about writing it. She was excited about the play and promised to have a rough draft of it ready in two weeks. With possible rewriting, they would then have six weeks to two months to learn and rehearse the performance. From past experiences, Amanda knew it would not be perfect, but it would give the children a sense of pride.

On Friday, Sue called and asked Amanda if she would like to ride with her to Williston on Saturday. This would be an opportunity for her to purchase some things to enhance her teaching, and perhaps to purchase snow boots and some warmer clothing for the upcoming season. They arranged to leave after breakfast on Saturday, in order to have a full day of shopping.

Amanda decided to make a visit to Miss Emma and see if she wanted anything from Williston. That afternoon she walked the few blocks to her home and knocked on the door. The older woman opened the door almost immediately, and the scent of fresh baked bread curled around Amanda's head. "My, I've not smelled home-baked bread since I went to my grandmother's as a child," she exclaimed.

"Come on in, and I'll slice some while it's warm. It's delicious with butter from the Hagen's ranch. Gladys has the best butter and cream around."

"I wonder if she's the one who gave me a pint of cream at my pounding. It was so thick that I had to thin it with milk in order to whip it."

"That would have been the Hagen cream," said Miss Emma. "I hope you don't mind sitting in the kitchen. I'll get our warm bread and butter. I also have some raspberry jam that Myrtle Mae made for me. They have rows and rows of raspberries."

"I don't believe I've ever had raspberry jam. They don't grow very well in Georgia. I think they need a colder winter."

"You may be right. Every part of the country has some sort of specialties. It makes our country a bit spicy!"

"You're right. It's nice to have a chance to try new things."

After enjoying the warm bread with butter and jam, Amanda asked, "Do you need anything from Williston? Sue Biscoff and I are going into town tomorrow."

"It seems there was something I wanted from town. Now what was it?" Miss Emma mused. "Oh yes! I need a spool of thread to match the dress I'm making for Ethel. I'll get some scissors and cut a snip of the fabric so that you can match it."

As Amanda left, she thought how nice it was to just pop in to see someone like Miss Emma. The visit had refreshed her, and the warm, fresh bread made her day special.

Saturday arrived with a brisk wind, chilling Amanda to the bone. Thankfully, Sue's station wagon was warm and cozy. As Amanda settled into her seat, Sue headed them toward Williston.

"Will you recommend a store where I can purchase some snow boots?" asked Amanda.

"Just about any clothing store carries them," returned Sue. "However, I'd recommend the North Face brand. They're a little more expensive, but I've found them to be the warmest for our weather. You don't want high heel boots for Stoney Butte. You want something that you can plow through the snow with. We can get some deep snow, but at the same time we'll have places where the wind has blown the snow down to the ground. Because of the wind, we have dry ground beside six-foot drifts. This seems strange to some people, but it's a common occurrence in this windy country."

During the trip, Sue asked Amanda how teaching was coming. With each comment, Sue smiled approval. "You are making an impression," she said.

"I just hope I will make a difference in these children this year. I've visited in several of the students' homes, and I think that not only gives me a better understanding of the child, but also helps them feel more at home with me."

"Yes, I've heard some parents speak of your visits. That's also a very good way to give the community an opportunity to get to know you better."

Amanda thought for a moment. "One project I've taken on is to have some people come into the classroom and tell about their work. Willard John has already visited and talked about his work as a mail carrier, and I'll have the Karrs come to the class and perhaps have the class visit their store. I've also asked Bill Bates to tell the class about his greenhouses and how he and Willis raise plants and ship them to the cities. We might make a field trip out of that too.

"That reminds me. I've intended to call and ask your help in finding a doctor in Williston who would come out and talk with the children. When I asked Marilyn what she would consider doing when she grew up, she said she'd like to do research, to try to find ways to help people who suffer from multiple sclerosis like her mother."

"Perhaps I can do better than a doctor in Williston, although you might like to have a general practitioner come in also. I had a friend in medical research. I may be able to get him to come for a visit next spring. You could have the Williston doctor talk with the class first, and then follow up with my friend in the spring. I haven't been in touch with him for some time. I hope he hasn't moved."

"That would be wonderful. I'd also like to have you talk to the class about a nursing career."

Sue slowed down for the next curve. "It's been many years since I was active in nursing, but I can certainly give them an idea of how rewarding it is. Hospitals are beginning to hire male nurses now also."

Excitement shone in Amanda's face. "Oh, great. Now I'll just have to locate a doctor in Williston."

"I can help you with that too. In fact, we can go by his office and talk with him this morning if he has time. His office is open on Saturday mornings."

Amanda appreciated Sue's help. When they got to Williston, Sue drove to Dr. Endive's office. True to her word, Sue introduced him to her and even explained just what the visit was about. The doctor was old enough to seem to know what he was talking about, but young enough to relate to the children. He agreed to work with his schedule and talk with the children. Amanda said she'd like to have Sue talk with them first, and then the doctor. All of them agreed to this plan. Dr. Endive gave Amanda his card and asked her to contact him when she had a better idea about a date.

The doctor's office wasn't far from the main street, and after Sue pointed out several stores, she left Amanda to shop on her own while she took care of her errands. They arranged to meet at a department store and eat lunch together at the Pizza Hut. Then they would stop at a supermarket on their way out of town.

Williston was certainly larger than Stoney Butte, but what most people in Atlanta would have called a small town. Amanda found an office store where she purchased several items for her class. Then she headed to the main department store in town and tried on several boots. She finally settled on a reasonable pair with false fur around the top. When the clerk learned she had moved from Atlanta, he suggested that she buy a small bag that she could use to carry her regular shoes in so that she could change into them when she went into a house. This was all quite new for Amanda.

Next, she wandered the aisles looking for some warmer sweaters and slacks. She realized that most Stoney Butte folks wore jeans year-round, but she didn't want to be quite so casual at school. She felt it important to show pride in her position as a teacher, but she wanted to also be casual enough that she didn't stand out as prideful. Thankfully, the store had some reasonable but warm clothing. These would fill out her wardrobe for the winter.

She had one more errand on her list, Miss Emma's thread. To her surprise, there was a Kresge's five and dime store across the street. Amanda reminisced her youth as she walked down the aisle. There were the nail polishes she had begged her mother for, and a little further down she saw the reading glasses that the older people bought. They never went to an optometrist, but simply bought glasses when they had trouble reading. And there was even an old-fashioned soda fountain. Such a temptation to enjoy a chocolate soda, but it was almost lunch time. Amanda felt as if she had stepped back in time to her youth as she remembered the five and dime stores. When she found the thread counter, she was amazed at the large array of shades of every color. She pulled out the slip of cloth that Miss Emma had given her and found the perfect match for the dress for Ethel. Reluctantly, she left the five and dime and walked to the department store where she was to meet Sue.

Lunch was a treat, since the little store at Stoney Butte didn't carry pizza. Amanda said, "I'd like to buy several pizzas to take home and freeze and have them as a special treat for the children one day. Do you suppose they would keep on the way home?"

"Oh, I always bring a large ice chest when I come to town, so we can put them in that. They will be fine."

"Great! Will we have time to wait for them to be cooked?"

"I have one more errand to run, so we can come back for them after that."

The clerk seemed quite surprised when she ordered six large pizzas to go. She decided to get enough for both classes, since she didn't want to outdo Ione. They had a good relationship going so far, and Amanda didn't want to ruin that.

Arranging to pick up the pizzas later, she went with Sue to the feed store for her last errand. Then after picking up the pizzas they headed for the supermarket. The large store excited her, but she was careful to only purchase things the Karrs didn't carry in their store. She wanted to support them and become a part of the community.

As they drove out of Williston, the most fabulous sunset of oranges and reds spread its arms before them. Although they were in North Dakota, Amanda was again reminded of the Montana slogan of the "Big Sky Country". She asked, "Do you always have such lovely sunsets? I guess I've never thought to step out of my trailer to see them."

"We often have them like this," Sue said. "Although Stoney Butte is small, the few houses in town often mar the view of God's glorious colors across the sky."

Crossing the bridge into her new hometown, Amanda felt an awe over the odd time of day – when the world seemed suspended between the day that was ending, and the promise of rest before the new day began.

"I've enjoyed today so much," she told Sue. "Thank you for asking me to go with you."

"It was my pleasure. And we had an opportunity to get to know each other. That made a bonus to a necessary trip."

Chapter Nineteen

The next morning Amanda awoke to a white world with a gentle covering of snow instead of the deep drifts that Sue had told her about the day before. Feeling prepared, she took her new boots out of the box. She planned to go to the little Methodist Church down the street from her house, but she also wanted to give Miss Emma the thread she had bought in Williston. Perhaps Miss Emma would like a ride to church.

Shortly after she cranked the phone, Bertha answered with a cheerful "Hello, who can I connect you with?" She wondered if Bertha was like this by nature, or if she just hoped to get in on some more gossip around town.

Within two rings, Miss Emma answered, equally cheerful. After Amanda identified herself, Bertha chimed in, "Isn't it a lovely day? I always enjoy the first snow. It makes me feel alive."

Amanda had to agree with her. She saw snow so seldom in Atlanta, and it always made drivers unhappy because they were not prepared for it. The least bit of snow brought the city to a near standstill.

After a few comments about the snow, Amanda heard Bertha disconnect. She asked Miss Emma, "Would you like to have a ride to church?"

The older woman replied, "Oh, that would be so nice of you. Ethel and Lloyd aren't coming home this weekend. There was a big football game on Friday, with the homecoming dance last night. I'd certainly love a ride." Amanda arranged to pick her up before the service and give her the thread.

When she arrived, she took the thread to the house and then helped Miss Emma to the car. She wanted to be sure that she didn't fall on the slippery snow.

After Miss Emma was settled in the car, she turned to Amanda and asked, "Would you like to stay for a little lunch when you bring me home?" Amanda welcomed the opportunity to get to know this wise woman better.

When they got to church, Miss Emma said she usually sat in a specific pew. "That way the preacher can be sure I'm here. If that pew is empty, our previous pastor would call to see how I was. However, I think Neil is afraid to call because he thinks we will get into some sort of theological discussion, and he knows that we don't agree on some things."

Amanda smiled, remembering that Myrtle Mae had talked about how this new pastor made comments that even her daughters didn't agree with. So far, she hadn't heard anything out of the ordinary from his sermons. But she continued to come to worship, if for no other reason than to become a closer part of the community.

One thing disturbed her, however. On several occasions Neil had asked her to go out to lunch with him after the service. He usually said he wanted to talk about the difference in a small town and bigger cities. He was handsome enough to catch the eye, and he seemed to have a gentle manner, but something just urged Amanda to turn him down each time. She usually found an excuse, primarily lesson plans or grading, but he continued to ask her.

Thankfully, he hadn't called her on the phone which would have spread rumors all over western North Dakota and eastern Montana.

Just before the service began, Bill Bates came in by himself. Miss Emma moved over to give him room on their pew.

Amanda felt her heart thump in her chest. This seemed strange to her. Certainly, he was handsome, but why should she be interested in this man with a life so different from hers? She had taken this year to get away from the immediate past, not attraction to someone who lived a completely different lifestyle. Besides, he had a mysterious side that he kept hidden about half of the year. No one seemed to know just where he went during those months. They just accepted that he was either gone or were happy to have him back. She thought to ask Sue about his mysterious trips, but she was afraid she would think Amanda was trying to connect with him. Maybe when she got to know Sue better, she could talk about it.

"Where are Willis, Wilda, and Jimmy?" Miss Emma asked.

"Jimmy came down with a cold yesterday, and they are keeping him home."

"That sounds like a good idea," said Miss Emma. "This early snow might make it worse."

"I hope he will be well enough for school tomorrow," added Amanda. "I will certainly miss him if he's not there."

Bill assured them that Jimmy was on the mend and would likely be in class the next day.

Neil's sermon was a bit different from his previous ones. Since Halloween was the following Wednesday, he spoke about it being the devil's holiday with witches, vampires, wizards, and ghosts. He even used several Old Testament commands to back up his beliefs. Amanda noticed that Miss Emma made notes of the verses he used.

After the service, Miss Emma invited Bill to join them for lunch.

"You know I will!" he exclaimed. "I always accept a meal that you cook."

"It's not a big meal," she said, "only some soup and a sandwich."

"That's great with me."

Amanda and Miss Emma drove to her house, and Bill followed. Amanda wasn't sure where Bertha lived and whether she could see that both cars were parked in front of the house, but she decided not to worry about any gossip.

The light lunch was delightful, and Bill and Miss Emma reminisced about their times at the ranch. After clearing the table of the dishes, Miss Emma suggested they have a cup of tea with some snickerdoodles. This delighted Bill, and he told Amanda how he used to help her make these favorite cookies of his.

"You should have seen him when we finished," Miss Emma remembered. "He stood on a chair to reach the counter, with a dish towel tied around his neck and gooey sugar from head to toe."

Amanda laughed at the vision of Bill as a little boy enjoying his time with this woman at his ranch. It was easy to understand how he loved her now.

As they enjoyed their tea and cookies, Bill brought up the morning's sermon. "I'm not sure I agree with Neil's idea about Halloween. We always made cookies to bring to town and share on Halloween. You even helped me make costumes for an evening stroll around town. Where does he get the idea that it's worshiping the devil?"

Miss Emma said, "I always look at Halloween as the dark side of the holiday. Most of the traditions come from the Celts before they learned about Christianity. They thought that witches and spirits brought about diseases, natural disasters, and other bad things. The bright side of the holiday is the next day, All Saints' Day, when we celebrate the good things that people who have gone before us did. You know, in The Methodist Church we also consider all who believe in Christ as being a saint."

Amanda said, "But Neil backed his statements with scripture passages."

"Let's look at his scriptures again," suggested Miss Emma as she pulled her notes out of her purse. "I believe they were from the King James Version. Did you know that this version of the Bible was written in Elizabethan English and it was translated from a translation, not from our earliest manuscripts? Since that translation, we have found many earlier texts of parts of the Bible, and new translations use those earlier texts. They also take into consideration how the meanings of our English words have changed. I have several translations of the Bible and we can read the verses in all of them. In the King James Version, the words from Exodus 22:18 commanded that witches be killed. There was no mention of how you knew a person was a witch."

"I remember from my history classes that the early Puritans in this country accused some women of being witches and killed them," said Amanda.

"Yes, and it also happened in Europe," said Miss Emma. "We have to remember that the writers of the Old Testament were trying to understand their world and just who God was. The Old Testament was written in Hebrew, and ancient Hebrew had absolutely no punctuation. We need to take that into consideration too."

"All of the scriptures this morning came from the Old Testament," commented Bill. "There was nothing positive about the whole service."

"The Leviticus 7:26-27 passage speaks of not eating blood, and Neil connected it to vampires," said Miss Emma. "Actually, this, and many other things in the Old Testament about what we should eat, were common health suggestions. Remember, they did not have refrigeration then, and if they were to keep meat it had to be dried. I think that the best lesson we can take from the Old Testament is to see God as one God and not a host of spirits."

Miss Emma took a sip of her tea before continuing, "You know, you can even look at the carved pumpkin in a positive way. Think of a pumpkin in the garden that God selects, washes all the dirt off, and opens it up to take all the gooey stuff out. Then God carves a happy face in the pumpkin and places a light inside to light up the world with love."

Amanda recognized the amount of thought and research that went into Miss Emma's statements. "How did you come to know so much about the Bible and your belief in God?"

"Well," Miss Emma said with a wink to Bill. "This man here got me started when he was a boy. He questioned everything, and I had to do some research to keep up with him. He's still questioning, which is good. You'll never learn everything, but you must keep your mind open to searching. I wouldn't know what I know today if Bill and I hadn't had so many talks in that big ranch kitchen."

That night, as Amanda worked on her teaching plan for the next week, she reflected on their lunchtime conversation. She had planned to let the older children carve out a pumpkin and give all of them opportunities to draw some Halloween pictures. Now, she decided that all of the pictures would be of happy pumpkins.

Chapter Twenty

Later that week Otto Gill, the church treasurer, was quite disturbed. The offerings at the church had fallen off, but attendance stayed about the same. He talked about this with his wife, Hannah, as they had dinner. She suggested, "It's just hard times for many of the people. You know, the church is usually what people cut from their budgets first."

Otto laid down his fork and seriously looked across the table. "But it shouldn't be that way. Last year many of our people fell on hard times, but the giving never went down like it has this year. I just think it might be something else."

Hannah pondered. "Well, what else could it be? The ushers take up the offering and it's brought to the front. After the service, Rev. Neil takes it home and then deposits it in the bank when he goes to Williston on Monday." After a pause in thought, she said, "You always go over the budget with him at least every month."

Otto answered with concern, "Yes, but we are barely able to cover our electric and gas bills and our share of Neil's salary. We had hoped to paint the church building this year. If we had as much offering as last year, we would be able to do it by next spring. I just feel that there is some other solution."

"What does Rev. Neil say about this?"

"He has the same answer you do, that people have fallen on hard times. He doesn't seem to be disturbed."

"Are you sure you did your math right? Have you checked with the bank about the deposits?"

With exasperation Otto said, "I've gone over my math until I'm blue in the face, but I haven't checked with the bank. I suppose that's where I should start."

The next morning Otto made a special trip to Williston and met with one of the bank officers. They looked over the deposits, and everything seemed to be in order. But Otto did notice that the deposits only listed checks made out to the church. There was no evidence of the loose offerings that people might give.

As he drove back through Stoney Butte, he noticed a light in Miss Emma's house. Many people in town sought out her wisdom. He had a nudging to stop and talk with her about this problem. He knew that she would never mention it to anyone else if he asked for her confidence.

When she invited him into her house, he noticed that she had her sewing machine out and was working on a lovely piece of material. "Miss Emma, I hate to bother you. You seem pretty busy."

Motioning for him to have a seat, she said, "Don't worry about that. I'm making a dress for Ethel. She and Lloyd are so nice to take me to church every Sunday that they come home. And do you know, the new teacher offered to take me to church last Sunday. I had a good visit with her and Bill over a light lunch afterwards. She has a good head on her shoulders."

"Yes, I've heard many of the parents speak about how much the children like her and how she's encouraging them to ask questions and to enjoy learning. She even gets along with Miss Ione, which many previous teachers haven't managed to do."

There was a pause before Miss Emma questioned him, "Well, what brings you to my door, Otto?"

"Like many people in town, I'm looking to you for advice. I didn't want to talk about it on the phone. You know how anything you say on the phone is public knowledge within the hour."

"You are right about that," she laughed. "Now, I don't claim to have a great gift of advice, but I'm willing to talk through your problem with you."

"As you know, I'm treasurer of the church. I've noticed that the amount of giving has fallen off during the last few months, and I can't understand why. The attendance has stayed the same."

"This is a puzzler. Maybe we need to ask God to think this through with us. Let's pray silently for a few moments."

After they had prayed silently, Miss Emma asked, "Do you take the offering money home with you each Sunday?"

"No. The pastors in the area have a luncheon meeting every Monday in Williston, and we have always had the pastor take the offering to the bank then. That gets it into the bank sooner and saves me a special trip to Williston."

"That's logical. And it has worked well to do this in the past?"

Otto responded, "Yes, the pastor then calls me to let me know how much he deposited, and when we meet once a month, he brings the deposit slips. I just made a special trip to Williston to talk to the bank about this, and I found something strange that I'd not noticed before."

"What was that?"

"There were only checks listed on the deposit slip, no loose change."

Miss Emma looked quizzical. "That does seem odd. Do you have any other thoughts on why this should be?"

"No, I've racked my brain, and have no other ideas."

Miss Emma led him with the question, "How do you suppose you can check on this?"

"It is awkward to suspect Rev. Neil, but I do wonder. He's the only thing that has changed since we have fallen behind in giving. The ushers who take up the offering are the same, and all my books balance."

"Hum, how do you suppose you could test this?"

Otto thought a moment. "Well, I can find an excuse to go to Williston on the next few Mondays. That way I can take the offering home and be sure it is all deposited. This is after harvest, and some people will give more because they want a tax write-off, but at least I could check on the loose change amounts."

Miss Emma smiled. "I think you have a plan there, Otto. Why don't you give it a try for the next few weeks and see how it goes?"

"I think I will. Thank you, Miss Emma. You always have good advice."

"I wouldn't say it was my advice. Remember how we prayed for guidance? Well, I think God gave you a plan. I'll not mention this to anyone, and you let me know how it goes."

Chapter Twenty-One

When Ione came into her room the day before Halloween, Amanda shared an idea. "I had a conversation with Miss Emma the other day. She said that the traditions of Halloween date back to the Celts and how, before Christianity came to their country, they believed that spirits, witches, and even black cats brought about illness and other calamities. She called Halloween the dark side of the holiday and the next day, All Saints Day, the bright side. When I went to Williston with Sue the other day, I bought enough pizzas for both classes and froze them in the top of my refrigerator. What do you think of our having the pizzas on Thursday, November 1st, and celebrating all the good things that people have done in the world? We can talk about what the early Celts believed, and how we now have hospitals, schools, and other things that help us. We can even ask the children to think of nice things that other children or adults have done for them."

"That sounds like a great idea. I'm so glad that we're doing things together with both classes. My children really enjoyed looking up information on the Pony Express before Willard John came to talk to us. I've never had a class so excited about using the encyclopedia.

"You plan to have Delmer and Leola talk with the children about owning a grocery store, don't you? Did you say they suggested a field trip to visit the store?"

Amanda picked up her calendar. "Yes, and we need to set a date for that. I've asked Sue to talk about nursing, and she helped me find a doctor in Williston who will come out some time to talk. She's also going to contact someone she knew in Missoula who worked in medical research."

"How about I talk to Melton Cazer about the lumber business?"

"That would be great. I also asked Bill to tell us about horticulture and his greenhouses. He suggested that we add a field trip to that too."

"This is going to be a great year. I enjoy working with you, Amanda."

On Wednesday, Halloween evening, Amanda decorated her door with the pumpkins the children had drawn during the week and left the porch light on. She was glad the snow had melted so the children could enjoy trick or treating.

Joel was the first child to come to the door, wearing a pirate costume. He exclaimed, "Oh, Miss Amanda, you put my picture on your door."

Amanda gave him a hug and a candy bar. "Your picture is special to me. It makes me happy with the pumpkin's big smile."

For the next couple of hours, every one of the children in her class who lived in town, and a few from the ranches, came to her door and received the same hug and candy bar. She mentioned that she was happy, because of each child's picture. Children from the older class also knocked on her door and received her hug and candy bar.

After the last child left, Amanda turned off the porch light and just sat in the dark for a few minutes. She felt she needed to reflect on her life for a while. This life was so different from what she left in Atlanta. She enjoyed her teaching. In fact, with such a small class she really got to know the children. She was simply glad to be back in the classroom too. Although her salary had increased when she took administrative jobs, the stress had also increased, especially when she became principal. The move had certainly eased that part of her complicated life.

But now Neil was pressuring her to go out with him, and she didn't think that was what she should do. Besides his good looks, there was nothing that appealed to her. She definitely was not looking for a relationship, and with some of his theological views, she knew that nothing would work out between them anyway.

She had spent many years away from the church, but she did enjoy attending worship with others from the community. It felt so right to sit beside Miss Emma on Sunday. And then there was the time after church when Bill joined them for lunch. The conversation challenged her to think for herself about her beliefs. No one had ever done that for her. When she was growing up, she had always been told just what to believe, somewhat like Neil's sermons. It was as if her thoughts didn't matter, only those of the one preaching or teaching. Even her parents pushed their beliefs on her. She wondered if they had lived longer whether she would feel comfortable talking with them now, as she and Miss Emma and Bill had done on Sunday.

Amanda had always challenged her own children and those in her classroom to think for themselves and work out their problems, but she'd never applied that to religion. Her husband was happy to relax at home on Sundays, and she made no effort to get up and go to church herself, or even take her children. Ashley and Kurt seemed to have turned out fine, even with their own little quirks.

She had just received a letter from Kurt, and he and Richard were in Peace Corps training. He wrote that the Peace Corps was based on Operation Crossroads Africa founded by Rev. James H.

Robinson, an African American clergyman and humanitarian. They learned that they were going to Zaire. He said they were learning to speak French and a little of some of the local languages. She had checked out the country in the encyclopedias and learned that it was a colony of France for many years, therefore the common language was French. She knew that Richard would be happy to be in the country of some of his ancestors.

Ashley went her merry way, climbing the corporate ladder after her graduate degree. She followed her father into his respected law firm and seemed to be enjoying her work. It did bother Amanda that she didn't do any volunteer work at some charity, but perhaps she was just too busy establishing her career. There was still time ahead for that.

Her mind kept going back to Bill, wondering just what he was doing during those months away from Stoney Butte. He had established his horticulture business well and gotten it into good hands for when he was gone, but just where did he go? He was a man of mystery. She was not only curious about the mystery, but also attracted to him as she'd not been attracted to any man since her husband's death. Was she ready for a relationship with someone who held a mystery?

The pizza party on the day after Halloween, All Saints Day, turned out to be a great success. The children came up with many suggestions of people who had made their lives better.

Timmy surprised Amanda when he said, "My Uncle Melton gave my daddy a job in the lumber mill. That was a good thing, and that makes us happy."

"It certainly was a good thing," Amanda replied. "All we have to do is think about our lives and think of people who do good things for us."

Mandy suggested, "The woman who drives the bookmobile does good things for us. She chooses good books for us to read and brings them out here every month. I like to read because I can imagine I'm someone else living a different life. Then I remember that I like my life right here in Stoney Butte."

Marilyn said, "We now have another day to celebrate, and it's a happier day than Halloween."

Several days after their All Saints Day Pizza Party, Myrtle Mae called to tell Amanda that she had the first draft of the Christmas play ready for her to read. She said she would send it to school with Mandy the next day. When Mandy gave the typed manuscript to her there was great pride in her eyes. Amanda knew the bond between the girls and their mother was firm, and she was glad she had asked Myrtle Mae to write the play.

Thankfully, she had very few papers to grade and was able to do that in a short time before heading home. She relaxed that evening with a cup of tea and the manuscript in her hand. Aggie insisted on sitting on her lap, but she was accustomed to that, and she began reading. The more she read the more excited she became. She was not only excited about the play, but also about Myrtle Mae's writing ability. She must be encouraged to write some stories for publication in children's magazines. Amanda tucked the thought back into her mind with a plan to talk with her about it after the family moved into their new home and the Christmas rush was over.

After Ione read the manuscript and they agreed on only a few small revisions, Amanda took it to Myrtle Mae personally. She also wanted to hear how the plans for their new home were progressing.

Once again, Marilyn and Mandy served her fresh cookies and tea. They listened as Amanda made a few suggestions about the manuscript. Myrtle Mae said that the adjustments would be easy to make, and she'd have it ready by the weekend.

After all the business of the Christmas play was settled, Myrtle Mae broke out in a big smile. "We have news for you. I asked the girls not to say anything until we could tell you together. We will move our house onto our lot next Saturday. Wenzel normally works on Saturdays, but he's getting that day off, and we have everything lined up. We won't move in right away because he's going to build cabinets in the kitchen. I can hardly believe it's going to happen. Our own house! Even this trailer isn't ours. We rent it from Mr. Cazer, the owner of the mill. Looks like we can really call Stoney Butte home."

Amanda put her hand on Myrtle Mae's arm. "I thought you looked pretty excited when I came in, but I didn't know it was more than excitement over the Christmas play. I'm so happy for you. Owning your own home helps grow your roots. I'll certainly be there to see the placement of the house."

Marilyn and Mandy joined in the excitement, saying that they would each have their own room, and how they hoped to fix it up. Marilyn said, "We'll have to put our mattresses on the floor at first until we can save enough money for beds. Momma has always made sure that we saved the money first before buying something."

Mandy added, "We saved money for Momma and Daddy to have a bed, because it's too hard for Momma to get up from the floor."

"Saving first is a very good habit to have," agreed Amanda. "If you learn that early you won't have the trouble that many people have by going into debt."

Before she left, Marilyn asked a special question, "Why did Rev. Neil talk about Halloween as such a bad thing? We just have fun dressing up and going to people's houses."

Amanda was glad for the conversation with Miss Emma. "You remember we talked about Halloween being the dark side of the holiday. That's sort of how people believed before they knew about God and Jesus. The bright side is when we realize that there is a God who helps us every day to do the right thing. Some churches have a service called All Saints' Day on the Sunday after Halloween. That's when we recognize all the good people who helped to make our world better. We also recognize that those of us who follow Jesus can be considered saints. I'm not sure whether Rev. Neil has planned such a service or not."

"All Saints Day is something like the time in class when we told about people who helped us," said Marilyn.

"Yes," answered Amanda. "I think you get the idea of being positive about things instead of looking at the dark side. It is fun to dress up for Halloween, but we have to remember how the tradition came about."

As she said goodbye to Myrtle Mae, the girls wrapped up several cookies for their teacher to take home. That evening, as Amanda enjoyed her cookies with a cup of coffee, she basked in the new friendship with such a good woman and her two daughters.

Chapter Twenty-Two

The following Saturday Amanda hurried to the lot that was to be Myrtle Mae's new home. Although she got there early, the men had already cleared and leveled the site and were placing the wooden forms for the cement base of the house. The whole town seemed to have turned out for the event. Men were helping; women were standing at tables serving coffee and coffeecake; children had found a sandy place near the tables playing with dirt-moving toys. Amanda noticed that Bill and Willis were in the middle of the activity. Thankfully, it hadn't snowed recently, but the clouds looked threatening.

Amanda accepted a cup of coffee, black as pitch. She added cream to tone it down a little and joined in the conversation about the new home for Myrtle Mae's family. As Amanda looked around, she saw a different type of family than she'd known in Atlanta. Here was a family of people, most of them not blood relations, joining in the joy of a new home. There was no big dirt-moving equipment, no bossing contractors off to the side barking orders – just a family of men and women working and celebrating this special occasion. And in the middle of it all was Myrtle Mae in her wheelchair, beaming from ear to ear.

As the morning wore on, several trucks of concrete arrived and poured the foundation as well as what would be the floor. When the cement trucks left, the house moving company came with the house from the nearby ranch. Suddenly the dark clouds came over them, and the men questioned whether the cement would be ruined if they had a heavy rain. They talked together and then spoke to Myrtle Mae. She nodded her head, and the process of moving the house onto the wet cement began.

First, they placed boards along the walkways to both doors. Then they let the house down into the wet cement. It sank about a foot, and you could see that the windowsills were only inches above the ground outside, but Myrtle Mae's bright face and smile made the clouds seem to disappear. However, as the men had predicted, it did begin to rain. Myrtle Mae was rushed to the truck, much to her regret. She hated to leave this, her new home.

After Amanda got home and changed from her wet clothing, she called Myrtle Mae. "I'm so sorry that the rain didn't hold off until the foundation was dry," she said. Myrtle Mae's cheerful voice assured her that she was happy with her new house, even if you had to stoop to get into the door. She said that the cement would have been ruined if the heavy rain had come before the house was dropped into place. She was just so happy to have a house of her own now.

The next week the Electric Cooperative came out to hook up their electricity and Wenzel began work on Myrtle Mae's cabinets at night. He used green wood from the lumber mill, because they could not afford to purchase dried wood in Williston. Amanda was concerned about the roughness of the wood and worried that it would warp as it dried. But Myrtle Mae assured her that the cabinets and countertop were fine with her. They would not bother with interior doors, so she didn't need to worry that they would not fit when the wood dried. Amanda made a mental note to purchase a large plastic cutting board for her the next time she went into Williston.

The next Wednesday, Amanda and Ione were scheduled to attend the school board meeting, giving information on how the school year was progressing. Ione assured Amanda that this was routine, and it would be a friendly meeting. She said they had nothing to fear.

When Amanda arrived, she remembered that Sue had told her that Bill Bates was a member of the school board. She thought, *He's certainly well considered to be elected to the school board even though he's out of town so much of the year.*

True to Ione's word, there was little business to come before the board, and all of the members seemed pleased with the report that they gave together on the year up to this point.

As they were leaving, Bill stopped her and said, "I saw you when we were setting the foundation for Myrtle Mae and Wenzel's house."

"Yes, I am so happy for Myrtle Mae. This is the first time they've owned a house, and they really saved their money to get it. I'm concerned, however, because Wenzel is building her cabinets and countertops out of green wood from the lumber mill. When I go to Williston again, I want to buy a large plastic cutting board that she can use on the counter."

Bill's eyes lit up. "I'm going into Williston this Saturday. Would you like to ride along?"

"Oh, that would be nice if it's not too much trouble. I'd also like to purchase a small filing cabinet for my classroom. Will there be room for that?"

"Sure, I have to pick up some fertilizer for the green houses this winter, so I'll be taking the pick-up. I plan to leave about 6:00 a.m., before daylight. Is that a problem for you?"

"I can do that. Should I come out to your house?" This brought a smile to Bill's eyes.

"That sounds like a good idea. If I pick you up in town there will be all sorts of rumors going around, even before we get out of town. You can just tell anyone who asks that you're going to Williston."

Amanda said, "I'm certainly glad I bought snow boots when I went to Williston with Sue. We've had some cold weather."

"You'll get used to our cold and wind if you hang around long enough. You think it's cold now. Just wait until January. It is the coldest month of the year and can average zero degrees in our part of the state. We can get freezing temperatures as early as September and as late as early May."

Chapter Twenty-Three

On Saturday Amanda decided to dress warmly. She wore warm slacks and her new boots and grabbed a pair of gloves as she left her home. She arrived at the Bates ranch just before 6:00 a.m. Bill already had the truck running to warm it up, although he was inside the house. As soon as Amanda knocked on the door he appeared, ready to face the chill of the early morning.

As they drove along the gravel road, Bill asked, "What was your impression when you first drove this road?"

"I was so tired at the time I just thought it was the most horrible miles I'd ever driven. Once I got to the bridge and looked at the town before me, I thought I'd come to the end of the universe. I was about to turn around and head back to civilization, and I might have if I hadn't thought about the long drive it would take to get to Atlanta. Of course, I also knew that I had committed myself to at least one year of teaching here, so I spoke some encouraging words to Aggie, my cat, and drove into town."

"And what do you think of our little town now?"

"I've found it very friendly, with some great people. The Biscoffs couldn't have been more welcoming. They set the tone for the whole community. And then all those people turned out to set up my trailer when it was delivered. I've even found the parents of my class very appreciative as I've visited them. I've never been in a more caring situation. It is quite different from life in the big city where people often don't even know their neighbors. I lived in an established subdivision, and our children grew up running through each other's yards. But as they grew older and left home, many of the parents moved to smaller houses, and younger families moved in. My career kept me so busy that I didn't make any effort to get to know them either."

Bill flashed a smile. "Yes, I realize now that this is a great place to grow up. I got the big city desire out of my system at the university."

They drove along in silence, a silence that was quite comfortable. Bill seemed to enjoy being with a woman who didn't need to chatter all the time. Amanda did ask some questions about the trees and vegetation that grew along the road. Bill told her that the trees in the creek beds were cottonwoods with seeds surrounded with a cotton-like fiber that flew with the wind. Bill mentioned some of the grasses that grew in North Dakota, but she was glad he didn't bore her with scientific names.

"What are the spiky bushes I see everywhere?"

"They are a form of yucca. They bloom on long stems early in the summer. There are various types of yucca that grow all over the world. I've seen them in Africa. In fact, there is a plant called cassava that looks very much like yucca. The Africans cultivate it and use the root much like we would use a potato."

"Have you eaten cassava?"

"Oh, yes, when I've been in Africa."

Amanda reflected on this statement for a while. Could Africa be where Bill goes when he leaves for long periods of time? She didn't dare ask.

"I'm so glad that you will talk to the students about your greenhouses," she said. "It is so important for them to realize that we can grow all sorts of plants here with a greenhouse."

After another lull of quiet, Bill asked, "Have you noticed how much the wind blows here?"

"I certainly have. It seems to blow every day."

"That's another thing that we could discuss with your students, how we can work with the wind to improve our ecology. From the early time of settlers in this country, wind has been used to pump water. Do you know that the first wind turbine to provide electricity was invented in 1888? We should have been using wind power for many years. Wind powered electricity will make a great difference in our environment since it doesn't pollute our air. The first electrical vehicle was developed in the mid nineteenth century. As batteries have reduced in size, we are looking at mass production of electric cars. If we would combine the wind production of electricity with new vehicles that run on electricity, we could really save our environment."

"Where did you learn all of this?"

"I've thought about it for some time and done a little research. Poverty stricken countries really need to look toward the use of natural resources, such as wind and solar power, to better their living conditions. It grieves me to see how we, in the United States, depend on oil and coal and aren't setting an example with the practice of reusable resources."

"It sounds like you enjoy research on energy."

"I guess I have to give Miss Emma credit for some of my thoughts on this. She keeps up on new ideas and always encouraged me to inquire about things and to research. When I was young, she would not let my questions go until I'd done as much research as possible with the encyclopedias we had and even magazines that she encouraged me to order. I spent more time in the bookmobile than most city kids spend in the library."

Amanda turned in her seat and was struck on the cut of his jaw. After a pause to put her thoughts back on the subject she said, "Maybe you can talk to the librarian when the bookmobile next comes to town and see if she can bring books that pick up on your talks with the students."

"I could do that. I'll check with Miss Emma and see if we still have the same librarian. If not, I'll call the library and try to arrange it. We'd better set up a time that I'll talk with the students so that the books are here soon after our conversations."

When they arrived in Williston, Bill left Amanda at the office store downtown to look for her filing cabinet. He suggested she arrange for them to pick it up when they were ready to leave town. They planned to meet for lunch at a small café.

Fortunately, everything was in walking distance, unlike Atlanta where most of the businesses were moving out of the downtown area, clustered around malls or what they called "big box stores".

Amanda found a small filing cabinet and browsed the office supply store for additional things that would be helpful in her classroom. She was glad to find a large dispenser for tape and a stapler. She had somehow missed these in packing her supplies.

After leaving the office supply store she decided to take her time along the main streets and familiarize herself with what was available. She found her favorite apple scented soap and shampoo, which surprised her in a smaller town, and checked out individual shops that might be important when she did Christmas shopping. She didn't want to shop for Christmas yet, because she remembered

Myrtle Mae's comment about the church fundraising auction where she bought many of her gifts.

She left the trip to the department store to get the large cutting board for last, because she didn't want to carry it from store to store. As she went through the department store, her eyes noticed the display of jeans. She'd seldom worn them in Atlanta, but since most of the women wore them, she decided to purchase a pair. When she tried them on, they felt strange after wearing soft slacks most of her life, but she supposed she would get used to them.

The sales lady said, "You don't seem to feel comfortable in those, do you? You must be from another part of the country."

"Yes, I'm teaching the lower classes in Stoney Butte this year. Most of the women wear jeans, and so I thought I'd try a pair."

"Well, they soften as you wash them. However, if you don't like them, just bring them back. We have a good return policy."

When Amanda got to the small café, Bill had already claimed a table and was enjoying a cup of coffee. "That certainly looks good to me," she said. Bill caught the eye of the waitress and ordered a cup for her. They both ordered soup and a half sandwich.

With their order complete, Amanda said, "On days like this, the main reason I drink coffee is to keep my hands warm."

Bill smiled at her as he took a sip of his coffee. "The January thaw that we have will fool you into thinking spring is around the corner. Then it freezes again, and we have to deal with ice."

"That makes me glad that I live right next to the school. I thought these first months had made me accustomed to the wind, but when the cold is added even a slight wind is fierce. I never envisioned this."

"Well, it is seldom calm on the plains. The average wind speed is 10-13 miles per hour. That may not sound so high, but it can grate on your nerves when it doesn't let up. Wyoming and North Dakota hold the highest suicide rates in the nation, and many speculate that this is attributed to the constant wind."

Amanda smiled, "I'm glad I didn't know about this when I signed my contract, or I might not have chosen Stoney Butte."

"I'd hate to have missed getting to know you. Our few times together have been a joy for this old bachelor."

Amanda raised an eyebrow at that. "Why are you calling yourself old? We're only as old as we feel we are. I actually taught long enough to retire in Georgia, but I couldn't imagine sitting back and doing nothing. I remember a friend, when I was first married, who said she looked forward to the day she could sit on the porch and say to herself, 'You did your job well; now sit back and enjoy life.' I don't think that's me at all."

"No, in the short time I've known you, I can't see you in that role. And it will take some serious illness to make me stop in my tracks."

"It sounds like you're making lots of tracks. I imagine those tracks go on even when you are out of town."

"Yes, they do. Maybe I'll tell you about those tracks sometime, but right now no one knows about them except Willis and Miss Emma. In fact, she is the one responsible for my tracks beyond our town."

Amanda felt comforted just thinking about the older woman. "I hope to get to know her better myself. I understand she has no children, but all the children in the area are like her children. That was evident at the Labor Day dance. The children all came up to her for a big hug at some time during the night."

"Well, she's a second mother to me. Always has been. I'm so glad that my dad hired her and her husband for the ranch. I loved my mother, and she spent a lot of time with me when I was young, but Miss Emma became my sounding board for all my questions and problems."

When their food arrived, Amanda happily found that the soup warmed her stomach. *Such a lovely meal with soup for my stomach and conversation to warm my soul.*

After they finished lunch, they drove by the office store to pick up Amanda's file and then stopped by the grocery store for Bill to pick up some frozen dinners. With the freezing weather, there was no need for a cooler chest to keep them frozen. They stashed the food items that Amanda bought in the cab of the truck and were on their way.

Most of the ride home was in a comfortable silence. It seemed to each of them that joy could come without a need to force a conversation. This was such a new experience for Amanda, and she realized just how much she appreciated the silence between Bill and herself.

When they got to Bill's ranch, he invited her into the house for a hot cup of coffee. Amanda so enjoyed their time together that she was happy to accept his invitation. As they sat at the kitchen table over their coffee, Amanda said, "Tell me a little more about your parents."

"They were wonderful parents. We had some great experiences together. Miss Emma's husband was good at keeping the ranch going when we took trips. When I worked at a greenhouse in Minneapolis after college and then returned home, I talked my dad into building the first greenhouse so that I could experiment with growing plants year-round."

Bill lifted his coffee cup to his lips as if deciding just where to go next in his explanation. "Dad had a small airplane and often took someone from the neighborhood to the hospital in Williston in an emergency. Mom and Dad were flying to visit some friends in Idaho when Dad had a heart attack, and the plane went down. Both were killed. All the times that they had used the plane to save people's lives, it was during a flight that they couldn't save their own lives. If I hadn't had Miss Emma here, I'm not sure I would have made it through that first year. She helped me see that God hadn't taken them from me, but that God would help me get through the grieving period. She taught me to journal my thoughts, just in order to get them out. She showed me many places in the Bible, mainly in the Psalms, where the authors screamed out to God in their frustrations and then ended the Psalm with praise to God, even in their dark times."

Amanda reached out and took his hand that lay on the table. "It must have been a very hard time for someone so young. On top of that, I imagine you had a sinking feeling about how you would run the ranch without them."

"Yes, I considered selling out and going back to Minnesota. I wasn't sure what I would do there, but it seemed there was no longer anything for me here. Miss Emma and her husband moved into the house with me, and then I learned that Willis was available to help out on the ranch. He has been a lifesaver for me. Eventually he found Wilda, and they are my family now."

"What happened to Miss Emma's husband?" she asked.

"Shortly after Willis came to help at the ranch, he fell off a horse he was trying to break, and never regained consciousness. I knew he was too old to get on a bucking horse, but I wasn't here when it happened. He was a determined old soul who felt he would never get hurt, and he seldom did. Miss Emma and I scoured the

Bible and mourned together over his death. I think we helped each other."

"I can see why she is so important to you now."

Bill looked into her eyes. "I know she's coming to the end of her years, and each time I leave I worry that she won't be here when I get back. But she is always in my heart, even when I'm away from Stoney Butte."

Amanda recognized moisture gathering in his eyes, and she said, "Well, I suppose I should get back to town." She added with a smile, "Bertha may see that my car is gone and wonder where I am."

This brought laughter to both of them.

Chapter Twenty-Four

The next day Amanda took Miss Emma to church. After the service, the older woman stepped out of the pew to talk to someone, and Amanda turned to find Neil almost in her face. Quietly he asked, "Will you go out to lunch with me today?"

Again, Amanda said she had papers to grade. Neil's face turned to steel. "Why do you always have an excuse when I ask you out?"

Amanda didn't want to tell him that she really had no desire to go out with him, so she said, "That's just the way it turns out. I went into Williston yesterday to buy a filing cabinet, and so I need to do my grading today."

"I saw how late you got home last night. Surely it didn't take that long to buy a filing cabinet."

"I had other purchases too, and I spent some time acquainting myself to the downtown shops. It's really a nice town."

"Maybe nice if you like little towns. I should think you would have been bored with it, since you lived in Atlanta."

Amanda turned toward the door. "I found the merchants very friendly and helpful. Actually, they were much more accommodating than those in Atlanta."

"If you continue to turn people's invitations down, you'll never have any friends in this small town, and you'll find yourself very bored."

With that, Neil left her and turned his attention to another person.

Thankfully, Sue Biscoff came up to talk to her. "Would you like to come out to the ranch this afternoon and help me harvest some tomatoes?"

"How can that be? We've already had a freeze. Surely there aren't any tomatoes left to pick."

Sue smiled. "You'd be surprised. We pull up the plants, pile them together, and cover them all with a tarp. The green tomatoes turn red, and we have tomatoes for another month or so, even if it snows."

"That sounds like an ingenious idea. I'm sorry, but I just turned Neil down for his lunch invitation, so I'd better stay home and grade papers."

"Did you not want to go out to lunch with him?"

"Not really. He just doesn't seem to be someone I want to be with."

"I can't blame you much there. I'll pick some tomatoes and bring them to you tomorrow afternoon. I need to come into town for some groceries anyway."

"Oh, I'd like that. Can you stay long enough for a cup of coffee?"

"I sure can. See you then."

As Sue left, Amanda found Miss Emma and took her home. Neil's sermon had again been one that Amanda had no problem with, but there was something that made her hesitant about being active in the church. If it weren't for Miss Emma, she didn't think she would have bothered to attend worship.

The next afternoon Sue and Amanda sat down to coffee and cookies that Amanda had baked the afternoon before.

Sue asked, "How are you liking our little town now, after almost three months?"

"I'm finding it not only friendly but also restful. I love the children in my class, and it doesn't seem near as taxing on me as my teaching jobs in Atlanta. Life runs at such a slow pace here. In fact, I often feel like I'm completely isolated from all that's happening in the world."

"You can be lulled into a quiet existence here. Don't let yourself become complacent. But then, I don't think I need to tell you that. I understand you're planning the Christmas play with the children."

Amanda took a sit of coffee. "Yes, Myrtle Mae has written a play for us so that we won't have to pay royalties for it. Ione and I gave her some suggestions, and she's revised it. We will begin practice later this week."

"That should keep you busy."

"The children are so excited that it should make the work easy. They are not only enthusiastic about learning and presenting the play, but they are thrilled that it's being written right here in our town by one of the mothers."

"I think we have you to thank for that. If you hadn't made a point of visiting in each of the homes, we would never have known that Myrtle Mae has the gift of writing."

When Amanda got up to pour another cup of coffee, Sue changed the subject. "Have you gotten to know Bill Bates very well yet? I saw you talking to him after the school board meeting the other night."

"He's an interesting guy. When I went out to visit Willis and Wilda, he and Miss Emma were both there. I got a tour of the greenhouses too." Amanda wasn't sure whether she should tell Sue about the other times she'd seen Bill, but she decided that she was trustworthy enough not to gossip.

"I also had lunch with him and Miss Emma after church one Sunday. He's quite a thinker."

"Yes, he's good at thinking things through. I really hate it when he's out of town and not at our school board meetings, because he keeps us on task, thinking through any decisions we need to make."

"He asked me to go with him to Williston last Saturday. It was a real Godsend for me because I wanted to buy a filing cabinet, and he was taking his truck. He brought the filing cabinet to the school after dark last night."

"Did you enjoy your trip to Williston with him?"

"Yes, we found that we had many things to talk about, but I also found it easy to just ride along in silence with him. That was even unusual with my husband."

Sue's eyes lit up. "It sounds like you've discovered just how adaptable he is."

"That's a pretty good word to describe him."

"Don't be afraid to get to know him better but be cautious about the gossip that can whirl around this town and the surrounding area. You know that Bertha enjoys passing on any gossip she hears."

"I'm aware of that. I drove out to his ranch early on Saturday and came home after dark. I was glad that his ranch is just off the road to Williston. Yesterday I just told Neil that I'd gone to get the filing cabinet."

As Sue left, she remembered the tomatoes she had promised and went to the car to get them. When Amanda opened the bag, she was amazed that the tomatoes were so big and red.

Chapter Twenty-Five

As the November days passed, Amanda and Ione worked on the Christmas play with the children. Once they began practicing on the stage at the town hall, Myrtle Mae occasionally joined them. Amanda could see the pride in their faces as they put together a play that was all their own, written by one of their own. This pride reflected in Myrtle Mae's face.

The play was about an early Christmas on the prairies of North Dakota, and this added to their excitement. They felt they were living the experience, since it was set in a similar setting as theirs.

Thanksgiving morning dawned with a light covering of snow, just enough to give that fresh, hushed feeling that all was right in the world. Wilda had invited Amanda to spend Thanksgiving Day with them. When she had asked what she should bring, Wilda suggested a salad. Remembering a cucumber congealed salad recipe of her mother's, she lamented that she couldn't get cucumbers at this time of year.

Wilda had answered with a delighted voice. "Oh, yes, we can have cucumbers! Our garden in Bill's greenhouse has cucumbers year-round. It's so nice to have those fresh vegetables right next door. I'll send as many as you need with Jimmy tomorrow."

As Amanda stepped out on the porch, she noticed that the trees looked like black spikes, softened by snow. The world had gone gentle and quiet. It occurred to her that this was the quietest world she had ever experienced, even with the occasional snowfalls in Atlanta. The tires of her car screeched in the quietness as they rolled over the fresh snow. The little river that she crossed at the edge of town rolled through a lacey fringe of ice on each side. She thought she had never seen anything quite so peaceful.

When she arrived at Wilda and Willis' house she was greeted by blazing flames in the fireplace and a host of joyful sounds. Bill had brought Miss Emma out the day before to spend the night at his house. They told her that having Miss Emma spend the nights before Thanksgiving and Christmas had become a sort of tradition. She always made it more festive with her smiles and cheerful voice. Amanda could certainly understand that.

The meal was a great banquet, with turkey raised right there on the ranch, and all the fresh vegetables you could imagine. After dinner they moved over to Bill's house where he soon had spiced cider, hot chocolate, and coffee ready to go with the traditional pies Miss Emma always made, both pumpkin and mincemeat. There was farm fresh cream for the pumpkin pie, whipped to perfection, with a sprinkle of cinnamon on top.

They sat by the fire, and through the large windows Amanda noticed how the sun caused the snow to sparkle like gems fallen from the sky. "In the south, we always think of cold weather as being dreary. Here it can be cold, but yet the sun glitters on the snow."

Bill responded, "Yes, we can have very cold weather and still enjoy a bright, sunny day. That's why I outfitted both of these houses with a solar system. Through the system the sun generates electricity, and any we don't use on the ranch we sell to the electric company. Then if we have a number of days without sun, we buy back our electricity. It's much more earth friendly than coal or oil."

Amanda said, "I've always taught my students that we need to use the earth's energy in ways that we don't pollute the air, but I've never known anyone who actually had a solar system."

Willis spoke up. "Well, it was quite an oddity when Bill had it installed. I think most of the county turned out to see the instillation. But now it's pretty accepted. I only wish that more people would install them."

Bill winked at him, "And my next big project will be windmills on the upper hill of the property across the road. That will probably bring the county out for another look."

Through the afternoon they played board games. Amanda thought, *How much nicer this is than sitting in front of a television watching a football game. We are actually getting to know each other better.* She enjoyed the light rivalry between the two men. Although they competed to win a game, their eyes told a different story, one of a deep concern and appreciation for each other. She felt privileged to be included in this close-knit group.

As the evening approached, Amanda felt she should take her leave, although she didn't really want to go. When she suggested it, Bill said, "Oh, but Thanksgiving isn't over yet. We always raid the refrigerator in the evening, and everyone makes their own supper with what they find left from our big meal."

Thankful to have more time with the family group, Amanda agreed to stay into the evening. On the way back to Willis and Wilda's house, the guys began to build a snowman for Jimmy. When it was almost finished, Willis asked him what was missing. Immediately the boy ran into the house and brought out a carrot for the nose and a stocking cap for the head. Everyone stomped through the snow to find rocks to form the mouth and eyes, and Miss Emma even pointed out two sticks that were great for the arms. Then there was a great discussion over a name for the snowman. After many suggestions, Jimmy wanted to simply name him "Frosty", which everyone agreed was the best suggestion of all. Jimmy immediately began singing the song, and everyone sang along. Again, Amanda marveled over Bill's clear voice.

As they finished the song, Amanda looked at the night sky and saw the biggest lightshow of stars she had ever seen. It seemed as though the heavens curved around their little group and held them in the palm of God's hand. She had never felt close to God. But the intimacy of the little group, along with the marvel of the created heavens, made her wonder if she had missed out on something all these years. She began to feel that instead of being at the end of the universe, she just might be in the center.

Chapter Twenty-Six

Just as Myrtle Mae had said, the church planned an auction at the Town Hall. It was a cold Saturday, but the pot-bellied stove heated the building well, especially after everyone crowded in. There were families from town and from the ranches in all directions. This was truly an anticipated occasion. Myrtle Mae sat proudly in her wheelchair with a girl on each side. Everyone who expected to bid on the items was given a large card with a number. Amanda took card 26, knowing that she wanted to be a part of this community event. She caroused wooden toys, needlework, cakes, pies, pickles, and other things displayed on tables in front of the stage. She decided on several she wanted to bid on.

As she found a seat along the side, where she could watch the people, Bill claimed the seat beside her. He asked, "Do you have something special you want to bid on?"

Amanda said, "I know I'll bid on the box of cupcakes, and if I get it, we'll have a party at school on Monday. How about you? What are you bidding on?"

Bill answered, "Oh, I have several items in mind. I know some people I'd like to share a bit of my hometown with."

Questions arose in Amanda's mind, but she decided not to voice them. *Could this sharing be with persons he's with when he leaves town for weeks or months at a time?*

There was a loud hammering sound, and everyone quieted down. To her surprise, Willard John stood on the stage with a gavel in his hand and began the auction, sounding like the auctioneers she had heard on television. In each case, he held up the item, describing it and then mentioning who had made it. She thought, *It's amazing how many talents that man has, yet he seems so bashful when you talk to him. Hidden abilities are part of this community. Perhaps that's what holds such a small town together; they all rely on the gifts of each other.*

As the auction proceeded, Amanda realized that the final price of each item often depended on who had made it, or on which persons were bidding against each other. Some items were sold for fairly low prices, but many went for much more than she would have paid for them in an Atlanta mall. Amanda did bid on a lovely crewel embroidered piece that said, "Merry Christmas". She decided that she could frame it as a reminder of her year in Stoney Butte. But to her surprise, the bidding began to climb. Finally, she gave up her bidding and just watched as two women bid back and forth until it reached $36.00.

Bill surprised Amanda by bidding on a collection of small needlework items. Some of them had tatting on the edges, a craft that had almost vanished in most parts of the country, but evidently not in northwestern North Dakota. He also bid on several small wooden toys, all made by Otto Gill. Amanda remembered seeing Otto at church and had met him at the dance. Amanda puzzled over why Bill had bought needlework and wooden toys. *There's more to this man than I know. He really intrigues me,* she thought.

Myrtle Mae bid on several items that Amanda assumed she would use as Christmas gifts. Perhaps she sent gifts back to their families in Minnesota. Each time she won the bid, one of the girls took the money up to the table and picked up the treasure.

Finally, Willard John held up the box of cupcakes for bidding. To her surprise, Miss Emma had baked them. This gave Amanda more incentive to win the bid. The final price made each cupcake worth $2.00 each, but she decided that her students were worth that. Little Jimmy was sitting in the front row with his parents, and Amanda gave him a knowing wink as she walked by to pick up the box. On her way back to her seat, Jimmy looked at her and ran his tongue around his lips. He had guessed what she planned for the class.

The auction was certainly a success in raising money for the church, and afterwards there were many treats for everyone to enjoy. As they munched on cookies and drank black coffee, Bill asked Amanda what she thought of their community gathering. Amanda smiled. "It was certainly interesting to see good friends bid against each other for the items. They seemed to do it without any argument. I think this is a happy occasion for the whole town."

"Yes, it is," said Bill. "We actually have very little conflict in Stoney Butte. Perhaps it's because we all know that we must rely on each other since we're so far away from most conveniences. I've seen that at other places too. This is a part of what keeps me tethered to this community."

The next few weeks passed quickly, and Amanda and Ione worked with their students as they learned the Christmas play. Ione took the lead in lining up parents to make costumes and props. Other parents planned the refreshments, and it all came together at the end of the second week in December.

When the curtain closed on the final scene, Amanda looked at Myrtle Mae and saw the pride in her eyes. Then Timmy came to the front with a lily plant. He beamed as he said, "We wouldn't have had this play if Miss Myrtle Mae hadn't written it. We're so glad that she is an author." He gave the plant to Myrtle Mae.

Amanda could see tears of pride glistening in her eyes. She turned to Bill and said, "Thank you for the lily for Myrtle Mae. It really made her day."

Bill replied, "I think it made your day too."

Amanda could only nod for fear of tears streaming down her face.

Chapter Twenty-Seven

Otto Gill knocked on Miss Emma's door. It was several weeks since his last visit, and he had found some excuse each week to go to Williston and take the Sunday offering.

Miss Emma invited him into her small kitchen. The scent of freshly baked coffee cake filled the air. After she made sure he had a piece of the cake and a full cup of coffee, she sat down herself and asked, "Well, how did it go?"

"Sure enough. Each Sunday we've had enough money, besides the checks, to bring our totals up to near what my records show from previous years. I have no doubt, but that Neil has been keeping the loose change. Now, where do we go from here?"

"Well," said Miss Emma, "who's the next in command in The Methodist Church?"

"I guess it would be the district superintendent."

"I don't think a phone call from Stoney Butte would be appropriate since everyone can hear the conversation. Do you have his address? Or you might call him from Williston on a pay phone."

Otto put his cup down and said, "I do have the address, and maybe that would be the best situation. When I was in Williston on Monday, I went to the office store and had copies made of the bank receipts for the past year. Each receipt has the name of the person who deposited it. I'll have Hannah type up a letter for me, using a carbon paper, so that we have a record of the correspondence."

"You did a good job of working with this, Otto. I'm not sure you even needed me, but I appreciate your confidence in me."

Otto took a bite of the coffee cake and said, "I may have done the digging, but you were the one who gave me the courage to follow through. You're much appreciated in this community, Miss Emma." He smiled. "And not just for your delicious coffeecake."

"Oh, pshaw," she responded. "I just listen to God's whispers and try to follow them. You do the same. You just needed a little encouragement to think for yourself. You and God were the ones who came up with the plan."

Within two weeks of mailing the letter to the district superintendent, Otto received a letter back, asking to meet with him at the Methodist Church in Williston and to bring two other leaders from their church, whom he felt he could trust. Otto asked Miss Emma and Bill Bates to go with him.

On the way to Williston, Otto explained to Bill just what had happened. They felt that the bishop would remove Neil from the position, but they did not know how they would manage the church without a pastor. Otto said, "Bill, you have preached several times when our pastor was on vacation. Do you suppose you could do it for a while if no one can come immediately?"

Miss Emma said, "Let's just be quiet for a few minutes and pray that God shows us the right direction."

Bill breathed a deep sigh and flashed Miss Emma a smile of thanks. He felt he needed to digest the situation. Otto had planted the seed in Bill's thoughts, and nothing more needed to be said about the matter.

When they met at the church, the district superintendent had the evidence laid out on a table. After reviewing it, he said, "It's not a matter of a few dollars, but rather the fact that Neil was stealing the money."

They all nodded in agreement. Then the district superintendent said, "I talked to the bishop on the phone and then sent copies of your letter and the receipts to him. He called Neil and asked him to meet with him at his office. In fact, they are meeting today. The bishop is asking Neil to resign, but we would like to do this in a way that will cause the least amount of disturbance in your congregation. Unless Neil makes the reason known, we will just treat it as if he has made other plans and is leaving the Methodist Church."

Bill said, "I agree that we don't want to make this a big ordeal for the church. Neil has made some good friends since he's been with us."

The district superintendent nodded and then added, "Although your church is small, we know you have a strong congregation. We know that you can handle things well. The pastor here in Williston has agreed to come out and assist with any weddings or funerals, and also have communion with you from time to time. There are several students in the mid-term graduation at our seminaries in Chicago and Denver, and the bishop will try to get one of them to come to Stoney Butte. In the meantime, we hope you can find someone in your church to lead the services and preach for a few weeks, until we can arrange for a replacement."

Bill spoke up, "We discussed this on the way over, and I have preached several times when our pastor was on vacation. I feel that God wants me to do this for the church during the interim. I'd like to involve other lay persons in the worship leadership, however, because I want everyone to feel that it is their church."

The district superintendent expressed appreciation for this and asked the Williston pastor to come in and meet them. Bill had met him before, but he introduced himself to Otto and Miss Emma.

The next Sunday, Neil broke the news to the congregation, telling them he felt God needed him in another situation and he would be leaving during that week. He told them Bill Bates would be preaching until the bishop appointed another pastor.

Bill was thankful that he made no mention of the real circumstances of his leaving.

Neil preached a sermon on forgiveness, and Bill hoped the preacher was taking the theme of repentance seriously himself. It bothered Bill that Neil had taken the money, and he took a moment of prayer to ask God for guidance for Neil as he tried to find his new direction.

After the service, Amanda followed Miss Emma out of the church. The older woman spoke to Neil, "I wish you well, Neil. God does have a place for you. Listen to God in everything that you do."

Chapter Twenty-Eight

That afternoon Myrtle Mae called Amanda and asked her to come over and see the new cabinets that Wenzel had just finished. When Amanda knocked on the door of their new home, Marilyn and Mandy jumped up and down with excitement. Amanda thought, *I'm glad to see that these girls still have the excitement of children, although they are much more mature in the obligations they take in their home.*

After she ducked to get in the door, the girls led her to the kitchen and proudly displayed the new cabinets. The newly painted white counter and doors competed with the bright smiles of Myrtle Mae and her girls. Anyone could see the pride they took in their new home. Wenzel had sanded the countertop well before applying the paint, and the cutting board that Amanda had given them held a prominent place. The tea kettle whistled, and four cups sat on the counter ready to be filled. Beside the cups was a plate of chocolate chip cookies, fresh from the oven.

After Amanda marveled over the new look in the kitchen, and the girls served tea at the kitchen table, Myrtle Mae said, "I must admit that there is more to my asking you to come and see our cupboards. Yes, I'm very proud of them. Wenzel worked hard every night and on weekends to finish them, but I wanted to talk with you about our pastor leaving the church. Of course, I didn't want to talk about it on the phone. Bertha would have it all over the county within five minutes after I hung up.

"I have to admit that I'm glad he won't be preaching here anymore, and that Bill Bates is filling in, but I'm concerned about who they might send to take his place. I don't want it to be someone who uses fire and brimstone to scare people into believing the faith."

Amanda took a sip of tea before commenting. "I don't think we'll hear that sort of thing from Bill since he will be the interim preacher. You might talk to Miss Emma about that. I think she would agree with you, and she's pretty wise about how to approach things like the replacement of Neil."

"I think she's the wisest woman I've ever known," said Myrtle Mae. "She lives close enough to our new home that maybe she would come over for tea sometime and I can discuss it with her."

Amanda smiled at Marilyn and Mandy, "You girls are wise enough to think things through yourselves or ask questions, and I think Bill's preaching will be a breath of fresh air."

The girls' excitement over Christmas filled the rest of their visit. They asked Amanda to accompany them the next weekend when they went to the butte to cut a Christmas tree. Since Wenzel only had a truck, Amanda would follow him in her car, and the girls would ride with her.

Amanda went back to her home wondering just what had changed Neil's mind about his assignment to Stoney Butte. She also felt a relief, because she no longer had to make excuses for not going out to lunch with him.

Late Tuesday afternoon, Bill made a trip into town for stamps and groceries. After stopping at the post office and leaving his grocery list for Delmar and Leola to fill, he walked over to Amanda's home. She answered the door right away, and Bill saw that she was in the middle of grading papers.

"I won't take much of your time, but I wanted to ask if you'd like to go with me to the butte on Saturday to cut Christmas trees. Willis, Wilda and little Jimmy will be going too. We thought we would make a day of it if the weather holds out. It will give you a chance to see the butte and maybe get a small tree for yourself."

Amanda replied in a sad voice, "I would love to, but Myrtle Mae and her girls invited me to go with them to cut their tree on Saturday."

Bill suggested, "Perhaps we can all go together. Wenzel and Willis can take their trucks, and I'll take my car. Myrtle Mae and Wilda can put a lunch together, and I know the perfect place for us to eat. It's sheltered from the wind, but quite sunny. It's also level enough for Myrtle Mae's wheelchair. The cold shouldn't be too bad, if the weather holds out."

"I want to contribute to the lunch too. I hope this will be okay with Myrtle Mae and Wenzel."

"I'll stop by their house after I pick up my groceries, and when I get home, I can call you to firm up our plans. Does the time we leave make a difference for you?"

"I can be ready any time. Have Wilda call and tell me what to bring for lunch."

It was late enough when Bill got to Myrtle Mae's that Wenzel was home. They all agreed on the outing, and Bill drove out of town excited about Saturday. He knew that Willis and Wilda would approve the plan.

Chapter Twenty-Nine

Saturday Amanda woke up to an unusually warm day for December in North Dakota. The two days before they had experienced temperature above freezing, and most of the snow on the roads had melted. She was glad she didn't have to drive on the slushy roads.

Bill had Marilyn and Mandy in the car when he picked her up around noon. "This is so exciting!" exclaimed Mandy.

"You will see the butte for the first time," Marilyn told Amanda. "I wonder why the trees grow on the buttes and not in the prairie."

Amanda said, "Perhaps we should check that out in our encyclopedia."

They met the others on the road just out of town. Soon they were away from the flat prairie and climbing a hill with evergreens on either side. These were smaller than those Amanda had seen in the Appalachian Mountains. She enjoyed the trees as they drove higher into the butte and realized how much she missed the mountains of North Carolina. It was exciting to be in the surrounding green after several months of prairie grass. She almost asked Bill to stop so that she could get out and hug a tree.

Bill pulled over at a rock outcropping. Willis's truck was right behind them, and as soon as it stopped, Jimmy hit the ground running. "This is a great place," he said. "We've never been here before, have we Dad?"

"No," said Willis. "This spot is special for Bill and me."

As they unloaded blankets and their lunch from the vehicles, Myrtle Mae was all smiles - glad to be out in nature instead of cooped up in a house. As Amanda helped spread the lunch on a blanket, she asked Myrtle Mae, "Are you enjoying this outing?"

Myrtle Mae answered in an excited voice. "I love being with such friends and a part of this special time. Some years it's been too cold for me to go along on a tree-cutting event."

Wenzel filled Myrtle Mae's plate, and Amanda sat on a blanket beside her wheelchair after she filled her own. "Do you get to come up here often?" she asked.

"Oh, no. We may come up once in the summer, but it's an altogether different world that I'm seeing in the winter. I'm glad that Bill knew about this place where I can use the wheelchair and feel like I'm on top of the world."

"It is lovely here," Amanda agreed.

As Bill sat down beside her he said, "Willis and I used to come up here when we were in high school and see how far we could throw rocks. Sometimes throwing rocks was just for fun, and sometimes it was a method of getting some frustration out of our system. It's always been special for me."

Amanda looked puzzled, "What caused your frustration?"

"Just different things," replied Bill. "Sometimes Willis was frustrated about breaking up with a girl. He was quite popular in high school, but no girl seemed to be right for him until many years later when he met Wilda."

"He sure found the right one then," said Myrtle Mae.

"Did you have frustrations too?" asked Amanda.

Bill threw a rock over the edge and said, "I think my main frustration was being stuck here in North Dakota. During high school I wanted the excitement of the big city. I hadn't grown up enough to appreciate the close-knit community of Stoney Butte."

After they finished eating, Bill challenged Jimmy, Marilyn, and Mandy to see who could throw the farthest over the edge. Bill kept the children entertained while Amanda, Willis and Wilda put the lunch items away, and Wenzel helped Myrtle Mae into the truck. Soon they drove off, earnestly searching for Christmas trees.

In addition to trees for their homes, they found a perfect tree for the church. Myrtle Mae remembered, "Several years ago we made Chrismon ornaments for our church tree. We carefully pack them away after Christmas."

Amanda asked quizzically, "What are Chrismon ornaments? I've never heard of them."

Marilyn was quick with her answer. "They are symbols that represent different things in the Christian faith. Some represent different people in the Bible. They make a beautiful tree."

Before they left, Amanda asked if they could cut some branches to decorate the school rooms. As they loaded the branches, Jimmy clapped his hands. "Oh! Let's not tell anyone about the evergreen branches and surprise the classes on Monday."

Bill threw the last branch into the truck. "I'll help Ms. Amanda put them up so that they will be there when all of you get to school on Monday and you can surprise them."

With the trucks loaded, they headed back to Stoney Butte. Bill took Mandy and Marilyn to their home first. When he parked at Amanda's place, he turned toward her with his arm on the back of the seat. "I certainly enjoyed our time together today."

Amanda smiled up at him. "It's been a wonderful day."

"I'd like for us to have more times together."

Her eyes sparkled. "I'd enjoy that too. It's nice to have someone who talks seriously and appreciates our world, but who is also open to listen to other people's ideas."

Bill said, "We'll just have to find more opportunities to get together. Right now, I suppose we'd better get these greens and tree unloaded." Their eyes locked for a few moments before getting out of the truck.

After unloading the branches, Bill helped Amanda place them around both classrooms. As they finished, Amanda said, "I'd better not call Ione ahead of time because the party lines would give Jimmy's secret all over town."

After they finished in the classrooms, Bill took the tree into Amanda's trailer, and then surprised her with a tree stand.

"Where did that come from?" asked Amanda.

"My parents had several trees each year, and I only put one up, so this is an extra one."

"Well, I certainly didn't think to pack one. Besides, in Atlanta I always had an artificial tree. This has certainly been more fun than going to a tree lot."

"And I imagine the evergreen scent will give you a better Christmas spirit."

"Oh, yes. We will enjoy the evergreens at school too."

As Bill bent over to screw the tree trunk tight, he said, "I don't suppose you brought any ornaments with you from Atlanta either."

"No, I just didn't think about decorating a tree. To be honest, I thought I'd be going back to Atlanta for Christmas. As it turns out, my son's in Africa, and my daughter just wrote that she will visit her boyfriend's family for Christmas, so I guess I'll stay here. I can make my own ornaments."

Bill smiled. "We'll just include you in our Christmas family like we did at Thanksgiving."

"I would like that," Amanda said with remembrance of the family feeling that was so evident at Thanksgiving. She looked forward to this opportunity to be with the same people at Christmas.

After the tree was secure and water was added to the tree stand, Amanda made coffee and brought out a plate of cookies. She turned the radio to a station that had seasonal music and joined Bill on the sofa, kicking off her shoes and pulling her feet up under her.

"Mandy and Marilyn were so excited to show me the butte," she said.

"They are two special little girls. I remember some other delightful girls."

"Was that where you were last summer?"

"Well, yes." said Bill. Amanda thought that he had almost let his secret slip out. "There are some lovely little girls everywhere, but these little girls of Myrtle Mae and Wenzel are really special."

Amanda thought, *I've stepped a little too fast toward Bill's secret.* She changed the subject. "What have you planned for your sermon tomorrow? Myrtle Mae was really worried about what Neil was saying in some of his sermons."

"I just hope I can do a good job."

"I have all the confidence in the world in you. I haven't known you very long, but I've heard you and Miss Emma talk enough to know you'll give us a good and helpful sermon. What is your theme for tomorrow?"

"I decided that the best theme would be to talk about the importance for us to recognize God's grace, that God loves us sometimes with a happy heart and sometimes with a sad heart, but God always loves."

"I think you'll talk in the language that children can understand."

"I believe most adults need to have things said in simple words too. I've learned that, everywhere I've been."

As Bill left that night, he grasped her hands and said, "You've made Stoney Butte really special for me this year."

Amanda responded, "And for me too."

After Bill left, Amanda realized that her hands still felt warm from Bill's grasp. She told herself she was too old to have such feelings, but they seemed to be there no matter how she tried to talk herself out of it.

Chapter Thirty

On Monday, the students looked around the room with wide grins as they entered. Jimmy, Marilyn and Mandy exchanged special looks. They did a good job of keeping the secret about the evergreen branches in the school room.

The children clamored with their requests to make ornaments for the branches, and so an art experience became the first subject of the day.

After the branches had received their art contributions, Amanda asked the older students to check out two questions in the encyclopedia. She wrote the questions on the board: Why do so few trees grow in the prairie? What types of trees grow on the prairie?

As they found the encyclopedias and began to search, Amanda quizzed the second graders on their multiplication tables while the first graders worked in their reading workbooks.

When Amanda asked the older students for their reports, one of them said, "The compacted soil has less air which limits the root growth, and trees often die during a drought because their roots can't absorb enough water to keep them alive."

Joel spoke up, "I remember two summers ago we got very little rain, and a tree we had planted near the store died."

Jimmy added, "I think our tree with the swing is a cottonwood. I know that they can grow very tall."

Marilyn reported. "We get temperatures over a hundred degrees in the summer and as low as fifty below some winters. That difference in temperatures gives us less rain. We get lots of snow, but the encyclopedia says that if the temperature is thirty degrees it takes ten inches of snow to equal one inch of rain. That's a lot of snow for one inch of rain. It takes even more snow when the temperature is lower."

This brought surprised expressions all over the room. Mandy said, "I just thought an inch of snow equals an inch of rain. Wow, was I ever wrong. I guess that's why we have encyclopedias."

Amanda suggested, "When the bookmobile comes again, you might ask the librarian to bring some elementary science books on snow.

"What else did you learn from your encyclopedias today?"

Another student said, "We learned that forests make up only 2% of North Dakota. Our state has the lowest number of trees per acre. The rest of the state is low lying hills and prairie lands filled with over 200 types of grass. There are wheat fields and other crops where they are planted, but the low rainfall makes it hard to grow these crops without irrigation, and that's expensive. That's why so many small farmers are selling out to big companies and leaving the area."

Marilyn said, "Thank you, Ms. Amanda, for showing us how to use an encyclopedia. It's good to be able to look up questions for ourselves, instead of just being told the answers."

"Yes, it's important for you to look up your own answers. It sticks in your mind better that way." Then Amanda asked, "Did you look up the second question about the types of trees that grow here?"

The children put their heads together looking for the answer to the second question as Amanda began to work with the first grade's reading assignment.

When the students found their answer, the whole class listened again. Marilyn reported, "First, there are many trees that can be grown if they have a good water supply. We have cottonwoods and even birches near the rivers. There are several evergreens on the buttes and on Killdeer Mountain, including juniper and ponderosa. They grow mainly on the north side of the buttes. We think the branches in our classroom are juniper. Poplar and Elm are popular around houses, but they've usually been planted there. We did identify the tree with our swing as a cottonwood. I wonder what types of trees Bill Bates grows on his ranch?"

Amanda said, "Since he grows them to sell, they will likely be trees that you find around ranch houses and in our towns and cities. Maybe we can make a field trip to his ranch and find out." This brought cheers from the whole class.

She affirmed them, saying, "You older students have done a good job of reporting, Thank you. We all learned something from your work."

When the children went out for recess, Amanda saw them gather around the tall cottonwood tree and investigate its bark, looking up into the bare limbs. They were beginning to take an interest in nature that was all around them. She was glad they were inquiring and thinking for themselves. She thought, *This is what learning is all about.*

Chapter Thirty-One

Friday morning, the last day before the Christmas break, each child came into the classroom with one or two Christmas ornaments they had made at home. Soon Amanda's desk was filled with the homemade decorations. Some of the older siblings even left ornaments on her desk before heading to their classroom.

Amanda could not contain herself. "Where did all of these come from?" she asked.

Little Timmy said, "We all got calls from Bill Bates asking us to make ornaments for your tree since you didn't have any yourself. He even said he had some paper and crayons if we needed them. We decided to make some for our tree at home too. We don't have any store-bought decorations."

Every child in the classroom bubbled with excitement over what Santa might bring them. Amanda looked at the students and wondered about how bare the Christmas trees would be of gifts for some of them. She knew that Myrtle Mae planned ahead for Christmas, and Jimmy's parents and Joel's grandparents would see that they got toys. But then her eyes fell on Timmy. When she'd visited their house, the furniture was sparse. She had seen the large bag of oatmeal behind the stove, suspecting that as their main staple meal.

On Friday afternoon she walked to Miss Emma's house and shared her concern with her. Miss Emma immediately picked up the phone and called Bill, asking him to come over. When he joined them at the kitchen table with his cup of tea, she explained Amanda's concern about Timmy's family.

Bill seemed to think for a minute, and then his smile brought a pair of curved lines, like parentheses, to his cheeks. Miss Emma said, "I knew you'd come up with an answer to the problem."

"I'll have to put in a special request to Santa for that family." Bill asked, "Amanda, would you like to be a part of this?"

"Oh, yes! What are your plans?"

"We'll make a trip to Williston a couple of days before Christmas," he explained. "You will be on Christmas break then. We can pick up some toys for the children and the makings of a Christmas dinner. We'll wrap the toys and leave them on the porch, along with the dinner supplies. If we're careful, no one will know where it all came from."

As they left Miss Emma's, hefty flakes plummeted toward them, plopping into their hair and eyelashes. Bill offered to give Amanda a ride home. Although it was only a few blocks, she took him up on the offer and asked him to come in and see her tree.

After they shed their snow-covered coats, Amanda turned to him with a smile. "Thank you for suggesting to the children that they make ornaments for my tree. I think they make the tree lovely, don't you? It speaks of the love that my students and I have grown together. I've never felt such love for my students."

Bill said, "Love seems to burst from you for everyone. I can see it every time I look into your face."

As they stood looking at the tree, Bill put his arm around her and pulled her close. Amanda felt comfortable in his embrace. She turned and looked up at him. "I do love the children very much. I've also seen love spill from you for everyone in the area. You told me that at one time you were just anxious to get away from here. Now the whole town seems to be a part of you, and it responds to your love."

Bill put both arms around her and whispered in her ear, "Miss Emma taught me to be content wherever I am, and I do love Stoney Butte." He paused a moment and then added, "And I think I'm beginning to love you, too."

With a hand under her chin, he tipped her head back and softly brushed his lips on her forehead, then her cheek, and finally her lips. Amanda knew that this was right, even though she was no longer a teenager or young woman. She leaned into his chest and enjoyed the simple kiss.

Amanda drove out to Bill's house early on the morning they planned their Williston trip. Again, she tried to avoid the chance of gossip across town. They had decided to get an early start.

When they drove into Williston, the first rays of sun touched the horizon, reaching pink fingers into the sky. Moved by emotion as she stepped out of the car in Williston, she said, "The colors of the sky at sunrise give me a real boost for the day."

Bill glanced at her, "I also love this time of day. Sometimes I get up early just to see the sunrise. Of course, in the winter you don't need to get up so early to see the colors. We do have long hours of darkness here. That's quite different from some places in the world."

Amanda wondered just what part of the world he referenced. *Just where does he go during those mysterious months?* She didn't dare ask. If he wanted her to know, he would tell her in his own time.

In Williston they found toys for the Cazer children and then went to the supermarket for the makings of their holiday dinner. As they drove home, Amanda asked, "When would be a good time for you to talk to the school children? Are you sure you want to combine it with a field trip?"

"Early April is when our summer plantings in the greenhouse begin to sprout. We could include an opportunity for them to plant some seeds in a sprouting pot to take home and put near a window."

"That sounds good. They would enjoy growing their own plants. After Christmas I plan to have Delmer and Leola talk to the students about running a grocery store. We'll also take a field trip and maybe have the children help replenish the shelves from a shipment of canned goods."

Bill ran a hand through his dark curls. "I remember, as a young child, wondering where they got the food they sold. The shelves of bright colored cans always intrigued me. It's interesting what little things come to your mind later in life."

"Sue will talk to the children about nursing in early February, along with Dr. Endive. Then we may follow that up in March with the medical researcher that she knew, if he's available. So, April is a good time to hear from you and visit the greenhouses."

"That will give their seedlings time to grow before we're sure the weather is warm enough for the plants to survive outside. We've had snow at the end of April before."

Amanda turned to Bill. "I understand that lilacs bloom profusely here. We have small bushes in Georgia that nurseries sell, but nothing large."

"You remember the large bushy plant in your front yard? It's a lilac, and it will overpower you with its scent. They bloom at the end of April and the first of May."

"I love the smell of lilacs. I don't think the scent will overpower me. I'm looking forward to its blooming. They have such delicate flowers. I'll cut some and put them in a vase. That way I can see them as well as smell them inside."

After a few moments of their comfortable silence, Amanda said, "In Georgia we have dogwood, cherry, and redbud trees that bloom before the leaves come out. That always puzzled me."

"By flowering before the leaves, those trees use the wind to move their pollen around. Later blooming trees and flowers must depend on insects to move the pollen because the flowers are often hidden by leaves. The contrast of cold and heat seems to have something to do with it, but scientists are still working on that angle. Most of our trees up here have both flowers and leaves coming out at the same time."

Bill paused as he took a curve in the snow-covered gravel road. "Some plants are a little different. Take for example the corn plant. It doesn't bloom until after it has grown tall and the leaves are well developed, but the bloom is right on top and our prairie wind does a good job of pollinating the surrounding plants."

"You explain things so simply that I know you will be able to talk to the children with words they understand."

Bill reached for her hand on the seat next to him. "I hope I can do that," he said with a smile.

When they got to Bill's house, they wrapped the Christmas gifts and found boxes for the dinner supplies and gifts. They made signs for each box that said, "Merry Christmas, Love, Santa." Now they only needed to wait until it was late enough for the children to be asleep.

As they waited, Bill placed logs in the large fireplace and put some kindling and a twisted paper below the logs. Striking a match, he lit the flame to the paper. The flame flickered delicately, and there was a first sharp whiff of smoke before the logs caught. Amanda was mesmerized by the flames. They seemed soothing in the comfortable living room. Bill suggested, "Shall we have a pizza and salad while we wait?"

Amanda hated the thought of leaving the fireplace, but she said, "Only if I help with the salad."

Soon Bill had the oven heating and the salad makings out on the center island. It seemed that their minds worked together, anticipating just what the other needed. The salad was finished just as the pizza came from the oven.

As they feasted in front of the fireplace, Bill asked her about her family.

Amanda began. "As you probably know, my husband was killed in an automobile accident four years ago. It was pretty tough at first, but I've learned to remember the happy times we had together. We had a daughter and then a son. My daughter, Ashley, is a lawyer, climbing the corporate ladder. She's always had goals for herself and she worked to attain them. My son, Kurt, graduated from college with an education degree but was an aspiring musician until this fall when he and a friend joined the Peace Corps. He's just been assigned to Zaire and is certainly getting his feet wet there. I think he will learn a lot about developing countries. We will have to see just what becomes of that experience."

"And yourself? I understand that you left a good position to come out here and teach in a two-room schoolhouse."

Amanda ate some of her salad, giving herself time to think through just what she wanted to reveal. "I've always loved teaching. After many years of teaching, I took a course in conflict resolution, thinking that would help me solve some of my students' problems. Actually, the training landed me in a job as principal of an elementary school where I had to deal with not only the discontent of students, but also the complaints of parents. You won't believe how the parents refuse to stand up for teachers. According to many of them, their children can do no wrong and the teachers all lie."

Bill raised an eyebrow, "And so you came out here to this tiny town. Have you found it any different?"

"Yes, I have. The parents are anxious for their children to learn and they cooperate with the teacher. At least that's what I've experienced so far. I've also enjoyed being back in the classroom again."

Bill picked up another piece of pizza and said, "I don't think that is the only reason you came to this little town."

Amanda was surprised at his insight. She had always been able to hide her inner thoughts from others, even her husband. This man seemed to read her like a book. Was that good or bad? She decided to put him off. "No, that's not the only reason, but I'm not ready to say any more yet."

Bill put his arm around her shoulders. "I understand. There are some things we keep to ourselves until the right time to reveal them."

"I knew you would understand because I think there are things that you keep to yourself too."

Bill smiled a knowing smile and kissed the top of her head.

By the time they finished their meal and cleaned up the kitchen, Bill said, "I think it's late enough that the children are in bed and we can deliver our Christmas surprises. Why don't you drive your car into town, and I'll pick you up? That way we'll only have one vehicle to conceal when we take the boxes to the porch."

When they got to the Cazers, they were glad that there were no other cars on the road. Bill turned his car around for a quick getaway and parked where a few shrubs hid it. They opened the trunk. Amanda took the lighter box with the toys, and Bill took the box with the dinner makings. He set his box on the ground and quietly closed the trunk lid.

"Be careful to walk in the tire tracks," cautioned Bill. "We don't want them to see our footprints."

When they got to the porch Bill placed both boxes in front of the screen door so that it would hit the boxes when they opened it. Then he said, "You go back to the car, and I'll knock and then run back to the car before they can get to the door."

The plan worked well, and Bill had the car started before the Cazers opened the door. They heard the boxes being pushed aside as they drove away.

"I hope we will just sound like someone driving down the road," Bill said. "At least it's dark enough they won't be able to recognize my car."

Amanda giggled, "I feel like shouting, 'A Merry Christmas to all. And to all a good night.'"

Chapter Thirty-Two

Since Bill had charge of the services for the church, he decided to have a candle lighting service on Christmas Eve. The little church had never had one, but his friend at the university had told him, in detail, about one he had attended. He announced it in church, and also asked Bertha to spread the word by telephone so that those who didn't regularly attend might come.

Ethel and Lloyd were home for the Christmas break, so Amanda did not need to drive Miss Emma. It was such a lovely night that she decided to walk the couple of blocks to the church. Her new snow boots were so comfortable she knew it would be easy walking. As she stepped out her door, she looked over the small town with the sky above. Out this far away from light pollution, the star-spangled sky looked limitless. She thought of the men who landed on the moon last year and wondered just how they had felt as they traveled through the heavens, seeing the earth among the stars. *Maybe there is more to this concept of God who created all of this than I thought before. No humans could make what I'm seeing tonight.*

As she approached the church, she saw a lit candlestick in each window. When she entered, the table in front of the pulpit was draped in white with a lovely creche in the center. There was a hushed atmosphere among the worshipers as the pianist played softly. There were many candles lit throughout the sanctuary. It was as if she had brought the whole star-studded sky inside the door with her. She was handed a small candle as she entered.

Quietly she found a seat just behind Miss Emma, Lloyd, and Ethel. She had never seen as many people at a service in this small church. Tears escaped her eyes as she blinked to hold them back. Suddenly she felt a real part of the community that gathered there.

Bill led the congregation in a few familiar carols, then read several poems, ending with the Christmas story from Luke. At the end of his readings he led the congregation in singing "Silent Night" and lit his candle from the ones beside the creche. Then he walked down the aisle, giving the light to the first person on each pew. Each one turned and lit the candle of the person next to them, and soon the little church was filled with light. From the back of the church Bill said, "You have each received the light of love. Now go and spread that light throughout our community, our county, our nation, and the whole world. This is what God wants of you."

When Amanda went through the door, Bill was nowhere in sight. She realized that he was not there to hear compliments on the service. He wanted them to quietly take the atmosphere home. It had been such a simple service, but one that drew the community together. She walked slowly home, carefully shielding her light from any breath of wind. When she got home, she immediately found a small glass, and dripping a little of the wax in the bottom, she set the candle in it. The one little candle lit up the whole room. She remembered someone telling her that darkness cannot conceal light, but light can overcome darkness. Was that what someone had told her after her husband's death? Perhaps. Now she knew that the darkness of her life in Atlanta had been overcome by the light of the people of this small town.

The next morning Amanda awoke before sunrise. Willis and Wilda had invited her to come to the ranch early for breakfast to see little Jimmy's joy over Santa's visit. Bill was to take Miss Emma out after the Christmas Eve service so she could spend the night at his house.

As she dressed in warm slacks and a cable-knit sweater, Amanda's thoughts went to the Cazer house. What sort of excitement might be going on there? Would Timmy like the puzzle map of North Dakota that she and Bill had picked out for him? Bill had driven by the house the day after they had left the boxes of gifts and dinner makings and knew that they had found them. It would be a great day for their family as they smelled the roasting turkey and opened their gifts.

She got to Bill's ranch at the appointed time and found the aroma of coffee and some sort of bread swirling through the house. Wilda said that their tradition was for Jimmy to stay in his bedroom until they were all gathered so that they could see his pleasure in Santa's delivery. Everyone took their cups of coffee and settled around the tree. Then Jimmy came in, all smiles and excited when he saw the gifts spread below the tree. After all the oohs and ahs, Willis said, "It's time for us to open our stockings."

To Amanda's surprise, there was a stocking for everyone, including herself. "How did Santa know I would be out here with you, Jimmy?"

He answered, "I told him, when I sent my letter to him. Santa really has lots of people to remember, but he didn't forget you Ms. Amanda!"

After a breakfast of fresh scrambled eggs and a Christmas wreath bread, Wilda said, "It's time to move back into the living room and open the wrapped gifts." Everyone found a place to sit.

It was obvious that they had left the love seat for Bill and Amanda. Jimmy parked himself in front of the tree,

"Can I hand out the gifts?" he asked.

Willis laughed. "You usually do. Of course, you can."

Amanda had brought something for everyone. The gift for Bill had been difficult, but she'd finally settled on a nice journal with a pen attached. He said he journaled from time to time, and his current one was almost full, so he was happy to get a new one.

Amanda received gifts from everyone. Miss Emma had made a quilted lap blanket for her. Wilda and Willis gave her a set of kitchen towels. Jimmy had made a story book about the different children in their class at school. Amanda was so pleased with it she said, "Jimmy, this is lovely. I will keep it on my coffee table so that I can look at it often." She was rewarded with Jimmy's bright smile.

She opened Bill's gift last. It was a silver bracelet with lilacs in a ceramic square. She smiled at him, remembering their conversation. He whispered in her ear. "You said you liked the delicacy of the flowers as well as the scent. This way you will have them year-round." Amanda was surprised that he remembered their conversation.

The whole morning was festive as the adults prepared the big meal, and Jimmy enjoyed his toys. Just before the meal was ready, Amanda walked into the living room to find Jimmy asleep, curled up in a big chair with the book she had brought him open on his lap. It had been an early morning for him. She knew he was tired.

When Wilda called out that dinner was ready, Amanda gently woke Jimmy and walked with him to the table. "I get to sit beside you and Bill," he said. "See. I made name cards for everyone and I got to put them wherever I wanted."

Bill winked at Amanda across Jimmy's head as they took their seats. They shared a real love for the little guy. He was very polite during the meal and asked each of them questions.

"Amanda, how did you celebrate Christmas in Atlanta?"

"Very much like you do here. My children are grown now, but when they were young, they were as excited about Santa as you are. We adults get excited about Christmas, but we don't expect toys from Santa."

Miss Emma spoke up. "Jimmy, do you remember when I told you that another name for Santa is St. Nicholas?"

"Yes, they call him that in some other countries."

"Well, there was a man, many years ago, with the name of Nicholas. He gave gifts to many people who didn't have much. Later he was made a saint in the Roman Catholic Church."

"That's a different church from ours, right?"

"At that time there was only one type of church. Since then many have developed, but we all believe in God and in Jesus."

"And Christmas is when we celebrate Jesus' birth."

"Yes, you are right, Jimmy. When this man named Nicholas died, the church made him a saint. That means that they thought he had done many wonderful things for people who needed help."

"We should all do good things for people who need help," said Jimmy. "Ms. Amanda told us about All Saints' Day that comes after Halloween. It's a better day than Halloween because it celebrates people who did good things."

"Yes," said Miss Emma. "We should all do good things for others."

Jimmy paused a few moments, then turned to Bill and said, "Uncle Bill, I don't know what you do when you're not here at home, but I think you must be doing good things."

Bill gave Jimmy a hug and said, "I always try to do good things for people. Miss Emma and my parents taught me that, and you learned that from your parents and Miss Emma too."

Jimmy smiled across the table at the little woman who was special to him. "You teach us some good things."

Amanda mused, *Bill ignored the question, but Jimmy seems to know nothing about Bill's absence. He just accepts it.*

Everyone joined in games during the afternoon while enjoying the roaring fire. Amanda felt a warmth that came in a different form than flames. She began to feel a part of this family as well as a part of the little community of Stoney Butte.

Chapter Thirty-Three

During the week after Christmas, Miss Emma called Amanda and asked her to have dinner with her. She decided to walk the few blocks to her house. Seeing Bill's truck in front of the house, Amanda was glad she had decided to walk. If her car had been noticed beside Bill's truck, there would soon have been gossip around the county.

After dinner, Bill brought up the subject on his mind. "You may remember that the President proposed a new agency last July. Earlier this month he signed an executive order establishing the EPA, or Environmental Protection Agency. This was then ratified by committee hearings in the House and Senate. I know that this is a political situation, but I believe that we have a moral obligation to take care of our planet. I wanted to talk with you two about how I can present the importance of this to our little congregation. Too often we feel as though we are just a little town out here in the midst of the prairie and have no obligation to anything or anyone else. Miss Emma, you taught me a different attitude about our place in the world, and I feel that this is my opportunity to share this with our church and community."

The older woman's eyes showed her pride in him. "You came to most of those decisions yourself as we talked together. What scripture do you think would be appropriate to share these ideas?"

Amanda sat back, taking the conversation in. She knew so little about scripture that she felt Bill was expecting more from her than she could contribute to the discussion.

Bill said, "First, of course, would be the passages in Genesis that God made our world and put us in charge of it. Then I've thought of using Psalm 24 that begins, *The earth is the Lord's and all that is in it, the world, and those who live in it.*"

Miss Emma nodded. "Yes, that's a good beginning. Take a look at the beginning of Leviticus 25 where God tells Moses to instruct the people to give their lands a time of rest every seven years. This is one way God wants us to care for the earth. You know that rotating cattle from one part of your land to another benefits the land."

"That's right. I've done it for years, and most of the ranchers follow that system." Bill turned to Amanda. "Do you have any suggestions of things that I should include?"

Amanda admitted, "I'm not very good about scriptures, but from a scientific point of view, I've been reading about how we are ruining our air and water in many ways. In the early 1800's scientists began noting what we now call 'global warming', but it was not until the 1950's that we began to pay attention to the data they were gathering to corroborate the global warming theory. That's when some red flags were raised about the dire consequences this could have on our earth. They say that the icebergs may melt and cause the oceans to raise, literally doing away with some of the islands. You know, it wouldn't even surprise me if global warming changed our weather patterns and even affected some of our plants."

He looked at his empty cup. "We may even find that the trees that grow our coffee beans can't live in the world we're changing."

Amanda laughed. "That would certainly ruin the morning for some of us."

Bill nodded in agreement with a smile and continued. "Most people take little interest in this, but if you look at the fact that God gave us the care of the earth, then we should consider all parts of nature.

"What are some of the simple things that people in our little community could do? I don't want people to just think about this, but they need to begin action."

Miss Emma was quick to respond. "Well, for one thing, we can share our trips to Williston with others and not put as many emissions into the atmosphere. Perhaps we can create a community bulletin board where people who plan a Williston trip can post the date and others sign up to travel together. Maybe that could be in the post office. Most people in town go there once a day. Or it could be at Delmer and Leola's store."

Bill chuckled. "I like that idea. Bertha will be happy to pass on any news of people going to Williston. Getting the word around shouldn't be a problem with our telephone system."

Miss Emma added, "We can also walk to houses around town instead of driving, and when someone comes to town, they can park at one place and walk to any of the other places they plan to go."

Bill suggested, "Perhaps we can invite people to park at our church when they come to town. The church is close enough for almost everything in town. We could even put up a sign that says, 'Save gas and park here for all your town needs.'"

Amanda spoke up. "My thoughts were along the order of saving water. I understand that we have some very dry periods in the summer. Perhaps we can suggest that everyone use a pail or some other utensil to catch water while they are waiting for hot water in the sink or shower. Then they can use that water in the washing machine or to water plants during the dry season. I never use hot water for washing clothes myself, and that saves on fuel consumption. I also read recently that it takes four gallons of water if you leave the water running while brushing your teeth, and only a quarter of a gallon if you turn it off."

Bill looked surprised. "I have been to places that were scarce of water, but I'd never thought about how much we waste just brushing our teeth."

In a short time, they had a list of simple ways that people in the community could save natural resources. Bill said, "I'll type these up and make some copies so that I can pass them out at the end of the service. I need to go to Williston this week, and I can make copies then."

Miss Emma beamed. "I knew you would preach sermons that were applicable to our everyday lives instead of dwelling on the negative and hell and damnation."

As they were leaving, Amanda told them how she appreciated being a part of the brain-storming session. Bill admitted, "I actually wanted Miss Emma to invite you because I thought you might have some good ideas, and you've contributed a lot to my own thoughts."

Amanda smiled her appreciation for his words. "I think I can weave some of this into our science lessons for a week or so. This is exciting, to think not only of informing the adults, but also getting in on the ground floor with the next generation. Who knows what they'll come up with as adults."

Bill added, "And some great things can come out of a little town of 92 people, especially with a teacher like you."

That Sunday Bill's sermon centered on our stewardship of the earth, and as he handed the lists to the parishioners, they thanked him for bringing some thoughts to their minds.

Chapter Thirty-Four

December thirty-first began as a cloudy, dreary day. Amanda stretched in her bed, waking Aggie who had been content between her legs. She told the cat, "It's a good day to work on my science lesson plans for climate control and conservation of water." She mentally developed ideas on how to help the children appreciate having accessible water. Suddenly, she sensed a quietness that could only be snowfall. Sure enough, the view out her window was completely white. She stood, mesmerized by the picture developing outside. Every tree was covered, and the wind pushed piles of snow against her trailer. Her Volvo looked like a ski jump.

Three short rings snapped her to the indoors. She rushed to the phone. Bertha was on the other end. "Just wanted to warn you that we're in for a real blizzard. We could have a foot or two of snow, according to the weather forecast. If you need anything, you can get it at the store. Delmer said they will keep it open. They can do that since they live there."

"Thank you for letting me know. I think I have anything I might need."

She had hardly hung up when there were three short rings again. This time it was Sue. "Are you alright? Bertha has probably told you about the prediction of this storm."

"I think I'll be fine. It's nice to have neighbors who check on me. It does look lovely outside, but I'm glad I have a warm trailer."

"I just wanted to check on you. The phone lines are likely to go out. At least you are close to Delmer's store, but don't go out into this if you can avoid it. People have become disoriented in the swirling snow and frozen to death, even in their own yards. We have already put up a rope between the house and barn so that we can hold onto it when we need to go from one building to another."

"Thank you for checking on me. I'll just stay put. You two take care of yourselves out there in the country."

Sue laughed. "We've been through blizzards so many times it's routine for us. We have the preparation down pat. We'll call when it's all over and see how you did."

After putting the phone in its cradle, she turned to view the spectacle outside her windows. Sure enough, there were already huge piles of snow with bare ground beside it, just as she had been told. It interested her to see how the wind in this prairie country brought this about. She made herself a small pot of coffee and sat down to watch the process of nature.

The blizzard lasted through the night, but in spite of it she slept soundly and awoke to the bright sun glittering off the snow. She decided to freshen herself with a hot shower, but she discovered that there was no water. At first, she became frantic, because she hadn't saved water. Then she realized that she could always melt snow. However, in the kitchen, she discovered that she had both hot and cold water. Puzzled, she asked Aggie, "How could water freeze to the bathroom but not to the kitchen? It's not a matter of frozen pipes leading to the trailer."

She washed up in the kitchen, dressed, and began a breakfast of oatmeal and coffee. Just as she finished eating and sat down for a second cup of coffee, she heard a scraping noise on her porch. Looking out the window she saw Bill's truck and snow flying off the side of her porch. She opened the door just a crack and realized that snow was piled high against it. She gave a knock on the door to acknowledge that she knew he was there. Then she sat and watched him out the window. Shortly, Bill opened the door and stomped his boots on the shoveled porch.

"The phone lines are down, and I was worried about you and Miss Emma, so I came to town. I went to her house, and she's fine. Is everything okay here?"

"I slept all through the night. The only problem here is that I have no water in the bathtub and shower. I have both hot and cold water in the kitchen, however. That's very strange to me."

"I'll take a look under your trailer when I can get the snow cleared away from the crawl space entrance. I think I smell the delicious aroma of coffee."

"Oh, how thoughtless of me. I should have offered you a cup as soon as you came through the door."

As she poured a cup for him, Amanda said, "Now I understand what you were talking about when you said snow can pile up six feet high and have bare ground right beside it. I'm sure I have six-foot drifts in the yard."

"Yes, you do. Willis has shoveled a tunnel in the snow drift from their house to the garage, and Jimmy is having a ball running back and forth through it. I hear that the road to Williston is blocked with packed snow as high as the cuts beside it. That means we may not be able to travel that road until they can blast it loose. Snowplows can't even clear it. Just how long it will be before they get to our road is a question, because there are families who don't have access to a grocery store. They will work on those first."

"How did you get into town?" Amanda puzzled.

"My truck has four-wheel drive, and there aren't any heavy blockages between here and home."

She felt pleasure that he had thought of her. "I really appreciate you checking on me. I can't believe that Neman will repair phone lines in this weather. It's hard to believe he can work on them at all since he's blind, but in this weather?"

"He'll get it done. They love that phone company so much that they will do anything to keep it going. Several larger companies have tried to buy them out, but they're here as long as they can do the work."

"Yes, Sue and Josh told me about that when I first came. You have to admire their determination, and the community seems to want to continue to support their company. At least, I've not heard any complaints."

Bill helped himself to another cup of coffee. "I think most folks want the party line convenience. It not only makes for good gossip, but it holds the community together. It's also helpful when there is an emergency, since we have no ambulance service here. Several years ago, we had a blizzard, not quite as bad as this, and one of the women went into labor. Bertha called all the ranchers on the road to Williston, and they all got out with their tractors, just in case the car got stuck. Tractors were lined all up and down the road and stayed there until they saw the car pass. Then an all-clear went out from Bertha, telling everyone that they had made it to the hospital in time and had a bouncing baby boy. Come to think of it, that little boy is almost old enough to go to school now. Do you have a boy named Ben Lowrey in your class?'

"No, I don't. He must not be old enough for school yet."

Bill's stories convinced her that he sincerely loved his town. She said, "Since you love this little town so much, why do you stay away for months at a time?"

Bill seemed reluctant to answer, but he did say, "I am convinced that God wants me to do other things that I need to do in person. I couldn't do them if I didn't have Willis at the ranch. He runs it very well, and that gives me the opportunity to follow God's calling."

Amanda could not understand why he kept the information of his trips from the community if he felt this was God's calling. Pouring herself another cup of coffee, she said, "I didn't mean to pry into your personal life. I'm sorry I asked."

He looked out the window for a few seconds before answering, "Maybe the time will come when I feel that I can share the other part of my life with you. I'm just not ready right now." She was more curious than ever and wondered just where their relationship was headed.

Reflecting on the reasons for her decision to sign the Stoney Butte contract, she said, "I guess there are many things we don't know about each other."

Bill reached for her hand. "That's true, but I do enjoy being with you. I hope you enjoy my company as well."

Holding her own secrets close, she looked straight into his eyes and acknowledged, "We do have some great conversations, don't we? Yes, I enjoy our time together. I hope we can continue them, but are you getting ready to go on another of your trips?"

"No, I've decided to stay here for a while now, at least until summer. Your contract is only for one year, right?"

She nodded. "One never knows what will happen between now and next summer. I do enjoy this little town and have come to love the people in it like a family."

Amanda felt his hand relax, as if he was pleased that she enjoyed Stoney Butte. He said, "Even when I'm away, I feel a connection to this community. There's something about this place that draws you into its fold."

Finishing his last sip of coffee, he said, "I think I'll shovel my way to your crawl space door and try to solve the puzzle of your water supply to the bathtub."

Bill put his coat and overshoes on again, grabbed his shovel from the porch, and disappeared around the end of the trailer. Soon Amanda heard noises under the floor and wondered just what he was finding there. Her thoughts of their conversation sent shivers racing up and down her spine. *Can this be happening to me? I feel like a teenager when I think of him.*

Finally, the noise beneath the floor stopped, and she heard the door to the crawl space close. Bill stomped his boots on the porch again, and she opened the door for him.

He came through the door, his eyes were jumping with merriment, holding one hand behind his back. "You won't believe what I found under your trailer."

"What? Frozen pipes?"

He pulled a yellow bloom from behind his back. "The first thing I saw was a dandelion, actually blooming in the middle of the ground."

"Really? Then the pipes couldn't be frozen."

"It's really very warm under there. The community did a good job of enclosing the space, so you must not have a heavy gas bill."

"Come to think of it, it hasn't been nearly as high as I expected. But why do I not have water in my tub and shower?"

"The builder of the trailer didn't put good insulation between the tub and the wall, and that's where the pipes run. I think if you filled the tub with hot water, it would melt the ice in those pipes."

Amanda cupped her face in her hands. "That was not too smart of them. They could have turned the tub around and not had to run the pipes between the tub and the exterior wall. Or they could have filled it with insulation."

"Yes, that would have been a better plan, but let's get some hot water in the tub and see if that works. Next time I'm in Williston I'll get some insulation to wrap around the pipes. If we have a hard freeze before then, you may want to leave the tub dripping a little in order to keep the water flowing through the pipes."

Amanda put the dandelion and in a small vase. Then she found the biggest pots she had. It took about an hour to fill the tub with hot water from the kitchen and bathroom sinks, heating some of it to boiling. By then it was late enough that she invited Bill to have soup and a sandwich with her.

During lunch, she asked him to tell her some stories of his younger days. He began, "I remember the year we had a ewe to drop her lamb early."

"I presume you mean a female sheep," she said. "When do they usually lamb?"

"In the early spring, but for some reason this one came early. We didn't have heat in the barn like I do now. We didn't want to bring the ewe into the house, but it was too cold for the little lamb to survive outside. It was even too cold for him to be on the back porch, so we ended up with a bum lamb in the kitchen."

Puzzled, she asked, "What is a bum lamb?"

"That's a lamb without a mother. Sometimes a ewe will ignore a lamb, and that's a 'bummer'. I guess that's why we call them bum lambs. Or a ewe may have three or four lambs and not have enough milk for all of them. Then the smallest lamb, or bummer, is pushed away. It's just the way nature works."

"How do you feed a bum lamb?"

He explained. "We use special bottles with large nipples. Bum lambs must be fed four or five times a day. I remember the time our pastor visited us, and a bum lamb came out from under the table. I thought the man was going to jump out of his skin, he was so surprised." Bill couldn't help but laugh with the memory. "He was rather new and had never been around such animals before. Of course, we explained why we had a lamb in the kitchen."

"Do you have sheep on your ranch now? I don't remember seeing any."

"No, Dad quit raising them when I was in high school. They really take a lot of care and sometimes are rather dumb. At least it seems that way. Last spring when there was a sudden late snow, Willis went out to help another rancher dig out a bunch of sheep because they had all huddled together in the corner of a fence, and the snow drifted and covered them. They are usually kept close to the barn in the winter, but this was after the grass had greened up, and the rancher had already let them out to pasture."

Amanda shook her head with a smile. "There are so many things about this way of life that those of us who grew up in the cities have no clue about. I'm learning a lot."

He began reminiscing again, "You know how Bertha enjoys being a part of the action." His eyebrows went up and his eyes twinkled. "I remember the time she called my dad and said, 'Willard John just came into town from his mail route and said there were a couple of male pheasants just west of town. I heard Otto talking earlier, and he said there were female pheasants near his house. Do you suppose we could get them together?'"

Amanda laughed. "What did your father say?"

"He said, 'Bertha, I believe that if they are in the same county, they will find each other one way or another.' When Miss Emma heard this, she said, 'That's just the way God planned it to happen. They'll get together, I'm sure.'"

"You told me about you and Willis going to the butte and throwing rocks over the cliff when you were frustrated. Did you do some foolish boy things when you were a kid?"

His eyes lit up with the memory. "We did take one of the rockers that the Bagleys keep on the porch of their cafe in the summer and tied it to the flagpole rope at school. We raised that sucker all the way to the top. This was in the summer, and since school wasn't in session, no one noticed that it was up there for several days. We got a big laugh out of that, but we finally admitted to our deed. Most of the town laughed about it, but our parents weren't very happy."

Amanda smiled as she imagined the young friends raising the rocker on the flagpole. "It sounds like you didn't lack for entertainment as you grew up. You just made your own instead of expecting it to be produced for you."

"You're right. Small towns and farms or ranches are places where children learn to entertain themselves much easier than in large cities. Have you watched your students at recess?"

The memory of her students on the playground brought a smile so wide it practically disappeared around the sides of her face. "Yes. They explore bugs and jump to touch the limbs of the big cottonwood tree. It amazes me how they can create a game that, to my knowledge, has never been played before. And they play together, no matter what the age."

"That's small town living for you, and we certainly have a small town here."

Bill helped clean up after lunch, and then he was on his way. He said he had some things to pick up at the store and needed to get home to help Willis with the chores.

Chapter Thirty-Five

Soon after the Christmas break, Amanda told the children that Delmar Karr would come and talk to them the next day. Then they would have a field trip to Delmar and Leola's store. Joel beamed with pride. At recess the children gathered around him and asked him questions about the store. They had all been to the store to shop, but they had no idea just what went on when they weren't shopping.

When Delmar talked with the students, he asked how many had been to the store, and of course they all raised their hands. Then he asked, "How many of you can add long columns of numbers?" A few of the older children raised their hands, but the younger ones were doing well to simply add two numbers.

"It's important to be able to add and subtract if you want to own a store," he said. "I have an adding machine at the store, but sometimes I have to do it in my head. What you are learning in school is important, whether you own a store or not. You want to be sure that a storekeeper gives you the right change."

Then he asked them to choose a partner. He gave each child a piece of paper with a store item and its price on it. He said, "I'm going to give each couple two dollars in change and two dollars in bills. You will take turns using the change and bills. This is pretend, and one of you will be the buyer and the other the storekeeper. The buyer will tell the other just what you want to buy and the price, according to the piece of paper I gave you. The buyer will also give the storekeeper both dollar bills. Then the storekeeper will subtract the price of the item and give the buyer change for the two dollars. When you have finished, we will take a break and then exchange with your partner so that you can each be a storekeeper or a buyer. You can use your pencils if you need to, but remember that this is why you need to learn to add and subtract."

As he handed out the money and papers, the room buzzed with excitement. Amanda had helped Delmer plan the learning experience, and she was pleased with the way learning about the vocation worked with their math experience. *This is true learning, having a real-life experience.* She thought about other opportunities to weld learning with vocations.

During the break, Delmer told them what to expect when they took their field trip to the store. "We have to keep track of what we have in the store and what we need to order. I will show you the records we keep and the orders we fill out for delivery of the items. Then we have several boxes of canned goods that need to be opened and put on the shelves. You older students can open the boxes, but everyone will have a chance to put some of them on the shelves. You need to remember to turn the cans or boxes so that the customers can see the labels properly. You will also need to count how many of that item are on the shelves and how many you have added from the box. Adding those two together will give you what we call an inventory. This way we know when we need to order more of that particular item."

When each student had been both a storekeeper and a buyer, they went next door to the store. None of the students seemed bored, even as Delmer showed them the ledger that he used to keep the records and the papers for ordering. He explained that some people kept what they called an account at the store and showed them the big book where they kept the amount people owed the store. "Then," he said, "when the person comes in to pay for what they owe us, we know exactly what it is. That's another reason we need to know math when we own a grocery store."

Delmer and Leola showed them how they weighed certain items on the big white scale and came to the correct price for the amount a person would buy. While they were gathered around the scale, Sue Biscoff came into the store to purchase some bread and sandwich meat. She said hello to the children, and they all greeted her. Amanda explained just what they were doing in the store and what they had learned in the classroom.

Sue smiled, looking each child in their eyes. "This is a good way to learn. Now you know just why math is important to know."

To Amanda's surprise, little Timothy responded, "Yes, this is a fun way to learn. Now I really want to study my math."

Leola weighed Sue's sandwich meat, explaining the process again as she did it, and calculated the amount she owed. Then Leola added the bread price to it and made the correct change.

To prepare for opening the new boxes, Amanda asked them to work in threes as they placed the items on the shelves. She said, "One in your group will take the items from the box. The second student will place it on the shelf, and the third student is responsible for keeping count of those you place on the shelf. An easy way to do that is to make a mark for each item. When you have made four marks, make a diagonal line across the four lines for the fifth item. Then, just as you learned, count by fives to know the total. You will take turns so that everyone has a chance to work at each job."

The students counted the number of their item on the shelves and wrote it on the paper that Delmer had given them. Then Delmer brought out the boxes and the students opened them. After they had emptied their box, they worked, adjusting each item just right so that the buyers could see what it contained. They added the numbers, in order to have an inventory.

Since it was the end of the school day, Leola gave each of them a piece of candy. Joel looked proud enough to pop the buttons on his shirt. This was *his* store and *his* grandparents.

After the students returned to the classroom, Amanda told them she had asked the bookmobile librarian to bring some books about stores on her visit the next day. She also suggested that the older students use the encyclopedia to learn a little more about storekeeping.

When the children had all left, Ione came into her room with a big smile, "Your idea of having people with different vocations visit the classroom has really worked well. I've never seen my students as excited about using an encyclopedia before. I actually had to shoo them out the door. They look up many things that we discuss in class, and they really seem to appreciate learning, even in history."

Amanda replied, "Owning their own learning will help them throughout their lives. I thought Delmer did a good job of getting them involved in math."

"He sure did, I would never have thought of combining math with keeping a store. I'm so glad you came to teach with me this year."

Amanda gave her a big hug. She appreciated the praise from the older woman, but she also knew that she was learning much from this small town too.

Chapter Thirty-Six

One Saturday in January Bill was in town and made his usual call on Miss Emma. He needed his downtime with her. It had been a busy week at the ranch, preparing to plant the flowers in the greenhouses that would go to the larger cities as spring arrived. On top of that he prepared a sermon each week. Now he wanted some good conversation with his dear friend.

As they sat down to snickerdoodles and coffee, she asked, "Have you had many opportunities to be with Amanda lately?"

Bill avoided her eyes. "Not as much as I'd like," he admitted. "She has been busy with her regular schoolwork, and recently she's been planning for Sue Biscoff and Dr. Endive to visit the classroom. Then they hope to have a research scientist that Sue knows who may make a follow-up visit. She certainly has made school more exciting for the children this year. I wish she would stay with us more than one year."

The old woman's face lit up with a knowing smile. "Is there another reason you would like for her to stay?"

"Oh, Miss Emma, you know me too well. I do have to admit that I really enjoy her company. I've never known any woman that I enjoy being with more than Amanda, unless it's you."

"Peshaw! I couldn't hold a candle to Amanda when it comes to your attraction. I can see it in your eyes every time you seek out her face as you lead worship, and even during your sermons. I think something great is happening between the two of you."

"Well, I thought I'd be a bachelor for the rest of my life, but now I'm beginning to wonder."

Miss Emma put her hand on his shoulder. "You always follow God's calling, and it appears to me that this may be a part of that calling. Have you told her what you do during your months away from here?"

"No, I've been afraid to. I don't know if she will understand it. She may think that I'm crazy to leave the country just to care for others. You know, she didn't go to church for years before she came here."

"That's true, but she has a caring heart. You know that as well as I. Make an effort to be with her more often, and God will tell you whether or when to reveal your secret."

"So far, our times together have been accidental or around planned gatherings. Maybe I'll ask her to visit Medora and the Teddy Roosevelt National Memorial Park with me. That would give us time together away from the prying eyes of the community."

Miss Emma's eyes lit up. "I knew you would come up with a plan. It sounds pretty good to me.

"Now, Bill, have you begun thinking about Lent and Easter Week? It may seem early, but I don't think the bishop will find anyone to fill our pulpit until Annual Conference in June."

"I thought for my main emphasis during Lent I would suggest that the church members do things for others instead of giving up something. I'd like to plan a program during Holy Week that helps people feel that they have been in the very shoes of Jesus or the disciples."

"I wonder if Amanda would have any ideas on that. She is so good at teaching through experience."

Bill agreed. "That seems to be right down her alley. I wonder when she will be free to talk about it."

"Why don't I call her and see if she can come over right now?"

Amanda was free and happy to walk over to Miss Emma's. When she walked into Miss Emma's yard, she felt a warm rush through her veins as she noticed Bill's truck in the yard. When she knocked on the door she felt her heart clatter around inside her chest, like a trinket rolling around in a box.

Bill answered the door instead of Miss Emma. Their eyes cradled each other in a loving embrace. Bill quickly turned to the kitchen table and invited her in. Miss Emma was all smiles. "Bill has some ideas about Easter Week he'd like to run past you. Would you like a cup of coffee with some of Bill's favorite cookies?"

"I'd never turn down your snickerdoodles, Miss Emma," replied Amanda.

When she sat down at the kitchen table and Bill poured her coffee Amanda thought, *This is so natural. I feel I've known these two people all my life, and I feel I belong here in this small community of loving people.*

Miss Emma began, "We thought you might help us flesh out his ideas."

Amanda looked at Bill. "What are you planning?"

"Well, I actually don't have much planned, but I'd like to do something that would help people understand just what it would have been like to be one of the disciples, or even Jesus during his last few days."

Miss Emma got up to get her Bible and turned to the Easter story in Matthew. "You know that all four gospels have different versions of the story, but we can pull out some of the situations and create learning experiences for everyone. We might call it 'The Way of the Cross' so that it doesn't sound too high church for our little town."

Amanda said, "It sounds like a series of learning stations, something like the stations of the cross, but maybe we could make it more experiential. I may be using too much 'teacher language' for you."

Bill looked pleased. "No, I understand what you're saying. We might begin with the story of Judas arranging to betray Jesus for thirty silver coins. We could have a bag with the coins spilling out on the table. Then have something about the Last Supper. Maybe the Williston pastor can help with that. Perhaps we can also include a large bowl and towel with the story about Jesus washing the feet of the disciples. This is getting exciting."

Miss Emma suggested, "Can we create a garden-like atmosphere for the time that Jesus went to pray, and his disciples fell asleep? Maybe we can have each person write prayers that they want us to pray over during the Good Friday service."

"Why not?" Amanda agreed. "We can type up the story for each station in common language and also have a Bible open for the people to read."

"What could we use to make his imprisonment and trial more experiential?" asked Bill.

Amanda thought for a moment. "Maybe the ropes that they bound Jesus with."

Bill added, "Then we have the story of the authorities mocking Jesus, putting a royal robe and a crown of thorns on him. They also lashed him with whips. We can suggest that people feel the whip and even put the crown on their heads. I know where some spikey bushes grow that we can use."

Miss Emma smiled. "Don't forget that Pilate washed his hands of the whole affair. Can we have a wash basin and towel for that part of the story?"

Bill said, "Sounds good to me. We can also get someone to make a large cross that people can try to lift and feel the weight that Jesus had to carry after being lashed with whips. I imagine that Melton Cazer or Wenzel can help us with that."

Amanda suggested that they use Q-tips that people could put in vinegar and taste, to remind them of what the soldiers offered Jesus on the cross.

"What would the closing station look like?" asked Miss Emma.

Everyone thought for a while. Then Bill said, "I'd like for it to be very meaningful. Maybe they can write something they want to say to God and nail it on the cross."

The room seemed alive with excitement. Miss Emma suggested, "Let's see if we can get several families involved in setting this up for us. We can give each family a different station to work on."

"I like that idea," said Bill. "We need to involve families more than just sitting in a service and coming to an occasional covered dish dinner."

He asked Amanda if she would help him write up the stories for each station. "I'd be happy to," she responded. "You can write up the basic stories, and I'll help you flesh them out."

When they left, he gave Amanda a ride home and they arranged a time to get together after he had written the stories. Before she got out of his truck, he reached for her hand. "I've really enjoyed planning this together. We have a lot more in common than I thought we would."

Amanda squeezed his hand, "I remembered more from my Sunday School days than I expected. Church here has become more meaningful to me than it ever was before."

"And you've become more meaningful to me. Can we get together away from the eyes of Stoney Butte after Easter?"

"I'd like that..."

"I want to show you Teddy Roosevelt National Memorial Park at Medora. You can see the North Dakota Badlands, which are quite a different landscape than any other badlands. Medora is also interesting, where they have restored much of the city to the Teddy Roosevelt era. During the summer they have a drama about the time that Roosevelt had a cabin south of there. In fact, you can even go to see the cabin, but that takes a long hike. We could just start with Medora and the surrounding landscape on a weekend. Would you like that?"

"Yes, I would enjoy it. What about your preaching obligation?"

"The pastor in Williston said he would come out from time to time. When I call him about The Way of the Cross, I will ask him if he can come out one Sunday after Easter."

Amanda found herself humming as she went through the door of her home. "Aggie," she said when the cat came to greet her. "I think I may be in love! But, you know, we do have to get past our secrets. Maybe a trip to Medora can bring that about."

Chapter Thirty-Seven

In February Sue and Dr. Endive talked with the classes about a medical career. Some of the children had never even been to a doctor. There seemed to be much that they didn't know about the field of medicine. Sue started the session talking about nursing. She told them about special schools that taught nursing.

"I found it a very rewarding career, because I really felt that I was caring for people and making them feel better. When we moved back here, I have been able to help people with minor medical problems. Some nurses work in a hospital and some work with doctors in their offices."

Dr. Endive said, "I have several nurses who help me in my office. If you've been to a doctor, a nurse probably weighed you and measured your height. One of the other things that they do is to take blood pressure and check your pulse rate. That tells them how many times your heart beats every minute. Look at your wrists. You will see what looks like blue lines under your skin."

He gave them time to look at their wrests. "These are what we call blood vessels. They do a lot of different work in your body. Can you guess how many miles of blood vessels are in your body?"

There were several guesses before he told them, "We have between 60,000 and 100,000 miles of blood vessels in our bodies."

Gasps came from the children as they automatically looked again at their wrists. Then he said, "One thing that blood vessels do is to carry your blood from your heart to other parts of your body and back to the heart. Some we call arteries, and some we call veins."

Marilyn raised her hand and asked, "What is the difference between an artery and a vein?"

Doctor Endive said, "That is a good question. Arteries and veins are both blood vessels. The arteries carry your blood from your heart to other parts of the body. The veins carry the blood back to your heart."

One of the eighth-grade boys said, "We studied a little about that is science, but I can never remember which is which."

The doctor answered, "You can remember the difference if you think of where the letters are in the alphabet. 'A' is at the beginning of the alphabet. The blood has been made healthy in your heart and begins its journey through the body. The letter 'V' is at the end of the alphabet, and the veins take it back to the heart to make it better again."

The children looked at each other's wrists. The doctor let them marvel over this for a while before telling them about their next experiment.

"We have blood pressure machines that measure how the blood circulates through your body. We've brought four of these machines, and Mrs. Biscoff and your teachers and I will show each of you how to use these. We taught your teachers earlier this morning, and they can help you. The strap that we put around your arm will get tight, but it won't really hurt you. You don't have to do this if you don't want to, but it will give you an idea of what happens when you go to see a doctor. This will also let you listen to the blood pumping through your blood vessels."

Most of the children were excited to try it. A few were hesitant at first, but eventually they all had their blood pressure taken and listened to their heartbeat.

Sue said, "You've been listening to your heartbeat through the blood vessel. If the heart beats 70 times a minute, it can completely cycle the entire blood supply through the body in about a minute. You can also check the number of beats per minute by holding the fingers of one hand on an artery in the wrist of the other arm. By doing this, the doctor or nurse will count the number of beats in a minute." The children tried feeling for the beats from their hearts.

Sue and Dr. Endive told them a little more about medical careers, including the fact that some doctors went into what they called research, where they tried to find out more about diseases. They welcomed their questions and answered them in simple words.

Mandy and Marilyn were very vocal about their times of visiting doctors with their mother. Marilyn had even done some research in the encyclopedia about Multiple Sclerosis. She told the students that MS causes you to lose the use of your muscles. "That's why my mother has to use a wheelchair. The research specialists haven't found a cure for it so far, but sometimes they can help slow it down. There are things that a person can do to keep it from advancing so rapidly. We always plant a large garden and can all our vegetables ourselves so that we know that they did not have chemicals during their growing period and when they are cooked before canning. Mother also takes lots of rests during the day. MS can cause problems with your vision, balance, and muscle control. That's why Mandy or I sometimes have to stay home with our mother."

Dr. Endive said, "There are many diseases that doctors need to know about, and it usually takes four years of college and then you will have three to four years of medical school. After that you must go through a year or more of internship in a hospital. If you plan to specialize in one specific area, you work in a hospital with that specialty. This is called your residency. It takes lots of study and can be expensive. But I will tell you that if you study well and make good grades, you can find scholarships that will help pay for it."

The researcher that Sue tried to contact in Missoula had moved and she was not able to arrange for another one, so she and Dr. Endive told them a little about a career in research.

When they finished, Amanda asked the children to thank Mrs. Sue and Dr. Endive for coming to talk to them. Several of the children talked to them during recess, and some of the children talked to Mandy and Marilyn about their mother's health.

Timmy came up to Amanda and asked, "Do you think that I could become a doctor?"

Amanda gave him a warm smile and a hug. "You enjoy science, and I'm sure that if you keep up your grades you would make a good doctor."

Chapter Thirty-Eight

Later that month, Milton Cazer and Mandy and Marilyn's dad were scheduled to talk to the classroom about the sawmill. Ione arranged for this, and her older children checked out all sorts of lumbering businesses in the encyclopedias and reported their findings to both classes.

When the date arrived, Wenzel began the conversation. "How many of you have been to the butte west of town?" All their hands went up, and Wenzel continued.

"Have you ever just sat among the trees where you could see nothing but trees?" Most of the hands went up on this question. "Well, that's what it was like in the part of Minnesota where we lived and I worked, before we moved here. There were trees everywhere. Some of the trees had been there for hundreds of years, and they were very large. My lumber company worked with the U.S. Forest Service to be sure that all the trees were not taken down at one time. When we did cut trees, we left some large trees so that their seeds could start new trees.

"Can any of you tell me why we need to have trees?"

One of the students from Ione's class spoke up, "We did some research on trees in our encyclopedias. Our cars and other machines produce carbon dioxide, and trees change that into oxygen which we need in order to breathe. They help to clean up the air."

Wenzel smiled his approval. "Yes, if we didn't have trees and other plants to do that, the earth would not have oxygen, and we would not be able to breathe. That's a part of the way our world is made. Plants are very important.

"How many of you raise cattle or sheep at home?" This time many of the children who lived on the ranches raised their hands. Wenzel continued, "I see that many of you know about this. When we raise animals, we need to move them from time to time. That way they don't eat the grass down to the roots so that it dies and doesn't come back each spring. The same thing is true with trees. They need to produce their seeds so that we continue to have trees to give us oxygen."

He began to open a bag. "I brought several pinecones that I will pass around for you to see. Some of these come from our butte just out of town. I brought some from where I used to work before we moved here, and some are from different parts of the country."

He held up two pinecones, one large and one small. "Notice that the large pinecone has open spaces in it. The spaces held seeds, but they have now fallen out. This smaller, tight pinecone has no spaces. A small pinecone you would think comes from a small tree, but it is from one of the largest trees in our country, the sequoia. I've never seen those trees myself, but a friend brought the cone back to me. This is what's interesting about the sequoia pinecone. The seeds are captured inside, and the pinecone will not open to release the seeds until it is exposed to excessive heat. That means that the cone protects the seeds when a fire burns through the forest, but afterward, when all other seeds are burned up, it opens and releases seeds to give us trees for oxygen."

There was a murmur of wows from the students. "I'll pass these pinecones around so that you can look at them. Next time you go to the butte, look for pinecones on the ground, and you may also see some green ones in the trees. They produce new pinecones every year to give us more trees and oxygen to breathe. As you learn more science you will understand about oxygen and carbon dioxide."

He began passing the pinecones to the students. "Did those of you who used the encyclopedias learn how many trees it takes to produce oxygen for one person each year?" The students shook their heads. "Take a guess."

Most of the students guessed one or two. Wenzel smiled, "You will be surprised to know that it takes seven or eight trees to produce oxygen for each of you each year." There was a gasp from the students. "That's why it's important for us to protect our trees and continue to grow new ones. Of course, other plants also produce oxygen, but we want to keep as many trees as we can and replace the ones we cut down."

Amanda was pleased that Wenzel brought science into his conversation with the children.

When Melton took over, he asked, "How many of you have climbed on the railings of the fence at the rodeo?" Most of the children raised their hands. Then he asked, "How many of you live in a house made of wood, like the schoolhouse?" All the children raised their hands to this.

"In the cities some people live in houses made of bricks, or even of concrete blocks, like our town hall. But most of the houses in and around Stoney Butte are made of wood. Wenzel and the men who work with him cut down selected trees and bring them to our mill just outside of town. We have big saws that cut them into boards or fence rails, like the ones at the rodeo grounds. We are a very small sawmill, compared to the ones Wenzel worked with in Minnesota and at other places where they have large forests of trees. The boards we cut are what we call 'green lumber'. The bigger sawmills have drying kilns where they dry the boards, or lumber. If the boards are not dried properly, they will twist a little or warp. Houses are usually made of dried lumber. That's why most of the wood at our mill is cut into fence posts or rails instead of lumber for houses...

"Another thing that we produce at the sawmill is sawdust. In fact, we have piles of it. The sawdust is tiny pieces of wood that fly out of the wood when it is sawed. Ranchers may use sawdust in the stalls for their horses. It can also be used to loosen up the dirt in gardens, but you need to know what trees the sawdust comes from for that. Some sawdust is not good for certain plants.

"Sometimes we use sawdust as insulation. We put it between two short walls under your teacher's trailer when we set it up for her. Some of you may have been there when we poured it in. Ms. Amanda, does the sawdust insulation keep your floors warm?"

"Oh, yes. In fact, it's so warm under my trailer that Bill Bates found a dandelion growing there when he checked my water pipes after the blizzard we had during Christmas break."

"You see," said Melton, "there is a purpose for almost everything."

The men gave the children opportunity to ask questions. One of the boys asked, "Where do they sell the boards that the big sawmills cut?"

Wenzel asked if any of the children had seen lumber being sold. A girl in the fifth grade said, "I went with my father to a big store in Williston, and they had lots of boards there."

"Yes," said Wenzel. "Sometimes they are sold in stores, but when builders plan to build lots of homes in a large city, they often buy truckloads of lumber from a sawmill company. You can see big trucks on the highways taking the lumber to different places. If you've been on the interstate highway that runs through Dickenson, you may have seen those trucks."

Timmy's brother raised his hand. "I saw those trucks when we lived in Dickenson. I think I'd like to drive one of those big trucks when I grow up."

Amanda said, "That's another career some of you might want to consider. There are lots of things that you can do when you are adults. But no matter what you choose, you need to finish school first so that you have all the knowledge you need to follow the career."

When all the questions had been asked and answered, Ione suggested that the children thank the men for talking to them about trees and the sawmill. They all voiced a loud, "Thank you!"

That afternoon Bill stopped to see Amanda and asked if she would like to go to Bismarck with him on Saturday. He needed to meet with the owners of several stores that would sell his plants. He also hoped to get a contract for plantings for the capital grounds.

He said, "Maybe you heard that there's a dance at the town hall Saturday night, and you may want to go to that instead. This will be an all-day trip, and we might get back late."

It was an easy decision for Amanda to make. "I'd enjoy going with you. It will give me a chance to see more of North Dakota. Shall I drive out to your ranch like I did before, to avoid gossip?"

"That would be a good idea."

Bill decided to take a back-roads route in order to see more of the Missouri River.

Near the little town of Arnegard, they passed a road that Bill said led to a large rock that had a folk history behind it. "During the winter, in the late 1800's, a group of cowboys were at a 'line camp'. That's a camp away from the main ranch where men stayed to watch over cattle. This group of men began to run out of food, and so a man named Jim, who loved to play poker, headed to town for supplies. He ran into a blizzard and got behind a big rock, blocking the wind. He gathered sticks to light a fire. He had waited too long to get off his horse, and he froze to death there by the big rock. When he didn't return, the men from the camp went out to find him. The ground was so frozen they couldn't bury him. Instead, they lifted him up into the rafters of a seldom-used shack. When the personnel of the line camp changed, they forgot to tell the new cowboys about Jim. The new guys decided to heat up the little stove in the shack and have some whiskey and a few hands of poker. As the blaze grew bigger and the bottle went down, the body began to thaw. Suddenly Jim dropped through the rafters, right in the middle of their poker table, sending the men out the door in a hurry."

Amanda burst out laughing. Bill continued the story. "No one knows exactly what Jim's last name was, but we remember him as Poker Jim. They tell this tale throughout the Dakotas and Montana."

As they continued their trip, Bill pointed out the Little Missouri National Grasslands which contains over a million acres. "Beginning in the 1870's people who wanted a farm could pay $18.00 filing fee and receive 160 acres. They had to build on it and produce their own living. The first year or two it usually went well, but then the nutrients were used and unless they could get neighboring property and afford to rotate their crops, the production went down. Some left after a few years, but others stayed on. My ancestors homesteaded our property. Then during the 1920's and 30's we had a terrible drought. Many just pulled up and left, returning the property to the government. The land had been plowed, so there was no more grass, and we had wind that blew much of the dirt away. You've probably read about the dust storms of the 30's."

Amanda looked out at the rolling hills of grass. "Yes, I studied that in high school and college."

"Most of this National Grasslands, as well as those in other states, were originally homesteads. Now the U.S. Forest Service manages most of the grasslands. Ranchers can pay an annual fee per head to run their cattle on the grasslands. The Forest Service makes sure that they rotate the grazing so that the grass is not destroyed."

Amanda reached over and put her hand on Bill's arm. "It must have been hard for the families to come to the Dakotas with such hope, and then to have to leave in a hopeless situation."

"Yes, I'm fortunate that my ancestors were able to hold onto their land. I know there is oil under the grasslands, but I certainly wish we could use the energy of the wind instead of depleting the minerals."

They continued their drive without much conversation until they drove along the Missouri River. Amanda said, "This really makes history come alive to me. This is actually the river that Lewis and Clark's expedition traveled as they explored this country and tried to find a river route to the west coast."

"Yes, they spent their first winter at what they named Fort Mandan, after the Mandan Indians," replied Bill as he followed the curve of the river. "The city of Mandan is across the river from Bismarck. There is speculation as to the exact site of their camp, because the river has changed its course several times, and we have built several dams on the Missouri River. Most people believe that the actual site is under water, between the small town of Washburn and Bismarck and Mandan."

Amanda said, "I've heard so many stories about Sacajawea, the woman who accompanied them from there into the mountains."

"She had given birth to a boy that winter of 1805. They named him Jean Baptiste. Sacajawea was the wife of a French-Canadian fur trapper, Toussaint Charbonneau, who also went with them from Fort Mandan. Sacajawea was Shoshone, and she carried her infant son on the trip. Lewis and Clark hoped that her relatives would be able to direct them to a river through the mountains. Of course, they weren't familiar with the continental divide, and didn't know that no river ran from one side of the mountains to the other, so they had to battle the terrain by foot. The whole ordeal must have been grueling. It amazes me that only one man died during that whole expedition, and that was before they got to North Dakota. It's now believed that he died from a burst appendix."

They stopped to view the Missouri River, and got to Bismarck in time for lunch. Bill was pleased with the contacts he made for his business before they headed home. As he predicted, they got to Bill's ranch quite late. She picked up her car and drove into town, expecting to see the town hall lit up for the dance. But there were only a few cars at the bar, and no lights in the building.

The next morning Amanda called Miss Emma to offer a ride to church. She said she had felt bad all weekend and thought she would stay home.

As Amanda walked the couple of blocks to church, she realized that most of the houses had clothes on the clothes lines, including coats. This puzzled her. After she found her seat, Sue turned to her and asked if she had been to the dance.

Quietly Amanda answered, "No. I actually went to Bismarck with Bill. He had some business to attend to. We took the back roads, and I saw more of the Missouri River."

"I'm so glad you had a good day, and you can be happy that you didn't go to the dance. We weren't able to go, but according to our news line, Bertha, a family of skunks moved in under the floor of the town hall, and when they heated up the stove, the skunks let everyone know that they were there."

"Oh, so that's why all the clothes lines in town have everything from jeans to coats hanging outside today. I'm certainly glad that I didn't go. Miss Emma didn't feel well, so she didn't go either. That must be why the town hall lights were out when I got back last night, and there were only a few cars at the bar. That is one time I made a good decision."

After the service, Bill asked Amanda, "Have you heard about the dance last night?"

She muffled a laugh. "Yes. Sue told me that Bertha spread the news. I suppose I'll get a call from her this afternoon."

Bill smiled as he said, "Guess we chose the right weekend to go to Bismarck. I understand they scared the skunks off, but there's no guarantee they will stay away. That place will need a real airing out."

Chapter Thirty-Nine

Easter was early that year, and before they knew it, they were preparing for The Way of the Cross, the program that Miss Emma, Bill, and Amanda had discussed. The pastor from Williston was to be a part of the communion station. Families were excited to set up the various stations, and the children cut out footprints that would guide persons or families from one station to another.

When the day arrived, it seemed that the whole town turned out to walk through the last few days of Jesus' life. Some of them even took the walk twice. Thankfully it was a nice day, and people stood outside the little one room church, waiting for their turn.

It was hailed as such a success that the families who set up the stations appointed themselves as a committee and decided they would keep the supplies, in order to make it an annual event. The Williston pastor asked if he could take the idea back with him to use the next year in his church.

Soon after Easter, Bill spoke to the classes about his greenhouses and how important it is to use our solar energy and keep the environment clean. He told them that he had solar panels put on his house, and that he would like to see the school board consider putting them on the schoolhouse.

He asked, "How many of you have felt the wind here in our state?"

Every student raised a hand. He said, "Someday you will see huge windmills above the grasslands and the hay fields. Wind is another way of creating energy. All of this is free and happens every day. We never run out of solar and wind power. I believe this will make your life better as an adult."

That afternoon they took a field trip to Bill's ranch and greenhouses. He first pointed out the solar panels on his house. Amanda noticed how little Jimmy stood tall with pride when Bill pointed to the solar panels on his house too. She heard some of the children ask Jimmy if they kept him warm in the winter. She didn't hear his reply, but his smile ran from ear to ear.

Next the students went through a couple of the greenhouses. Bill explained how he and Willis planted the seeds in the individual containers and showed them the various stages of growth. "We plant them at different times so they begin to bloom and are ready to sell in Williston and other cities as they need them. This way people can have blooming plants earlier than if they planted the seeds in the late spring or early summer."

When they finished the tour of the greenhouses with plants in various stages of growth, Bill took them outside to the tree farm where he grew trees for people to plant in their yards. He said, "In the cities new houses are being built every day, and the owners want trees in their yards. We grow the trees that survive in this colder part of the country. Willis and I start the trees, and then we wrap the roots in burlap. A truck takes them to the cities. Besides Williston, our trees and flowers go down to Rapid City, to Bismarck, and even to Fargo and Minneapolis."

After the greenhouse and tree farm tours, the children came back to the first greenhouse where Willis had seeds, dirt, and containers for them to begin their own flowers. He explained to them just how long it would take their seeds to sprout and that they needed to put them near a window to get sunlight. Jimmy spoke up, "Remember, you can't plant them outside until we're sure we won't have frost or a freeze."

Willis smiled at him. "Jimmy has tried to plant his seedlings outside too early, so he knows what he's talking about.

"One more thing you need to remember, you can kill a plant with too much water as easily as you can kill it with too little water. We will water them well before you leave, but periodically you must feel the dirt and if it's still wet it's too early to water the plant."

Ione had arranged for some of the parents to drive the students, and they helped the children plant their seeds. As they left, most of them thanked Bill and Willis for the tour and their future plants. The parents who drove were particularly grateful for the tour. They had seen the building of the greenhouses some years back, but most of them had never been inside.

True to his word, Bill arranged for books on horticulture and greenhouses to arrive with the next bookmobile after the field trip to his ranch. He also arranged for books on wind and solar power, since he had talked with the students about that.

Chapter Forty

Amanda anxiously awaited the trip to Medora. She was curious, checking the encyclopedia. She found that in 1883 the Frenchman, Marquis de Mores, built an elaborate hunting lodge in the area. He established a beef packing plant and was one of the first to use refrigerated railway cars to send his beef east. Marquis de Mores named Medora in honor of his wife. He and Theodore Roosevelt were good friends. When Teddy Roosevelt found the area, he bought a ranch, built a cabin, and named it Elkhorn Ranch. The ranch lies between the north and south units of the North Dakota Badlands. She found Medora on the map in the southern part of the Badlands.

The encyclopedia information whetted Amanda's interest in Medora and the Badlands. When Bill picked her up after school on that Friday, she could hardly contain herself. "I read up on Medora," she told him.

Bill chuckled at her enthusiasm. "You do sound excited. When I called for reservations, I realized that the only hotel in Medora isn't open this early. I did get reservations in Dickinson, however, which is close by. We can still see the town, and I especially want you to see the Badlands. Did you come through the South Dakota Badlands on your way up?"

"No, I took the interstate through Minneapolis and then to Fargo."

"Well, they are completely different in structure from what we'll see. In fact, I'd call them the opposite. In South Dakota they seem to rise from the ground. However, in our state you'd never know they were there until you were on the brink, looking down into the huge cavern-like area. The Little Missouri River winds through it, among tall sedimentary rocks of various shapes and forms."

Amanda turned in her seat. "I suppose this happens by erosion, but why just at these places?"

"The amount of soft clay influences the erosion. In North Dakota we have very little rain, but when it does rain it comes as if buckets of water are falling from the sky. The Badlands have soft clay that soaks up rain like a sponge. As it dried over the years, cracks were exposed. The next heavy rain washed particles away, forming gullies and channels."

Amanda surmised, "So what is left must be the strange peaks."

"Yes, those peaks are composed of tiny grains of sediments, cemented together over the years. We do have large rocks that have broken loose at places where the ground washed away, leaving piles of these huge rocks. We call these cannonballs."

"Have they found fossils in the area?" Amanda asked.

"Oh, yes. People look for them, but some folks are afraid to accept the fact that these might change our understanding of the literal Biblical interpretation of the amount of time since the earth's creation."

Amanda turned to him. "That's one thing that always puzzled me. How can people stick to the literal Biblical interpretation of time when there is scientific evidence that our world is older than that?"

Bill smiled. "I can see the science training coming out in you."

"Yes, that's one of the reasons I quit going to church."

"Many people get their faith in a great God mixed up with beliefs, and I see them as two different things. The Bible came from years and years of oral tradition before it was written down. We don't even know if they kept time as we do. You just must recognize that some people will never change their ideas and accept them for how they are. That's what Jesus did. Even though people didn't agree with him, like the Samaritan woman at the well, he still loved them. Sorry, I'm beginning to put on my preacher mode."

Amanda put her hand on his arm. "No, it's more like a teacher mode. You're helping me understand. That's what I like about your preaching."

In the west the sun glowed a deep, burnt orange as it sank to the prairie, painting the sky with lavenders and grays. Soon it was dark, and they drove in silence for a bit.

Amanda spoke some of her thoughts. "Speaking of science, there's a great big universe out there, and our earth is only a tiny speck in it."

"Yes, and what matters is that God created it all."

After riding through the dark for a while, Amanda said, "The sky looks like endless frost sprinkled over a deep blue/black backdrop. I have grown to appreciate the night sky out here away from the bright lights of the cities."

Bill just nodded in agreement, recognizing her depth of thought.

They turned south and then drove through some curvy roads. As they came over a hill, a small town appeared. Bill pointed out the name of the town as they drove by, Grassy Butte. "That's a very unique town," he said. "All of the buttes are usually grassy around here, but this little town has a post office that is made of sod, like they once made their homes on the prairie. If we leave early enough on the way back, we will stop and see the outside of it at least. Of course, it won't be open on Sunday, but the unique building form can easily be seen from the outside."

When they got to Dickenson, they were ready for dinner. After checking into their rooms, Bill suggested a steakhouse he liked. As they entered, Amanda felt she was in the old wild west. There were steer heads on the walls with cowboy hats and spurs dangling from the longhorns. She looked around and saw pictures of notorious early western characters.

The hostess called Bill by name and led them to a corner booth. He asked Amanda if she had a preference for wine. She said, "Perhaps white. Sometimes I wake up and can't go back to sleep if I drink red at night."

After the waitress poured the wine, they opened the menu. Amanda was surprised to see buffalo steak on the list. "I didn't know that people actually ate buffalo," she exclaimed.

"There are ranchers in the central Dakotas who raise them for sale. You should try it. There's not much difference in the taste of buffalo and beef."

Amanda looked quizzical. "I'm not too sure."

Bill laughed. "You never know until you try it. I think you'll like it. Consider it an adventure."

Amanda spread her napkin on her lap. "I guess I'll give it a try."

After Bill gave their order, they sipped on the wine. Bill admitted, "I had an ulterior motive in bringing you here. I'd like for us to get to know each other better without the prying eyes or listening ears of Stoney Butte."

"I'd like that too. I really enjoy being with you, and this sounds like an exciting weekend."

Bill began. "Tell me a little more about your family, and I'd like to know more about your husband too, if you don't mind talking about him."

"No, I don't mind. He was a good man and a great father. We married right after I finished college, and I truly loved him. He established a prestigious law firm in Atlanta and was considering politics when he had the automobile accident that killed him. However, we each lived our own lives and the children were the glue that held us together. We seldom talked about things like you and Miss Emma do. I appreciate you including me in those conversations. After my husband died, I was somewhat lost for a while, but I had the children, and I threw myself into my career. Kurt had just graduated from high school and Ashley was following in her father's footsteps with a law degree. She's in her father's firm now and doing well for herself. I've told you about Kurt's music ambitions and then his decision to join the Peace Corps."

"What have you heard from him lately? Is he in Zaire yet?"

Amanda's eyes warmed with the thought of her son. "Yes, they had a real crash course in French, which wasn't too hard for Kurt since he took it in college. They also learned a bit of the native language where they are living and working. That will come along better when they've been living with the villagers for a while."

"What will they be doing there?"

"From what I understand, they will do some teaching once they learn the local language better. In the meantime, they will help people learn more about growing their food. Kurt was always the gardener, and they were also trained in tropical gardening before going to Zaire. I haven't heard from him since he got to the villages where they will work."

Bill smiled suddenly. "That sounds interesting to me."

"I thought you might like that, with your horticulture background."

"In what part of the country is he working?"

Amanda thought for a moment. "I believe it's the province of Katanga, or something like that, in the southernmost part of Zaire."

The waitress arrived with their meals, and the conversation turned to the food. After the first bite, Amanda commented, "You are right, this is really good. It's a little sweeter than beef, and it's amazingly tender for such a large animal. No wonder the Native Americans went on big buffalo hunts."

Bill seemed pleased that she liked it. "One reason it's so tender is that bison are usually grass-fed. The amount of acreage it takes for raising one bison depends on the forage and water available. Some of the Native Americans on the plains burned the grass every year to prevent trees and help the grass grow to attract them. This burning tradition left six feet of topsoil.

"You have to force cattle to move from place to place so they don't kill the grass. That's why we have cowboys. However, bison are natural rotation grazers. You just need to keep them on your property. The park has fencing to keep the bison out of the neighboring pastures. It also keeps the cows out of the park. If a bison gets out of the park, they usually shoot it because there is no way to lasso it."

Amanda questioned, "Are bison and buffalo the same?"

"People often call them either name, but we actually have no buffalo in America. They look very much the same, but the bison have the big beard, making them recognizable."

Bill asked, "Remember the large skull with horns over my fireplace? That's a bison."

Amanda nodded. "I thought that was a mighty large cow."

Bill laughed. "Nope, it's a buffalo skull. A bison can jump a six-foot fence from standing still."

"I'd never have guessed that from the size of the animal."

Bill recalled, "I have a park ranger friend who called and asked if I wanted the skull of a bison they had to shoot. They staked the head over a large ant hill so that other animals wouldn't drag it off. Then the ants did a good job of cleaning it out."

Amanda shuddered as she imagined thousands of ants crawling over and through the head of the bison.

Bill continued, "I can testify that they can jump. One year I rode with my park ranger friend when they were doing a roundup, and one of them literally jumped over the hood of the truck."

"I imagine that really startled you!"

"Yes, I thought he was going to come through the windshield, right into my lap."

Amanda laughed. "That would have been a big lap puppy."

They returned to the hotel after finishing the meal and went into the bar for an after-dinner drink. Bill led her to a secluded corner booth, and Amanda kicked off her shoes, tucking her feet under her.

She moved close to Bill and said, "Now it's time for you to tell me something more about yourself."

Bill put his arm around her shoulders and drew her close. He seemed to take a moment to think. "You know that I grew up on the ranch and had Miss Emma as my second mother. I had great parents, but they were so involved with the ranch that they didn't spend a lot of time with me. Mom also had responsibility with the church, and so Miss Emma filled in. I was happy there as a child. We had all sorts of animals, and they were my playmates since I had no siblings. I would chase the chickens, which provoked my mother to no end. She told me that chasing them gave them stress. Of course, at that age I had no idea what stress meant, so I went to my great source of knowledge, Miss Emma. She gave me a simple definition, that stress meant being extremely upset. Now *that* I understood. Then she told me that chickens often didn't lay their eggs if they were stressed."

Amanda imagined young Bill chasing chickens around the yard. "What other experiences did you have as a child?"

Bill's eyes gleamed in merriment. "I'll tell you one if you promise not to tell anyone. I guess some folks know, but it was so long ago they don't talk about it now."

Amanda crossed her heart. "I cross my heart and promise not to tell anyone. It must be funny."

"Yes, it's funny now, but it wasn't funny when I was in school. It happened when I was just a toddler and with my parents in the pasture. I came up to Mom with a dried cow pie, saying 'Cookie, cookie.'"

Amanda couldn't control her laughter. Bill laughed too until he looked around and saw that others in the bar were staring at them. He squeezed her shoulder and shushed her. It took a while for her to bring her laughter under control. Bill said, "The word got out about my mistake. It was funny until I went to school, and then the kids started following me saying, 'Cookie. Cookie.'"

After wiping the grin from her face, she asked, "When did you first meet Willis?"

"I've known Willis for as long as I can remember. His parents had a ranch near us. You know that we went to school together. We even roomed together when we were in high school in Williston. We stayed with the Methodist pastor there. They had a large parsonage and only one young child, so they had plenty of room. That pastor made a significant influence on me too. I guess he filled in for Miss Emma, as far as not being surprised at my questions about God and life. Like Miss Emma, he made me think through for my own answers. He also helped me realize that beyond our national boundaries much of the world lives in poverty.

"Willis couldn't afford to go to college. He had lots of brothers and sisters, and he settled down, working with his father. Willis found joy in working with the animals, where I wanted big city life. His family fell on hard times and sold out, heading south to retire. That's when he took over the management of my ranch."

Amanda sipped her drink. "So, you went off to Minneapolis to find some excitement."

"I've told you I finally realized that the city life didn't really fit me after all. I did stay long enough to get my degree and recognize my interest in horticulture, working at a greenhouse for a while."

Amanda questioned, "Did you come back to Stoney Butte then?"

"Yes, I felt like I was a dog, coming home where he belonged, with his tail between his legs."

Amanda took his hand. "We all feel like that sometimes. We just learn from our mistaken ideas and adjust to it. Maybe that's a part of why I'm teaching here too. Like you, still hanging onto your interest in horticulture, I still believe in what my own children say I'm running away from."

"And what is that?" he asked.

"Well, as you know, I was principal of an elementary school. I saw welts on two sisters' backs and believed that they were being beaten at home. I'll admit, the girls sometimes gave us trouble at school. I'm sure the lack of love they received at home had something to do with their actions. I did, however, report it. Although the officials stood behind me, I had not shown the welts to the nurse or anyone else. Of course, the parents denied it. The rest of the year many of the parents seemed to turn against me. Perhaps I should have stayed on as principal, but I saw the ad for the Stoney Butte position, and I applied for it."

Bill sat quietly and Amanda cast her eyes downward. "I could have asked to be moved to another school, but I just didn't think I could put up with another year of people shunning me at the grocery store or when they saw me on the street. My mistake was not showing the welts to the nurse and thereby having another witness. I guess, in a way, I am a run-away mom."

Bill reached over and kissed her ear. "Just look what you ran to," he said in a whisper.

She looked up and returned his smile. "I am happy here. It's so good to have so few students that I can really get to know them. And I've been so welcomed into the community, especially by you and Miss Emma. I enjoy being included in your family."

"And I can certainly speak for myself. I'm so pleased that you replied to our ad and came to Stoney Butte. Otherwise I would never have met you."

Amanda put her head on his shoulder. "And I'd never have known just what I missed, especially you."

After a few minutes of silence, Bill suggested, "I suppose we'd better get some sleep before tomorrow. I want to show you Medora and the Badlands. Is eight o'clock too early for breakfast?"

"Sounds fine to me. I'm generally an early riser."

At the door to her room, he gathered her into his arms for a kiss. Her lips quivered at first, but as his kiss deepened, she leaned into his body, feeling that she had found a home there.

Chapter Forty-One

The next morning Bill knocked on Amanda's door, and they went to a nearby bakery for breakfast. Then they headed west toward Medora. As they drove, she suddenly said, "Look at those cute animals. What are they?"

Bill pulled the car off the road to give her a better look. "Those are prairie dogs. Prairie-dog towns spread out over several acres. Their holes are yards apart, almost like a town laid out in streets and avenues. The little animals sit on their hind legs over the doors of their houses, barking and shaking their tails. They have the most complex language of any animals."

Bill saw the excitement in Amanda and continued, "They're cute little critters. If you watch them for long, they show a lot of personality. I've spent hours watching them scurry about, ducking in and out of their holes in the ground. They communicate with each other with high-pitched noises, warning of danger. I rate them pretty high on the cuteness scale."

"What do they eat?" Amanda questioned.

"They mainly eat seeds, stems, roots and leaves of flowering plants, grasses and weeds."

"No wonder they are here. This land has plenty of grass and weeds."

Bill put his arm across her shoulder and pointed to the mounds and holes in the ground. "When you see a multitude of those, you know you've found a prairie-dog town."

"What do they do in the winter when it snows? Do they hibernate like bears?"

"No, they scurry around except when it is very cold or snowy. Then they may go into a light hibernation-like sleep for a few days, cozy in their burrows."

Amanda's eyes shone with excitement. "There is so much about this part of the country that I don't know. I just thought North Dakota was like a northern desert."

"Oh, you've seen the trees in the buttes. You'll see even more when we walk down into some of the Badland valley. Anywhere there is water, you can usually find some sort of trees. For true, the water sources are few and far between."

After a few miles, Bill again pulled off the road at an overlook. Before them lay a canyon, deep and wide. They looked down on the glittering tops of cottonwoods with a river snaking its way from one end to the other. Amanda drew a deep breath. "I'd never have guessed that this was here. I can't see across it, but I can see the many layers of sediment that you said were laid down over thousands of years. That river has cut its way right through it."

They were quiet for a while, just looking at the majestic scene before them curling around the Little Missouri River. Then Amanda asked, "How did the Badlands get its name?"

"The French traders first called this the Badlands, maybe because they were so hard to get across. They soon learned to follow the bison trails around it. I'm sure it frustrated them to have to take that detour. Theodore Roosevelt came to the area in

1883 to hunt bison and fell in love with the rugged lifestyle and what he called the 'perfect freedom' of the west. I told you that he built a cabin called the Maltese Cross. We won't be able to see that today because it's quite a hike to get there.

"The bison go down into the Badlands from time to time, and there are also other animals. South Dakota has wild burros, but we have wild horses. They are skittish and hard to see. We also have coyotes, elk, antelope, and white-tailed deer. Sharp tailed grouse and wild turkeys show up from time to time, and you may be lucky enough to see a golden eagle feeding her young,"

Amanda turned to him with excitement in her eyes. "I'm so glad you brought me here. If I'd come along this highway alone, I'm afraid I'd have just driven right by without so much as a glance to the side of the road."

Bill laughed, "Yes, that's what many people do. I'm glad that President Truman established this area as the first and only National Memorial Park. We hope someday that it will be listed as a regular national park and included in that list. Maybe more people will realize it's something special to see."

When they arrived at Medora, Bill could see that Amanda felt like she was in a real old west town as she turned in a circle. Bill imagined her in a long calico dress with a bonnet over her lovely hair. The buildings had fronts of saloons and shops right out of the Old West.

Bill watched her. "It does put you back in history, doesn't it?"

"Who had the vision to bring this reconstruction about?" Amanda asked.

Bill answered, "In 1965, a man named Harold Schafer came upon Medora, and he loved this area like President Roosevelt had.

He set out to renovate Medora so that others would come to enjoy the unique place too. Besides history here, they have a musical telling the background of the community and the area. Of course, that's only run during the summer, but there are a few shops open year-round. Would you like to visit one?"

Amanda smiled in amusement. "Only if I can get there without dragging my 'calico gown' in horse dung.'"

Bill laughed. "That's one thing I like about you. You have an imagination, and it transports me with your mind."

Inside the shop, Amanda found mementos of the Badlands. She seemed most fascinated with the fossils. "I think I'll buy a few of these for my classroom. They will certainly interest the students."

"If it were later in the spring or summer, we could search for fossils ourselves." Then Bill suggested, "I think in the future it will be illegal to own fossils and certain types of rocks, so you had best keep your receipt to prove when you bought those."

As they left the shop, Bill said, "If you are still here after they begin performing the historical musical, we'll have to come back for that. We can also do some hiking, and maybe see the unusual rock formation called the Hoodoo Rock. In that area you can see pillars with cap rocks on them. They are beginning to do geological research here, and they speculate that it was once a swamp, much like we find in Florida. The Little Missouri River, as well as most of the Missouri River, definitely ran through North Dakota millions of years ago."

"Wow!" exclaimed Amanda. "There is certainly more to Medora and the park than I read in the encyclopedia. I guess it takes getting involved with the whole park to really appreciate it.

How do you know so much about it when you're often gone half a year?"

"I've not been so involved in recent years. After I came home from Minneapolis, I really became interested in it. We were using scoria rock as a ground cover near the house, and I just had to find out how it was formed. Turns out it's a volcanic rock formed millions of years ago."

Bill suggested that they take a short hike on one of the trails. "Do you mind a trail that's a little steep? It isn't long, but it will take us to the highest accessible point in the park."

"I'm all for it. I wore comfortable hiking shoes."

They bought sandwiches and drinks from a vendor and set out to explore. Along the way, Bill stopped to comment on a plant just poking through the ground or a bush beginning to show greenery. "North Dakota has its different seasons. Most people seem to think that it's only a dry prairie. You've experienced winter in North Dakota, but you should see the park at that time of year. The peaks and cap rocks sometimes look like icing on a tall cake. At other times they have no snow on them but piles of snow below. It all depends on the wind. We have a saying, similar to yours, 'I'll be there if the creek don't rise'. We say, 'I'll be there if the snow don't blow.'" They both chuckled over the sayings.

When they reached the top, Amanda looked around as if she were on top of the world. They found a flat rock to use as a table and spread their lunch.

Bill suggested that they have a blessing over the meal. He took her hand and prayed, "Our God, we thank you for this wonderful world - not just here on this high ridge, but wherever we may find ourselves. I particularly thank you for bringing Amanda into my life. And now we thank you for this food before us. Amen."

Amanda looked at him with appreciation. "Thank you. I should thank God more frequently than I do. It's so easy to get out of the habit."

"We often think of our 'religion' as more about information than an intimacy with God. Miss Emma taught me that we need to work toward intimacy with God, twenty-four/seven."

"She's such a wise person."

"And remember, she's hardly been out of the county since she came as a bride many years ago. It proves that there is more to wisdom than book learning. I think you are teaching your students that. You help them relish in finding answers on their own."

Amanda took a bite of her sandwich as she seemed to think. "You were so fortunate to have her as your second mother."

"She has much to do with my long trips away from home."

Amanda kept quiet as she ate and looked at the beauty before them. Bill knew that she hoped he would open up to her about his mysterious trips but didn't dare to ask. She had come close to trampling on his thoughts before.

After a few minutes of silence, Bill said, "I think I know you well enough to be sure you won't talk about it elsewhere if I tell you a bit about where I go when I'm away from Stoney Butte."

Amanda reached out and squeezed his hand. "Yes, you do know me that well. I'd never say anything you didn't want me to pass on."

Bill held onto her hand and looked at the vista before them. "Where I go is very different from here, in many ways. But maybe I should start at the beginning."

Amanda let him take his time.

"About ten years ago the ranch and greenhouse businesses were functioning well. We were even shipping plants to larger cities. I'd made contacts with some college friends who had nurseries in Minneapolis and St. Paul. Willis was with me then, although he hadn't met and married Wilda yet. I enjoyed being back home. I loved the people, and I loved the solitude. But for some reason I was restless. I felt that there should be more to my life than managing a good ranch and growing and selling plants. I went to Miss Emma with my thoughts."

Amanda's eyes encouraged him to continue. "Of course, you would."

"Her husband had taken a drastic fall about five years earlier while breaking one of our horses. He never regained consciousness. I asked her how she could continue with such a cheerful attitude. She said that it was because she felt God within her, and that she knew God had a plan for her to help others, including myself. She told me that there is little in the Gospels to suggest a sharp division between the earthly things and the spiritual. This approach was prized by Christian history. She's done a lot of reading about Christian history."

Amanda said, "She seems to have done a lot of reading about many subjects."

Bill smiled. "Yes, she never misses the bookmobile, and she always has a list of books she wants for their next trip."

They sat quietly for a few moments. Then he continued, "I told Miss Emma how I felt restless, even though I enjoyed my work and being home. She asked, 'Have you thought about something else that God may want you to do?' I was rather taken aback. I told her that I tried to live close to God, and that I'd even contributed to several African missions after checking on their budgets. She just nodded, her way of encouraging me to go on. I was really stumped as to how that related to my restlessness. Finally, she said, 'What else do you suppose you could do?'

"I sat silent for a while. I can feel very comfortable thinking silently with her. Then I said, 'Maybe I should go to Africa and see the missions for myself.' She just squeezed my hand and said, 'Maybe that's God talking to you.'"

Bill picked up a small rock and threw it down into the canyon. "So, I arranged for Willis to take control of the ranch and greenhouses, and I booked a flight out of Bismarck to Kinshasa. I didn't want the community to know just what I was doing. I suppose at the time I was afraid they would laugh at me. Now I keep my trips secret because they are something private between God and me."

There was another lull of silence. Amanda just sat quietly with her hand in his.

Bill gave a big sigh. "Miss Emma and Willis are the only ones in Stoney Butte who know about this. After checking out the agencies I'd been contributing to, I decided I wanted to not only know where my money was going, but also to be personally involved in the work. I chose a village, and I've spent part of my year there ever since, getting to know the people and their needs. I've learned their native language and carried their children on my shoulders. I built a little hut for myself there.

"The villagers and I have drilled a well so that the women don't have to walk four miles and carry as much as five gallons of water, usually on their heads. We are now repairing some of the houses and have plans to build a church. I really feel that the restlessness I felt before was God nudging me to be personally involved in helping others. I know I could have helped here in our country, but when I went to Africa, I experienced a stirring to work there. I guess I believe more in God working within me than I realized."

When Amanda didn't comment, Bill asked, "Do you understand?"

"I think I understand more now than I would have last fall. I'd been away from the church, and for that matter any thoughts of God, for so long that it would have been foreign to me. I've really done some thinking since being a part of your conversations with Miss Emma. I can't believe what a deep but open thinker she is. And, as you said, she's hardly been out of the county since she moved here as a bride. Such a jewel of a woman."

Bill kissed her on the cheek. "You are a jewel yourself. One I've just discovered."

Amanda turned, and his arms went around her and drew her close. It seemed so natural to him when she buried her head in his chest. After a few moments he pulled away enough to look deep into her eyes. Then he tipped her chin up and kissed her. Amanda wrapped her arms around him, and the kiss deepened. He had never felt so close in spirit to anyone in his life.

Amanda said, "Bill, you have just given me something that you've given to few people. You've given me your confidence in keeping your secret mission. Such a treasure."

Chapter Forty-Two

The next morning Bill asked if Amanda would like to attend a different worship service on their way back to Stoney Butte. He said, "There is a group of Old Country Ukrainians that live just north of Dickenson. The ancestors of this community came here in 1910, and only recently has the younger generation sought out customs of their heritage. It's a Ukrainian Orthodox Church, but I think you will enjoy it."

"It sounds interesting," she replied. "I'd like to worship with them."

On the way to the church, Bill told Amanda about the Ukrainian Easter customs. "After the Lenten time of fasting and penance, the day celebrating the resurrection begins just before sunrise with a processional around the church. They circle the church three times with the sacrament, symbolizing the three women who came to the tomb, as well as the three days before Jesus' resurrection. Then as the sun comes over the prairie, they sing 'Khrystos Voskres', Christ is risen! The priest, holding a golden cross, opens the door for everyone to enter."

Amanda's face shone with excitement. "What a way to start Easter Day."

Bill took his eyes off the road long enough to smile at her. "Then after the mass, the people gather on the lawn with baskets of food they brought with them. The priest blesses each one, and they take the blessed food home for their Easter breakfast. The baskets are filled with *'paska'* a special bread, hard boiled eggs, ham, sausage, cottage cheese, horseradish and beet relish, a macaroni dish, butter, and special eggs called *'pysanka'* which they have covered with a design of Christian symbols.

"The egg is hand painted with wax between a series of dyes. In the early years they used a traditional writing instrument called a *kistki*. It holds wax which they warmed over a candle flame. Now many of the women use an electric stylus that keeps the wax at an even temperature. They first place the wax on the part of the design they want to remain white and dip the egg in the lightest color they plan to use. Then they apply the wax to the places that will have the next lightest color. And on it goes, using as many coats of wax and colors of their plan."

"Do they have books or something that they use to draw the designs first?" Amanda asked.

"Women who have done this for years don't draw the design on the egg beforehand. It just goes from the mind of the creator to the egg. When the design is finished, they place the eggs in a warm oven to melt the wax, and then they polish the egg with a soft cloth."

"That takes a lot of practice and a steady hand, I'm sure."

"And lots of time. Even an experienced artist will take about four hours to create one *'pysanka'*."

Amanda's eyebrows raised in a questioning way. "How do they take the insides out of the egg? If they don't, I think that it would soon smell pretty terrible."

"Some do make a pin hole in each end and blow the contents out. That makes the egg even more fragile. Others use the uncooked egg with the yolk and white still in it. After removing the wax, they apply a coat of varnish to preserve it. Over time, the yolk dries to a lump and the white dries to dust. If the insides are left in the egg, it must be turned periodically so that the yoke doesn't settle at one place. When cared for, they will last for many years. Miss Emma still has one that I gave to her when I was a teenager."

As they entered the church, many people greeted Bill. He introduced them to Amanda. After they were seated, she said quietly, "You seem to know many of the people here."

"Yes, I often stop to worship with them on my way to and from the airport. I've even enjoyed the thrill of the Easter morning ritual and then had breakfast with one of the families."

As they drove away from the church, Amanda said, "You amaze me with your interest in different people and different religions. What religions have you found in Africa?"

"Although most Africans are either Christian or Muslim, there are many ethnic religions. Most of these, however, do believe in a creator god. They may add other gods to their beliefs."

Amanda turned in her seat. "In your work in the African village, do you try to teach them about Christianity?"

Bill smiled. "I try to follow what St. Francis reportedly said, 'Preach Jesus, and if necessary, use words.'"

"That sounds like you. It is certainly a better way of approaching it."

Bill took a few moments to think. "I don't know if you would actually call what I do a mission, since I'm not sponsored by a church and have my own foundation for my trips. You know, when nations colonized Africa, they tried to force the people to adapt to the western world."

Amanda nodded. "We also tried to do that with the Native Americans."

"Yes, we took away their self-dignity by doing that. Thankfully, missionaries today realize that much of the people's culture can be woven into Christianity."

After a few moments, Amanda said, "It would be interesting to see your relationship with the people you work with in Africa."

A smile spread across Bill's face.

As he had promised, they stopped at Grassy Butte. They pulled up to an old building, and Bill got out and opened the door for Amanda.

"We call this a sod post office," he explained as they walked toward the structure. "It is actually constructed of mixed materials. The Ukrainian man who built it incorporated both earth and timber, as they did in the old country. The community hopes to get it listed on the National Register of Historic Places."

After walking around the post office, Bill suggested that they take the gentle climb up Grassy Butte. At the top they found interesting rock formations and great views of the surrounding countryside.

Amanda looked out with sad eyes. "I guess this is goodbye to the Badlands."

Bill drew her close. "Yes. Goodbye for now, but we'll come and see it again."

There was little talk the rest of the way to Stoney Butte.

Chapter Forty-Three

When they parked in front of Amanda's trailer, Bill reached to the back seat for a package. He pulled out a beautifully wrapped box and handed it to her. Surprised, she asked, "What is this?"

"It's something special for you. Open it."

As she pulled the top off the box, she saw a bright-colored Ukrainian egg. She drew her breath in and exclaimed, "Oh, how lovely! I had no idea just how exquisite they are. When did you get this?"

"When we were in the shop at Medora."

"Well, I must have missed that section of the shop all together, because I would have been mesmerized by them. Look how intricate the wheat is on the egg. I recognize that as a symbol representing the bread that we use in communion."

"Yes, it is," he said with a smile. "Wheat is often used as one of our Christian symbols."

Bill gently put the egg back into the box and drew her to him. "Giving a *pysanky* is considered a token of love. This is my way of saying I've fallen in love with you." Amanda felt a quiver shoot through her.

As he bent to kiss her, she thought, *It doesn't matter if the entire community of Stoney Butte sees us.* When they parted, she looked deep into his eyes, and her voice caught as she said, "I've fallen in love with you too. Thank you for this token of love."

After he took her small suitcase into her home, she asked if he would stay for dinner. They cooked together, stopping at times for a refreshing kiss. When the meal was over and the dishes washed and put away, Amanda took the *pysanky* egg out of the box and discovered a unique, clear holder for the egg. She placed it on a high shelf. Turning to the cat, she said, "Aggie, this is definitely a no-no for you." Aggie cocked her head as if she understood.

Amanda made an after-dinner coffee, and they sat together on the sofa reviewing some of the pamphlets they had collected in Medora. "I definitely want to go back again," she said. "I'd like to take the hike to Teddy Roosevelt's cabin. I'm beginning to understand his statement about the Dakotas giving you a feeling of perfect freedom."

Bill smiled, "I'm so glad you've come to enjoy our Dakotas. When I'm away, I have a pull to return. The villages in Africa don't have the traffic and frustration that our cities have, but it's always a breath of fresh air to return."

Amanda turned on the sofa to face him. "Tell me more about the people you work with in Africa."

Excitedly, Bill told her about several families in the villages where he had worked. Amanda found herself totally engrossed in his stories. She suddenly realized just why her son had signed up for the Peace Corps.

She said, "I know I'm helping the children of Stoney Butte, but it seems that helping those you are working with can also make a difference. We have so many people in our country who could make changes for good if they did the sort of things you are doing. You're truly changing lives that could eventually change countries. I knew there was a reason I came here. That urge that I felt back in Atlanta brought me to meeting you. You and Miss Emma have taught me so much about living in the world, as a whole, instead of just in my little corner.

Bill looked into her eyes and said, "Would you like to be a part of my experiences? Would you marry me?"

Amanda caught her breath but didn't hesitate. "I realize that working in Africa will always be in your life. I want to be a part of your life too. I also like your ranch family, along with Miss Emma, and the community of Stoney Butte. I enjoy the times we've spent together, and I know I'm in love with you." She was quiet for a moment. "Yes, I will marry you, no matter where that leads me."

Bill kissed her on the ear and then whispered, "I never thought I'd find a woman like you. I thank God for bringing you into my life."

Amanda pulled back a bit with a smile that lit up her eyes. "And I'm glad I answered that ad for the teaching position. I never knew that love could be so simple and yet so real as this."

Bill pulled Amanda up from the sofa. Giving her another hug, he said, "Let's go tell Miss Emma. She's the closest thing I have to a mother."

They walked to Miss Emma's house as a full moon emerged above the horizon, giving the world a golden glow. Amanda felt she was walking on air. As soon as Miss Emma opened the door, she gave Bill a wink. "I'm so glad you two had time to be alone. Your faces are as bright as a shiny penny!"

Bill put his arm around Amanda and drew her close, "They should be bright. This wonderful woman has just agreed to be my wife, even though she knows it will involve periods of time in Africa. And I thought I'd never find such a woman as this."

Amanda delighted in the approval on Miss Emma's face. She invited them in, starting a pot of tea and putting a plate of snickerdoodles on the table. "This certainly calls for a celebration, but all I have are these cookies."

Amanda smiled. "Snickerdoodles will always be a celebration for us because you are a part of them."

As they sipped their tea and enjoyed the cookies at the kitchen table, Bill told Miss Emma just what they had done over the weekend. She grasped both their hands, bowed her head, and said, "Our God, I thank you for these lovely people, and I am so happy that they found a way to come together. They both have such a yearning to follow your guidance. Give them joy as they walk this walk together." She paused a moment and then said, "Amen - so be it." Amanda blinked back the tears of joy.

Bill smiled at Miss Emma and said, "Thank you. You are such a mother to me. We wanted you to know about our decision first."

Miss Emma's eyes also sparkled with a hint of tears. "You waited a long time to find such a woman. Your parents would be proud."

Then she went on to say, "I know it's early, but you will have to make some decisions, not only about your wedding but also about where you go from here in the future."

Amanda thought for a moment and then agreed. "Those will be some big decisions. I know that I've grown to love Stoney Butte and I'd like to call this my home base, but I'm also excited about what Bill is doing in Africa. I think we'll just have to take this one step at a time. I'm afraid my daughter will be shocked out of her high heels."

As they left Miss Emma's, the moon was full and bright overhead. The stars that Amanda had seldom seen in Atlanta seemed to create an arbor for their path ahead. As Bill left her at her door, he gave her one last kiss and then smiled into her eyes. "We each need to pray about where God leads us together. We can talk about plans another day. I know it's been a busy weekend and you need your sleep since you have school tomorrow."

"It will be a pleasant sleep, if I can only ignore my thoughts about how we will go about this happy future of ours."

Chapter Forty-Four

The next morning, after Jimmy had gone to school, Bill went to see Willis and Wilda. As they sat down for coffee, Wilda said, "You seem excited about something, Bill. You must have had a great weekend."

Bill's face turned a bit red, and it wasn't from the rising dawn. "Yes, it was a great weekend. I was able to introduce Amanda to our Badlands and some of the history of the area. We also had time to get to know each other better. She told me just why she left Atlanta, and can you believe it, I actually told her what I do when I leave Stoney Butte?"

Willis said, "That sounds risky to me. Will she keep your secret?"

"I trust her with it. In fact, she will probably be taking the trips with me. She accepted my proposal for marriage."

They both jumped up and gave Bill a big bear hug. Willis smiled at Wilda and said, "It took a bit longer, but I think he found the right woman for himself."

His wife responded, "She's not only the right woman for him, but also the right woman to fill out our ranch family. I enjoy her so much that I feel as though she's the sister I never had."

Willis settled down into his chair. "Now, tell us more about the weekend. And how did you come about asking her?"

Bill said, "She was so excited about the Badlands and all the history behind it. We even went to a worship service with the Ukrainians on the way home. We both knew that there were secrets about our lives that the other one didn't know. Friday night after supper she explained her circumstances behind looking for a position away from Atlanta and applying for our teaching job. Then the next day, as we ate lunch on an overlook, I shared some of my experiences in Africa. She was so excited about it that she said she would enjoy being a part of my work there. That's when I knew that I had to ask her to marry me. I knew that I could not think of leaving her and heading to Africa alone. Strange how I've always felt I was independent and never needed anyone with me, and now I even have trouble leaving her for a night."

Willis' eyes met Wilda's, "That's just the way I felt about Wilda once I truly realized that I loved her. Now, can I ask you when and how you asked her?"

"I had bought a Ukrainian egg, and I gave it to her when we got back to Stoney Butte, telling her that it is considered a token of love. Then I asked her to be a part of my life. After her answer, we walked over to tell Miss Emma. As you can guess, she was as pleased as peach. She's the one who suggested that I find a way for us to be alone, away from the town gossip. I'm sure that some of our secret is out if anyone saw me kissing her at her door and realized that her car had been parked in front of her trailer all weekend."

Wilda laughed. "Oh, you can be sure of that. News travels fast up and down our party lines. I guess it's okay now for folks to know, since you two have made the decision. It will be a big celebration for the town, something to talk about for a long time."

In a serious tone, Bill said. "We still have to make decisions about our wedding, and about whether we'll spend the school year here so that she can continue teaching or whether the school board will have to search for a replacement. I could probably cut my time in Africa and get someone to work with us, carrying on after we leave each year. I feel it's up to her as to whether she wants to continue teaching or not. I'm certainly not going to make that decision for her. She enjoys working with the children so much, and she's very inventive of ways to help them learn."

Before school that morning Amanda was having her own thoughts and questions about the future. Her main thoughts were of her love for Bill. This brought a smile and a warm glow from head to toe. The weekend had been wonderful for her, as well as revealing. Bill's long trips to Africa and what he did there were important.

She also knew she loved teaching. There were some teaching opportunities in Africa. But she felt she had gotten to know the children of Stoney Butte and their families so well that she hated to throw a new teacher their way. She saw that her first obligation was to tell Sue Biscoff of their plans to marry. Maybe she could talk the situation over with Sue, although she had little time now before going to school. Miss Emma might give her some insight too.

Lifting the receiver of the phone she realized that she would not only be telling Sue, but the whole community. If anyone realized that her car was left while she was away and then saw them kiss at her front door, the party lines, starting with Bertha, would give their engagement away. With confidence she asked to be connected to Sue.

After she told Sue the news, Amanda could almost hear her smile. "I'm certainly happy for you, and for Bill too. You will make a great marriage, I'm sure."

Then she asked, "Will you go with Bill on his travels? Does this mean you won't be signing a contract for next year?"

"We're still thinking that through," Amanda assured her. "I love teaching here, and we will just have to weigh through our decisions."

"Maybe Bill could limit his trips to the summer, and you could still teach in Stoney Butte. The children and the families have certainly grown to love you."

"And I love them too. I can't believe I've found such joy in this small town."

Sue said, "You know that we'd like to keep you in the classroom. You are giving the children a love for learning as well as simple facts."

"Thank you. I need to get over to the school now. I'm sure the word has gotten around town, but I wanted you to hear the true version from me right away."

Sue closed out the conversation. "We will keep you in our prayers as you consider your decisions."

"It will take prayer to make the decisions. Please don't pray for God to lead us one way or another. Just pray that we follow God's guidance."

When Amanda got to school, Ione came into her classroom. "I've heard some rumors about you and Bill this weekend. I don't want to be nosey, but I'm sure the children have heard them too."

With a smile as wide as her desk, she said, "Yes, I think the rumors are somewhat true. We spent the weekend enjoying the Badlands and getting to know each other. We've found that we not only enjoy each other's company, but it goes deeper than that."

A knowing sparkle came to Ione's eyes. "Well, our primary source of news, Bertha, even made calls to several hotels in Dickenson and found out you had separate rooms. That made her feel better about your trip."

"I'm not surprised. Other times, when we've gone to Williston for the day, I always drove out to his ranch early and left my car there so as not to raise suspicion. This time we left on Friday after school, and I was so excited about the trip that I guess I threw caution to the wind and had him pick me up in town. I'm sure the whole county knows that now. I will simply tell the students that we are thinking about marriage."

As Ione left for her classroom she said, "I've learned so much from you that now I'm not sure I want to retire. I do hope you can continue teaching with me if I don't retire."

"And I've learned from you too. I've specially learned to love the children of this small town. When I first drove across the bridge into town, I thought I had come to the end of the universe. Now I know that the universe centers around you, no matter where you are."

As Amanda expected, the town was full of speculation. Even the children asked about her relationship with Bill. She simply said that they enjoyed each other's company, and that they may get married. This brought such shouts from the class that Iona stepped into her room and gave Amanda a wink. "I guess it's okay to tell my students that you two are seeing each other."

Ignoring the blush that crept up her face, Amanda said, "Go ahead. Bertha has already spread the news on the party lines."

Chapter Forty-Five

Bill and Amanda set their wedding date for the Saturday after school was out. The pastor in Williston agreed to come out to wed them properly, and Bertha let it be known that the whole town, indeed the whole county, was invited. They decided to have it outside at Bill's ranch since they knew that all the guests would not fit in their tiny church. Amanda's daughter agreed to come to represent her family. Kurt would not be able to come, but Bill assured her that he would plan their trip to Africa to include a visit to the village where he was working.

Soon spring bloomed on the prairie. One day in mid-May they wandered to the creek that ran through his ranch. Bill pointed out many of the wildflowers. They spread a blanket on the bank of the creek where they had come several times since the weather began to warm. As they looked out over the prairie, they heard the gentle mooing of the cattle across the rustling water.

Amanda thought of her first view of the prairie as she had driven to Stoney Butte at the end of last summer and how different it looked now. "I don't know whether the spring prairie is that different or that I've come to love the peace and solitude of this area."

Bill drew her close and smiled. "I think it's a bit of both. I have always seen the difference in the late August prairie and that of May, but I also think that the prairie grows on you if you allow it to."

"Yes, I remember hearing two women in the post office talking. One of them said, 'I hope North Dakota doesn't work on tourism too much, because I like it just the way it is - a wide prairie with few people.'"

Bill laughed. "I don't think we will ever have crowds like the big cities. I will say, however, that there are other lovely places in the world too. I've certainly seen many of them in Africa."

Amanda cuddled her head on his shoulder. "I'm so looking forward to seeing those places with you. I'm glad that we were able to adjust our schedules so that we can make the trips in the summer and be here the rest of the year, at least for a few years. The day may come when I'm ready to give up teaching in our little schoolhouse, but I look forward to continuing it for now."

"And you should," said Bill, kissing the top of her head. "You have made a difference not only with the students, but also in the town. We've never had a teacher like you. Even Miss Ione can see it, and most of our previous teachers had trouble getting along with her. She said it's because of you that she's putting off her retirement. Stoney Butte needs you to continue."

"I've been thinking about how I can help the students recognize that our nation is definitely a part of the whole world after our trip to Africa. Will you mind if I speak of where we will go during the summers? You've kept it a secret for so long."

"Having you with me makes it altogether different. Now I can see just how important it is for Stoney Butte to realize that we are a part of a larger world instead of keeping the two parts of my life separate. Yes, I'll be happy for you to use our experiences in Africa as part of your teaching. The children will be all the richer for it."

A few days before the wedding, Ashley flew into Williston, and Amanda picked her up. She seemed shocked at the distances between towns and the sparse population of the countryside. The daughter had taken her mother's advice about leaving her high heels at home and dressing very simply. She seemed comfortable when they stopped at Bill's ranch for dinner at Willis and Wilda's.

Amanda had sent pictures of Bill to both of her children when she told them about the engagement. After dinner Ashley drew her aside and said, "You wrote about this man, but he's much more than I expected, even from your letters. I'm very happy for you that you found him. I just can't believe he came from such a small, out of the way place."

Ashley also seemed charmed by little Jimmy, which surprised Amanda. She had never seen her daughter around children. Miss Emma joined them for dinner, and Ashley later said, "She's the type of grandmother that I've always wanted." During the next few days Ashley spent most of the school hours at Miss Emma's. Amanda had never seen her daughter so happy.

Bill asked Wenzel to help build an arbor for the wedding, and they used vines grown in the greenhouse to cover it. The arbor looked out over a field full of wildflowers, but most of the guests would be able to sit under a canopy of trees. Although Bill rented chairs from a company in Williston for the older guests, each family was encouraged to bring their own quilts to sit on the grass, and a side dish or dessert to share.

Willis began a pit bar-b-que the night before, and as the guests arrived all the side dishes and desserts were placed on long tables made with boards and sawhorses. Some of the community had never had an opportunity to see the greenhouses up close. The men who worked with Willis proudly organized tours. The school children acted as tour guides, telling the adults just what they had learned about growing plants in greenhouses and growing trees that were adaptable to North Dakota.

True to the predictions, their wedding drew a large crowd. Amanda wore a simple gown, typical of what the early settlers had worn, and she carried an armful of wildflowers. Ashley stood beside her and Willis next to Bill. Miss Emma's eyes sparkled with tears when she was presented with a bouquet of wildflowers, being told that she was considered the mother of the bride and the groom. It was truly a prairie wedding and a celebration for the whole community.

Bill and Amanda spent their first night in his home, and as the last guest left, Amanda thought of her world now in the small town in North Dakota as well as her previous home in Atlanta, and all the problems of the past few years. She had come to what she thought was the end of the universe, but now she realized that ends are only new beginnings. Anywhere with Bill was the center of the universe.

The End

About the Author

Delia Halverson lived for 13 years of her adult life in the Dakotas where her husband was ranger on the National Grasslands. She uses some of her small-town experiences in the novel. She is the author of 26 published non-fiction books, including devotionals and books for parents and church leaders. She has also written numerous magazine and newspaper articles and columns, and a large amount of church curriculum. For years she led workshops and seminars throughout the country, as well as in Africa. After 24 moves from Key West, Florida, to Northern Idaho, Delia now lives in Woodstock, GA. She and her husband enjoy living near their children and grandchildren.